Blind Witness

By

ALYSIA S. KNIGHT

Heart Dreams
PRESS

Blind Witness
By Alysia S. Knight
Published by Heart Dreams Press
Layton, Utah
Copyright © 2014 Alysia S. Ricks
Cover design: by Kelli Ann Morgan @
www.inspirecreativeservices.com

ISBN:1942000014
ISBN-13:978-1-94200001-3

Also available from
Alysia S. Knight

Letting Love Win

Past To Die For

Temperature Rising

Kare for Me

To my family with love,

Alysia

Chapter One

Beemmmp

The single tune caught Rachelle's attention as Lois, the other person in the small office, transferred the incoming call to her terminal. Rachelle picked up the headphones sliding them on with practiced ease.

"Clairbourne Industries. Mr. Clairbourne nor his personal assistant are available at the moment. If you would like to leave a message, I will make sure it is brought to their attention." She waited. If it weren't for the faint breathing sounds on the line Rachelle would've thought, whoever it was, had hung up.

"Who is this?" The words when they came were curt and demanding.

"This is Clairbourne's executive answering service. If you would like I can redirect your call or take a message."

There was another long pause. Rachelle shifted in her seat. For nearly two months she'd fielded calls for the executive levels of Clairbourne Industries. She hadn't felt this uneasy since her first days, and then it was out of concern over her own abilities to handle the job. She forced a swallow to relieve the dryness that settled in her throat while her hands remained poised over her computer keyboard waiting to input every word exchanged.

"May I ask who is calling?" she asked to break the silence.

"You have a beautiful voice." The words came back, startling her. Her fingers paused for a second over the keyboard then the voice continued and so did she. "Are you as beautiful as you sound? Soft, sweet, innocent, an angel, Clairbourne's going to need an angel. He's going to die."

Rachelle's lungs tightened, tensed with the rest of her body, but her fingers continued to type. "Sir, may I ask whose calling?" She tried to keep her voice from shaking as she forced the words out.

"Tell him he's going to have to pay the price. Clairbourne, who is all-powerful, who has everything. It's time. He's going to pay. I'll take everything from him. He won't have anything left. I'll destroy him and everything he cares about. I'll take it all away. I can do it. Only I can. No one will be his friend. No one will stand by him. I'll destroy him. He will pay."

"Please, can't I help you?" Rachelle voice trembled unmistakably now.

"You're frightened." The cold rambling voice changed to confusion. "Don't be frightened, Angel Voice. I won't let him harm you. I'll protect you."

"Protect me?"

"From Clairbourne. He'll die. He has to. But not yet, he has to suffer first. Pain, I want him to feel pain. I want him to hurt like I've hurt. Then he'll die and only I'll know when. I can get him anywhere, anytime. He must know that. He'll be helpless, but you'll be safe just … just don't go near Eastbourne Shipping then you'll be safe. I'll take care of you, Angel Voice."

The words stopped. The line went dead, but Rachelle's fingers remained frozen over the keyboard, waiting.

"Rachelle." The voice that came to her next was warm, female and from in the same room.

Rachelle jumped in spite the reassuring familiarity of it. "Rachelle is something wrong? You look pale." Rachelle could hear Lois' slender body shift around, but when she turned to the voice only darkness greeted her eyes. It was the same darkness she'd been fighting to adjust to for almost nine months, since the accident when her sight was taken from her.

"Will you get me security, please?"

Only a moment passed before the headset came alive again.

"Security."

Automatically, she turned back to her computer. "This is Miss Harris, executive answering." Rachelle's voice sounded foreign, too calm for what she felt. "I just received a death threat against Mr. Clairbourne."

"Please give me the details." The voice that came over the headset seemed bored or matter of fact. It disturbed her, causing her to hesitate.

"I'm sure he was serious," Rachelle stressed, fighting the wave of dread that left her feeling sick.

"I'm sure he was. If you'll just give me the details, we'll check it out. Start by giving me the number trace."

Rachelle felt foolishly chastened, like a small child or rather an air-headed bimbo. Feeling the sides of the keyboard, she moved her finger in position and made the request.

"No listing available," the computer generator voice answered. Puzzled, Rachelle re-entered the command. The same answer greeted her.

"The computer says there's none available." She heard a muffled curse, taking the image of 'air-head' to another level.

"Can you play me the recording?" The gruff voice held little patience.

"Yes, sir," Rachelle answered seriously, grimacing at her attitude. The recording began, but the only thing that came through was her voice and a strange mechanical hum.

"What's that, where's the recording?" The voice through the phone passed well beyond annoyed.

"I don't know. I don't understand." Rachelle tried to work with the recording, her fear now combining with frustration. Her stomach churned, leaving her feeling nauseated. Tilting her head forward, she pushed her fingers into her hair and forced herself to take a deep breath before once more placing the command only to receive the same fouled recording as before.

"I don't understand. It's not here."

A harsh line of swear words came over the phone making her flinch.

"Do you think you can tell me what the man said? I'm assuming it was a man from what you previously said?"

"Yes, it was a man. But wouldn't you …"

"Just tell me what he said." The man cut her off.

"Yes, sir." Rachelle fought to firm up her voice. "He said he was going to kill Mr. Clairbourne. That he was going to destroy him and everything he had. He mentioned specifically Eastbourne Shipping and to stay away from it."

"Anything else?" The voice sounded bored again.

"He said a lot. Kind of rambled, but that was the gist of most of it, stressing that he was going to take everything, and then he was going to kill Mr. Clairbourne." Hearing the doubt over the phone, she wasn't quite sure what to say to make the man take her seriously.

"Rambled, like bragging to you?"

"Well, yes, I suppose so."

"I see, thank you, Ms. Harris. I'm sure it was just a prank, but we'll check it out."

"But, wouldn't you like–," for the second time in a matter of minutes the line went dead in her ear, "the printed transcript." Rachelle finished to herself, slumping forward.

"Rachelle, are you all right?" Not having heard Lois cross the room, she jerked as Lois' hand settled onto her shoulder. "Sorry," the woman said gently.

"It's all right. I just feel a little shaken. He sounded so serious." Rachelle raised trembling fingers to her lips.

"What all did he say?" A gentle hand squeezed her arm, showing warm concern besides the curiosity that was evident in Lois' tone.

"Mainly that he was going to kill Mr. Clairbourne. He was so cold, so … he kept saying he was going to destroy him and that only he could do it." A shudder raced through her body.

Lois' hand tightened on her arm in another reassuring squeeze. "Well, security will handle it."

"I don't know. I don't think they took it very serious. The man seemed to think I was a flake."

A small chuckle escaped Lois. "Only you would say that. No matter, they'll still check it out, so just relax and forget about it. I've answered a few calls that were threats before and nothing's ever happened. You did what you were supposed to do in reporting it. So don't worry about it."

Rachelle managed a nod. "I need a minute, would you cover for me?"

"Sure, take what time you need but don't let it get to you. As I said, it's nothing. Just some jerk trying to be a big shot."

Rachelle made her way to the door and moved down the hall, touching the wall lightly with one finger. Hesitating for a moment when she realized she hadn't kept track of her steps. She moved the hand from her side to just in front of her. Even though the people in the offices around hers knew she was blind, she hated to look as if she was groping her way. She hated to feel helpless, fought against it with all her being. Maybe that was why the call bothered her so much. It made her feel helpless. No matter what Lois said, or the security man thought, the man on the line was serious. She could hear it in his voice, in his cold irrational words. He was going to do something.

She jerked as her hand touched cold metal. Using her other hand, she caught back her long hair and leaned forward letting the water trickle over her lips, to run down her throat. It was cool, refreshing, but did nothing to soothe her anxiety within.

The hours past torturously slow. Every time the phone rang Rachelle jumped, half expecting the chilling voice once again to reach across the line. By the time the day was through she was such a nervous wreck that when Lois offered her a ride home she accepted, knowing she couldn't face the trial of making it to the bus and home.

Closing the door of her apartment, she turned the deadbolt, and with a satisfying click, shut out the world. Her apartment had become her refuge. For two months after the accident it had been her dark domain, where her frustrations were handled on her own, away from too helpful family. Where bumps, knocks and bruises faded, until boredom set in, and she was ready to venture out. Now, it was where peace soothed her tormented nerves.

∽∾

The next morning, the lobby at work was in as much turmoil as her dreams had been. People milled around, talking in excited voices. It took all of Rachelle's concentration just to make it to the elevator. The relief that came from the doors closing lasted only until they opened four stories up, where the room buzzed with conversation. She let out a sigh as she stepped into her office, but again her relief didn't last long.

"A bomb exploded last night at building three's loading dock. No injuries but part of the awning came down on a truck." Lois' words were spoken gently but left Rachelle cold. "Security will be here soon. They want to talk to you about the call."

Without a word Rachelle nodded and made her way to

her chair. Her eyes closed tight though it made no difference in shutting out the world. *I'll destroy him, I'll kill him. I can do it, only I.* The words echoed in her mind. He would do it just like he said. She'd known it. It was in the tone, in the pitch of every curt word. In the voice she knew she would never forget.

"Rachelle, would you like me to get you something?" Lois' mothering tone was as evident as the cruel promise in the caller's, helping Rachelle to force out a smile as she shook her head.

"I have to check the executive messages." Rachelle turned on the computer before settling the headphones in place. Her fingers moved over the familiar keys.

⋈

Britton Clairbourne had never been down to the message center, always letting Darrel, his assistant, handle any dealings his office had with it. Today was different. Today, he would handle things personally. When someone attacked his company, his people, it was very personal. It had been sheer luck no one was injured in the explosion. He wanted whoever was behind it, and he wanted them now.

Clenching his fists, he strode down the hall. Ahead, he saw Theodore Laslow, head of security, disappear through a doorway. The gravelly old bear of an ex-policeman had a sizable chip on his shoulder, but he was still a good man who knew how to get answers. Following him into the room, Britton stopped just inside. His alert senses took it all in.

There were two desks in the small office, two tall plants, and a cluster of seascapes and a calendar adorning the walls. The first desk held a computer, phone bank, an array of pictures undoubtedly of family, and a huge coffee cup that announced #1 MOM, which fit the older, petite, brown-haired woman that sat there. The other desk was barren save the computer and telephone system. A woman sat at the desk with headphones settled amongst long, brown hair that shimmered with golden highlights. Quick fingers moved over the keyboard.

Theodore Laslow rested on the corner of her desk. "Well?" His voice boomed, making the woman at the keyboard cringe.

"I'm trying sir, I don't understand." The voice was soft, strained to nearly breaking.

The man could be intimating, Britt thought. As if sensing his arrival Laslow turned, setting down a coffee cup by the computer, he extended his hand.

"Nothing yet, Mr. Clairbourne, I just got here and she hasn't brought the conversation up," Laslow said as they shook.

Behind the security officer, the woman turned her chair his direction, but didn't look at him. Still, he felt a punch to his system which took him by surprise. She was young, maybe mid-twenties. Her cheekbones were high, delicate; her nose small, pert. Her mouth was a perfect bow, lips slightly too full, giving an invitation to be kissed, promising lush, sweet, softness. He wondered where the thought had come from. It had to be that her lips were the only features on her face to show any signs of make-up. The rest of her face was fresh and clean. Dark lashes shaded her eyes, giving her a shy look.

How could someone so pretty, be that self-conscious? The thought cut through his anger, startling him so that he growled out the command. "Let's get started then." At the sound of his voice, her head lifted, and he found himself lost in depths of blue. *Not pretty, beautiful.* Then the eyes were turned away from him as she swiveled back to the keyboard. The motion brought her arm around connecting with Laslow's coffee cup.

"No, my computer!" The cry came almost before the cup tipped. Without hesitation her hand came down on the desk in an effort to keep the spill from the computer then it pulled back as the hot liquid burned. At the same time Laslow stood, the other secretary moved to the desk with a towel which mysteriously appeared in her hand. Pushing past the burly man, the woman dropped the towel over the spill.

"It's all right, Rachelle. I have it." Carefully, the older woman caught the younger woman's wrist turning her hand over. "You burned yourself."

"Did the computer get wet?" The soft voice almost pleaded for assurance, and for the first time, Britton realized the beautiful blue eyes, in the turned-up face, didn't see him or anything else.

"No, it's all right," the woman assured. "But, you should go run some cold water over your arm."

"Yes." She stood, took an uncertain step toward the door before she stopped. "If you'll excuse me, I'll be just a minute." Again her steps were hesitant as she moved forward, giving time for the others in the room to move out of her way.

"I'll help you," Britton offered as he stepped to the side of the doorway.

"It's not necessary. I can manage." Her hand came out to touch the doorframe following it around into the hall.

Britton watched her move down the hall with more confidence, stopping just in front of the drinking fountain. She wrapped her arms in front on her.

He moved to her. "Here, let me help."

She jerked when his fingers closed on her wrist, but instead of releasing her, he moved her hand under the stream of water.

Her tiny gasp drew his eyes to her face. Though she was tall, she barely reached past his chin.

If he leaned forward he could press his lips to her forehead. "It doesn't seem too bad," Britton said, shaking aside the strange thought.

"No, it'll be fine, it just stung a little. I'm usually a lot more careful than this, and never let anything near my computer that might spill."

"It wasn't your fault," Britton reassured.

She removed her hand from the water, tilting her head away. "I'd just got in and Lois told me about the bomb yesterday, then Mr. Laslow came in and startled me. Gruff people tend to do that because I can't see it coming, and now Mr. Clairbourne is in there. He must think I'm totally incompetent, but I'm not. I really can do my job."

"I'm sure you can, but maybe I should introduce myself. I'm Britton Clairbourne."

Her head shot up, her eyes searching as if to see him. Her breathing turned rapid. He'd startled her.

"You don't sound like I thought you would. You're younger, less gruff." The words seemed to slip from her.

"I'm thirty-four; will be thirty five next month. And, as for being gruff, after yesterday I should be able to give an ogre a run for his money." Britton couldn't keep the first smile in two days from creeping across his face.

"Oh," the groan was almost silent but it made his smile deepen. "I didn't mean to sound, I mean that … I knew you weren't old, it's just … I knew you weren't mean, I mean you okayed my working after the accident, but." She finally stopped to take a deep breath. "You just didn't sound like I thought you would."

"How did you think I'd sound?" His curiosity forced him to ask.

Her brow crinkled slightly. "Hard, forceful, dominant, demanding." She dipped her head then jerked as he touched a finger under her chin, tilting her face back up.

"And how do I sound?"

Every emotion showed on her face, stunned, shy, hesitant, and an almost visible compulsion to answer that seemed to leave her breathless. "Strong, but smooth, warm, like rich mahogany." Her words sent more pleasure through him than they probably should have, but when she swallowed and whispered. "Sexy." Britt lost his own breath. He didn't stop her when she tilted her head away off his finger, wondering for a moment who was shocked more by the last revelation.

"Mr. Clairbourne, I can't get anything to come up on her computer." Laslow's gruff voice came down the hall, shattering the silence that had fallen.

The call! He pulled back. She didn't resist when his hand cupped her elbow heading her down the hall.

Britton watched as she slid past Laslow into her seat, as certain as if she could see him. Her fingers reached instinctively for the headset, sliding it into place, then touched the keyboard, settling into position. She took a small breath before her fingers set to work moving over the keys with confidence.

Her fingers stalled. Her brow wrinkled as she concentrated on the headset. With a slight shake of her head, her fingers once more flew over the keys. This time, as her brow wrinkled, her teeth caught her bottom lip. Frustration showed in every expression.

"It's not coming out right. I don't know what's wrong."

Laslow's grunt brought out a whispered. "I'm sorry." The tremor in her voice pulled Britton from the wall where he'd leaned while he watched her. When his hand settled on her shoulder, he felt her muscles tighten. With a will of their own, his fingers squeezed in reassurance, though he felt frustration at the loss of their only lead.

"You can't find the recording at all?" Laslow's words made her jump.

"It's here. Or at least part of it is. It's …" She chewed her bottom lip fighting her obvious nervousness.

Laslow tended to have that effect on people, and though he was good at his job, Britt just wished he would ease up on her.

"Only part of it's here."

"You erased it," Laslow snapped in disgust.

"No!" she said defensively. "I don't understand this, it has never happened on any other message."

"Why don't you play it for us?" Britton cut off his security chief before he could snap at the young woman again, squeezing his hand down.

"Yes, sir." Her voice trembled. Pushing the speaker button, she again typed in the command. In the next second, her voice came over the speaker followed by a familiar electronic whine, then her voice again. By the fourth time fear was unmistakable in her tone. Britt also noticed she didn't seem overwhelmed as she tried to reason and keep whoever it was talking, trying to gain more information. If only they could hear the other part of the conversation.

A string of curses burst from Laslow carrying Britton's sentiment exactly.

"That's it, I'm sorry. I don't know what's wrong. I just can't seem to get what was said to me. It's never done that to me before."

"I'm sure it hasn't, and you have nothing to be sorry about. What's happening to the recording isn't your fault. You couldn't record his conversation because he scrambled it," Britton informed grimly.

"But I could understand him." She turned his direction.

"You're supposed to. You shouldn't have heard anything unusual, but any recording or tracing of the line is quite impossible."

"I'm not responsible."

He knew she was voicing a concern. "No, if anyone is, I am. I designed the scrambler. Whoever it is has access to Clairbourne classified technology, and is using it against me." A heavy silence hung in the air as Britt exchanged looks with his security officer. Clairbourne Industries was well known in the security and electronic world, and something like this would be hard to cover up and didn't speak well for the company.

"Miss." For the first time he realized he didn't know her name.

"Harris," Laslow supplied.

"Miss Harris." Britt squatted down beside her chair. Reaching out, he took her hands in his. A jolt of awareness hit him. Her hands were delicate, with long thin fingers that trembled in his hands. The knowledge that the large stunning eyes held no sight added to the gentle image he longed to shield, but he needed her. She was his only link. "Do you think you could remember any of the conversation, what was said or anything else you could pick up that might help?"

She nodded without hesitation. "I'll never forget that voice."

"Good, let's start with that. You described me, now describe him."

"He was a baritone. The voice was cold, hard; sharp in the delivery. Sometimes it was like he was forcing the words out, though he was rambling." A shudder vibrated through her body as if chilled. She released his hands, sank back in the chair and wrapped her arms around her waist, as if holding herself together. "You could hear the hate in his voice. I knew he wasn't lying. He's going to try to hurt you."

The tear that formed in her eye shocked him. The words were spoken as if she truly cared. He swallowed deeply. Laying his hand over her arms, he gave another reassuring squeeze.

"Very good, now can you remember what he said?"

"Yes, but you have the transcript?" Puzzlement showed on her face.

"Transcript?" Britton echoed her puzzlement.

"Yes, I make a transcript of the entire conversation of every call as it goes on then send the message up from there. The transcripts are in case the person receiving wants to read all that was said. The messages are just recorded in case I make an error or miss something. It's a precaution mainly."

"So you have a copy of all that was said?"

Instead of answering his question directly, her fingers once again moved over the keys with assuredness. At the same time the computer screen filled with the script, the printer came to life. "The phone transcripts are kept in the computer for two weeks unless requested to be transferred to a file. Otherwise they're cleared," she informed, using her job to push back the tumult he observed moments earlier. As the printer stopped, she reached up taking the two pieces of paper and handed them to him.

His heart chilled as he read the first few lines of the conversation. "Can you run me three more copies of this then have the file transferred to my personal file?"

She nodded her fingers once more on the move. He was amazed watching her do it without sight of what was happening under her fingers or on the screen.

"What would you like it filed under, so you can recall it?"

"Clairbourne, threat."

Chapter Two

"Angel Voice."

Rachelle fingers froze. Her chest tightened. Since Mr. Clairbourne and the security chief had left the office three days before, she had been trying to convince herself it was over, that it was an isolated case that would never happen again. But no matter how much she had tried, deep down inside she knew it wasn't. Now the harsh voice over the phone testified to the fact.

"Who is this, please?" Even as she asked the question she knew who it was. She would have known even if he hadn't called her Angel Voice. She shuddered.

"Thank you for giving Clairbourne my message. I'm sorry he came to see you. You shouldn't have to be around him, but I won't let him hurt you. But he has to be punished."

"Please, you have to stop this." Rachelle cut him off.

"I can't. He has to know pain, deep inside. He has to feel what it's like to have everything ripped away. Agony, before he dies."

"Why?" Rachelle felt tears slide down her cheeks. Her trembling fingers continued to move over the keyboard.

"Because he has to pay." The voice roared through the

head set.

"But someone could get hurt."

"Then that's what they get for being around Clairbourne. But don't worry." The voice softened. "You'll be all right. I'll love you. I'll take care of you. You're my angel. You must not go to the warehouses. Promise? Promise!" The voice repeated harshly when Rachelle first failed to answer.

"Yes, I promise." The words trembled out.

"Don't be frightened, my Angel Voice. I'll take care of you. I'll love you. But Clairbourne dies."

Rachelle sat still, as the silence filled the air. She wasn't sure how long she sat there before she felt Lois' arm around her shoulder.

"There, there sweetheart, it's all right. I called security, they're on the way."

০৪৪০

Rachelle Harris looked pale when Britton stepped into the message center. As he drew closer, he could see the evidence of dried tears on her cheek. He was shocked by the overwhelming urge of wanting to punch the wall, via the face of the beast that put the fear and sorrow in her eyes, eyes that might not see, but mirrored her innermost emotions.

Since he had met her three days before, he had learned a lot about Rachelle Harris. In the past year, she had known enough pain. She didn't need this. Her file had told of a bright, intelligent young woman who had started to work for Clairbourne while in college. Even after she graduated, she had continued to take classes in the evening to move up to an executive secretary. She worked hard, and her advancements showed her progressing to her goal until nine months earlier, when there was a notation of absence due to a car accident. Then dated nearly two months ago was another notation of return to work and listed under disabilities was <u>blind</u>.

Seeing her sitting there trembling made Britton ache to shield her from what was happening. Unfortunately, she was caught in it again.

"Laslow?" He kept his questioning tone soft, the tension within him at bay, not wanting to upset Rachelle Harris any more.

"Another call, same jamming equipment; no trace, no recording."

Britton, unable to help himself, laid his hand on the slender shoulder of the woman in front of the computer. He felt the tremors within her as he tightened his hold. He had realized the first day it wasn't normal for him to touch his employees as he had done, and now again his hands found their way to her almost unconsciously.

"Can you print me a copy of the transcript then send it to my file?"

She nodded but didn't speak as her fingers moved over the keyboard. His fingers lingered on her shoulders before he gave her a pat and moved them. He picked up the printout, reading over it. "I want security at each of the warehouses, and the buildings cleared. See about getting hold of the police for some dogs to sniff out explosives."

"We're talking about five holding bays and three warehouses?"

"I'm aware of that, so get on it. I'm heading out to the warehouses."

"Mr. Clairbourne." As he turned to leave with Laslow, his soft-spoken name called him back.

The gentle face, like before, was void of all make-up except for a soft shade of off-red lipstick which made her lips look full and kissable. Her face was turned up to him, urging him to want to do just that − kiss her.

"Will you−" Her words faltered.

Coming forward, he crouched in front of her taking her hands in his. "Don't worry, it will be all right." The words came out followed by the prayer that they would be true.

⊙੩ᔆ೦

"It's all clear, Mr. Clairbourne. They just finished the sweep. It's clean. You can let your people back in."

Britton shoved his hands back through his hair in frustration. His first instinct was to ask if they were certain, but he knew they'd been thorough. They had combed the buildings with dogs. There was no trace of a bomb. It was the same at all the warehouses, but it did nothing to alleviate the uneasy feeling within him.

"Thank you, Captain." He shook the man's hand. There'd still be forms to fill out and other paper work, but he would handle that later.

"Okay, Michael, you can get them back to work." Britt watched silently as the last police car pulled away, then moved through the huge open doors of the docking bay.

Steepling his index fingers together, he tapped them to his lips as he looked over the warehouse. It still didn't feel right. There were too many places to hide a bomb from the massive metal shelves stacked with crates to the high girded ceiling. He didn't like it. The thought of his workers being in danger, or the thought of someone after what he had worked so hard to build. And he especially didn't like the thought of being toyed with. There was no doubt that was what the lunatic was doing. Britt cut back the urge to curse.

Above, the overhead crane rumbled to life, swinging along the girders forty feet in the air, before lowering to snag a waiting crate. It was funny how in just a matter of minutes, everything seemed back to normal.

"Mr. Clairbourne." Laslow's gravelly voice sounded behind him. He turned to the man and waited for the security chief to approach.

"I just left docking bay four. Everything's cleared there. Since it was the location of the first attack, they checked it close, not even a dust ball. Talking to the captain, so far they've found nothing helpful. The bomb was basic. It could have been made by anyone with a little know how and the Internet. Not much chance to trace, but they're staying on it. As for today's threat," Laslow paused. "It's likely he just wants to see us squirm."

Behind them, there was a sharp grinding sound. Britt turned with Laslow, eyes going to the ceiling. The first pop echoed through the building, followed closely by the second, giving everyone in the area just enough time to dive for cover as the last crack came, and the crate swinging overhead plunged forty feet to the concrete floor.

Silence and dust settled as the men in the bay began to move.

"Is everyone all right?" Michael, the foreman, rushed out of the office.

"Yeah," Britton's confirmation was echoed by five other men. Everyone moved to the crushed debris that a moment earlier had been state of the art electronic equipment.

ಋಞ

Rachelle knew she was foolish. She should never have waited around to hear what happened. Now, she'd missed both of the buses she normally took. Which meant neither Harold nor Mr. Jenkins would be there to call to her, so she would know the right bus. Worse, she really didn't find out anything except there was an incident at one of the warehouses, but it was hush, hush, because of the police investigation.

She finally learned no one had been injured. That was what was important. She could go home knowing that, trying not to single out the fact she knew Mr. Clairbourne was all right. It wasn't that he was more important to her than any of the others. It was just, she knew him, and she liked the way he treated her. Not like she was helpless or even incompetent at doing her job. It made her feel good. That was all it was. That's what made her anxious about him, appreciation.

Rachelle heard a bus coming but when it didn't slow down until the next stop, she stepped back under the canopy of the waiting area. She listened to several groups of people walking down the sidewalk, and shifted nervously. This was the hardest thing for her, waiting when she couldn't see what was around her. She wondered if she ever would get used to it, or the inkling of fear that something was going to happen.

She heard the car brake sharply. It pulled to the curb in front of her and she took another step back. The door opened. Rachelle could barely hear the man's voice offering to give her a ride over the roar of a large truck passing and the other bus leaving.

"No, thank you." She pulled back further and bumped into the bench.

"I promise you, it's no trouble." This time she heard the voice clearly, without the street interference. "In fact, I wanted to talk to you."

"Mr. Clairbourne?" Rachelle asked timidly.

"Sorry, I should have introduced myself." He had come around the car and was directly in front of her now, standing close.

"The truck passed, it made too much noise to recognize your voice."

"Of course, can I offer you that ride now?"

"It's not necessary. My bus should be here anytime." Rachelle shifted, embarrassed.

"Yes, well, it isn't any trouble, and as I said, I really would like to speak with you. I swung by the answering center on my way out. The room was empty. I obviously just missed you. Please, let me give you a ride." He reached out and took her hand. She didn't pull back, instead let him draw her forward.

"Are you sure it's not too much trouble?" She wished she could see his expression.

"Not at all." He opened the door and held it while she settled in before closing it and going around to the driver's side.

The rich smell of new leather surrounded her with an added musky smell she was beginning to associate with Britton Clairbourne. It was a pleasant smell, not overpowering. She wasn't good at identifying men's colognes, but whatever it was, she liked it. Trying to get her mind off the direction her thoughts were going, she fumbled with her seatbelt, getting it done up about the same time he settled in the seat beside her.

"All set?"

"Yes, thank you."

"Great, you'll have to give me your address."

She recited it.

"You're right on my way. I only live about five minutes from there."

"Oh."

"Yes, I have an apartment in The Heritage."

Rachelle knew the area where a group of charming old buildings that had been renovated into upscale apartments. She often admired the architecture of them before she lost her sight. "I heard they did a nice job on their remodeling. I always thought they were beautiful buildings."

"Yes, Steve did a wonderful job on them. Then again, his wife Cassie is a stickler for details."

"You're friends."

"I've known Steve for years. He and Cassie met while he was doing the renovating. It's quite a story. I'll tell you sometime, but right now we have our own psycho to deal with."

CB&EO

Britt cursed himself for bringing up the trouble when

Rachelle tensed in the seat beside him.

"You said you wanted to talk to me," Rachelle asked in a soft voice.

"How about we talk over something to eat?" He tried to make the suggestion sound casual.

"That's not necessary." Her head tilted away. The shy action caught his attention.

"I know it's not necessary. I just thought it would be nice."

"I should be getting home," Rachelle came back, her shyness still visible.

"Of course, I should have realized you had plans. I'm sorry to keep you." He felt bereft at the thought she had a boyfriend.

"Oh, no, that's not it." Her correction came fast. "It's … I hate to take up your valuable time."

"Don't worry about it. If you don't have anything planned why don't you join me?"

"I, I haven't been to restaurants much since my accident."

"Then it sounds like the perfect time."

"You don't understand. I might embarrass you."

"You could never embarrass me."

"A lot of people feel uncomfortable being around people with disabilities."

"I don't."

ᏨᏏᎣ

Rachelle realized what he said was the truth. He never treated her any different. "I'm trying to give you an out here."

"I don't want an out. I want to go to dinner with you."

She fell silent. "I still don't feel very comfortable going to restaurants yet."

"This from a woman who handles a computer better than I could ever dream of."

"That's familiar territory." She shrugged it off.

"How fast do you type?"

"Approximately a hundred and ten words per minute. That usually isn't necessary in most conversations though."

Britt shook his head. "Incredible, I get in the thirties, forty if it's a good day. Let me guess you play the piano too."

"Yes, how did you know?"

"That quick of fingers, you're kidding." He could see her slight blush brighten her cheek and he longed to reach out and run his finger along it. Rachelle Harris was a very compelling woman to him. "How about pizza?"

"Excuse me."

"How's pizza for dinner? It's a good finger food, and who cares how you eat it?" When he could see a slight hesitation, he pressed.

"Come on, I know a great pizza place near here and I'm starving. I'll even let you choose, as long as it has no anchovies."

"Awe gee, and just when I had my heart set on little fish swimming in tomato sauce and cheese. All right, if you're sure." She sounded slightly breathless which was like a flash of electricity to his heart.

"I'm sure." He hadn't meant to say it aloud, but when her blush deepened, he was glad he had.

Two minutes later he pulled into the parking lot. Rachelle waited while he came around to get her. Her hand reached for his and he helped her out, before placing it on his arm. Instead of hesitating steps, she moved fluidly with him, giving her trust to him to guide her.

Inside, the place was packed with people. Rachelle pressed closer to him as they were bumped into while waiting to be shown to their table. Instinctively, Britt slid his arm around her waist and was surprised when she turned slightly into his sheltering stance.

"Busy night," he said by her ear.

"Friday night, date night," she said back.

"Yes, of course, I forgot."

"You didn't have plans, did you?" she asked, tilting her head up toward his face.

"No, just a quiet evening trying to unwind, but this is much better."

The edge of her bottom lip caught between her teeth but before more could be said, the hostess came to show them to their table.

"If you'll follow me." The woman headed off leaving them to follow.

Britt wasn't certain how to move through the crowded room without Rachelle being tripped up, but she solved it for him. Shifting behind him, she rested one hand lightly on his waist. He reached back and caught her other hand, leading her around and through the crowded area with little trouble. She ran into his back once when someone stood in front of him making him stop short.

"Sorry," she apologized.

"Not your fault. Someone stood up." He shifted her around the table, away from the man blocking the way totally oblivious to their presence.

The table they were led to was out of the way, in a quieter corner as Britt had requested. He let Rachelle slide in the curved booth then slid in beside her.

CR80

With a sigh, Rachelle settled back into the seat, relieved to be out of the main noise and commotion. What had she been thinking, accepting his invitation? She knew the answer, though. She wanted to spend some time with Britton Clairbourne. It was foolish, but since he had come into her office, she couldn't stop thinking about him. Earlier when he'd laid his hand on her shoulder, she had felt the contact to her soul. It had calmed and excited her. Yes, it was foolish to think a man like him might be interested in her, especially now. But, for one night, she could dream and enjoy time with him.

"Name your toppings. If I don't agree we'll do a half and half."

She heard the menu open and said. "Since we already ruled out anchovies, I better tell you, I'm not big on pepperoni or sausage either. Weird, I know for a pizza lover."

"I can live with that. How about a Hawaiian or they have a BBQ chicken that is really good?" he suggested.

"All right, let's try the chicken, if that's okay."

'Thick or thin crust?"

"Thick, please."

"The lady has good taste." He gave the order when the waitress came up, then turned back to her. "Well, tell me about yourself. Are you from here?"

"No, I grew up in a little town about an hour south of here. My parents still live there and my two sisters and their families."

"Any brothers?"

"One. He lives just across the river. He's the oldest and the bossiest."

"And where do you fit in?"

"I'm third. The odd one of the bunch, both my sisters got married not long after high school."

"You went to college before coming to Clairbourne?" he asked, taking a sip from the drink the waitress set before him.

"Yes, to State. I started working at Clairbourne toward the end of my sophomore year."

"I guess this is putting you on the spot, but did you like it?"

"Very much, everyone was great. And my senior year I was accepted for the tuition assistance program so you paid for most of it."

"That says a lot for you. You have to be a good worker

and show great promise." Britt knew the competition for the program and what was required to make it. It was just one more thing to be impressed by her.

"I wanted to be an executive assistant."

"So we would've met eventually anyway," he said. Though he wasn't a strong believer in destiny, he wondered if it wasn't that he was to meet her. "I looked at your personal file. It said you were in a car accident."

"Yes, it was nice of your company to find a place for me. I'm very thankful."

"You're welcome. Do you like working executive answering?"

"Very much, Lois is wonderful. She mother's me, but not too much. She lets me do my job and is a good friend. As I said, I'm glad for the opportunity. I know it was a risk for you to hire me."

"I can't take credit for that. I didn't know about it, but I'd say the man in personnel deserves an award." His hand moved across the table taking hers.

"Actually, it was Mr. Goodsell, my old boss. He had faith in me and pressed for it. I don't know what else I would've done."

"You would have found something," he said, as Rachelle shook her head.

"Maybe eventually, but I needed something then to help me get my life back together. I had come about as far as I could go, just living on my own. My family was really pressing me to come home so they could take care of me. At first, I wasn't the easiest person to handle. I know they were trying to help but—"

"You needed to know you could do it by yourself." Britt got the drift of what she was trying to say. That drive was similar to the one he had. At age twenty-four, she'd become blind. At twenty-four, he'd taken over his family's electronics company and turned it into what it was today. He had overcome a lot of skeptics, who were stuck in the glue of the old ways of doing things. The people whose minds he could change, he did. The others he'd bought out, sinking almost every penny of his inheritance from his mother's family to do it. If he'd been wrong, he would've lost everything, but all his sacrifices had paid off. Clairbourne was exactly where he wanted it, and his investment had multiplied ten-fold.

Britt hadn't realized he was telling Rachelle all about it until she asked her next question. "Do you think that's who is behind these attacks could someone be jealous of what you've accomplished? Maybe one of the people you bought out?"

"I don't know," he said slowly. "I hadn't thought of the possibility. Listen, I'm sorry. I didn't mean to talk about that." He wanted to move the conversation back to about her.

"But you said you wanted to talk?"

"It can wait. I don't want to ruin dinner. The pizza should be here any minute."

"I'd just as soon get it over." Rachelle shifted his direction.

Britt wondered if the action was intentional. "I wanted to warn you, the police are planning to contact you."

"About the incident today?" She shifted again. "I heard no one was hurt."

"That's right. A cable broke, there was some property damage, but that's it."

"And the bomb?"

"There's nothing to worry about," he added quickly. "It's just you're the only one who's talked to this guy. They want to see if police psychologist can generate a profile, or maybe even come up with a clue about him."

"I put everything in the transcript, but I'm willing to talk to them if it might help."

"Thank you, I appreciate it. They'll call you sometime tomorrow. I'm sorry you got caught up in this."

"It's not your fault. I want to help if I can. I'm afraid someone's going to get hurt."

"Me too, I've added extra security, but he's managed to get into both places without anyone knowing. Anyway, let's talk about more pleasant subjects. What's your favorite flower?"

Rachelle laughed at his obvious change of subject.

"Oh, like most women, I like roses, but I'm also a pansies and sweet peas fan. Sweet peas have a beautiful smell. I like lilies. Actually, I like most flowers."

The pizza arrived, and the subject changed to music. They continued to talk while they ate. They lingered, stretching out their time until the waitress came over a second time after they finished eating and had boxed up the leftovers, to see if they needed anything else.

"I think that's a hint to leave," Rachelle observed.

"I'm enjoying myself," he said, reaching for her hand.

Rachelle followed Britt out the same way they came in. They were moving along extremely well until they neared the front entrance, where the area grew louder with a particularly large, boisterous group. Bodies became congested, bumping and jabbing into them.

Rachelle tightened her hold on Britt, but it didn't do any good when the next person instead of just bumping into her, fell against her knocking her away from Britt, to the ground. Pain jolted her body. Fear raced through her as she felt unknown hands grab at her.

Chapter Three

"Hey, beautiful, sorry about that."

The alcohol breath was so heavy in her face, Rachelle about gagged. Turning her head to the side did nothing to help.

"How about I buy you a drink to apologize, then maybe we can get to know each other better."

The words slurred over her like his breath on her neck. She cringed, but there was no escape from the weight pinning her down. It was the hand on her hip that released her panic. Swinging out the best she could, she hit him. Smashing her fists against him, not trying to calculate where the blows landed, or caring. There was swearing, then the man rolled off her, but the fear didn't end. A scream welled in her throat. When a hand touched her, the scream came out as a squeak, then the familiar voice feathered into her mind.

"Rachelle, it's all right. I have you." Britt's hand rested on her arm. Once he had her attention, the hand closed and he lifted her off the ground. Rachelle collapsed against Britt, wrapping her arms around him, clinging to him like he was her life line. Aware, that besides a few drunken laughs, the room had become silent.

Rachelle could hear someone asking Britt if she was all

right. Rachelle presumed it was the manager because he offered an apology before she heard him approach the drunk and ask him to leave.

ങ്ങ

Britt slid his hand up to her face, cupping her cheek, tilting her face to his. He knew she couldn't see him, but he hoped it would help her to focus on him. Fear was so alive on her face he could feel it. If it wasn't that Rachelle needed his attention, he'd liked nothing better than explaining a few facts to the creep the hard way. But right now, Rachelle was all that was important. She needed him.

"Are you hurt?" he asked taking care with each word.

There was a pause before her head began to move back and forth. "N ... no." It seemed an effort to get out.

When the manager's hand reached out and touched her arm, she jerked, pressing closer into him.

"It's all right," Britt said as his arm curved around her back, pulling her in even tighter.

"Sorry," the manager said. "Is she all right?"

"She'll be fine." He could tell the way the manager stared at Rachelle and shifted uneasy, that he just figured out she was blind.

"I ... I need your names for an incident report."

Britt gave their names then his office number. Again the man apologized. Britt brushed it off, excusing them. Keeping her held snugly to his side, he maneuvered them out. Fortunately, the people parted the way for them, because this time she was no longer steady on her feet.

Outside the door, he paused. "Rachelle, I want you to put your arms around my neck."

"What?" Her voice trembled, but as he moved her arms up, they circled his neck. "It's all right," he said as he slid his arm behind her knees. "I'm going to lift you up," he warned just before he did it.

He heard her gasp and her arms tightened on his neck.

"This isn't necessary," she said but her arms didn't loosen. "I'm feeling steadier now that we're outside."

The trembling had left her voice, but Britt had no desire to put her down. She felt good in his arms. "I know, but it will only be for a minute until we're in the car."

He headed down the steps.

cs≈so

Rachelle knew she was safe. Britton Clairbourne wasn't going to let anything happen to her. She also knew that any dream of ever going out with him again just ended after such a wonderful example of what going out with a blind woman was like. Britt was used to grace and beauty that drew attention, not being the center of attention while everyone was thinking 'what a shame for such a handsome man.' She heard the car door open and he settled her into the seat. His hand on her arm startled her, but she didn't jump.

"Rachelle." His voice was low, thick with concern.

"I'm sorry, I ruined your evening."

"You didn't. I'm sorry that happened."

"It wasn't your fault. The guy was drunk."

"It wasn't yours either."

"Yeah, but I didn't need to panic," she said downcast.

"Panic, I think you did well. Most women I know would have been screaming their heads off for the police and a lawyer."

"I guess I'm not much of a screamer." She shrugged.

"No, you're a fighter and the quiet, cuddly type. Which is okay, it's what I prefer, though I can't say I've had a lot of experience."

cs≈so

Britt wasn't sure what she would say if he said he really liked having her in his arms and that she was welcome there whenever she wanted. He didn't think Rachelle was the kind of girl that usually ended up in a guy's arms on the first date. Then again, this wasn't a date technically, and after what happened, his chances for a first date were pretty slim.

Her building wasn't hard to find. It was plain but seemed tidy and well-tended. After he came around to help her out, she turned his direction.

"Thank you for the pizza and the night out. It was nice to talk with someone for a while and I really appreciate the ride home."

"I'll see you to your door."

"That really isn't necessary. Once here, I can find it easily."

I'm sure you can, but let's say I'm old fashioned." Taking her hand, he placed it on his arm before she could object further.

Rachelle's apartment was on the third floor. Instead of taking the key from her, he waited while she unlocked the door then stepped inside with her. Other than being in the dark, the first thing he noticed was the sweet but gentle smell of raspberries. Rachelle stepped aside, taking off her jacket and hanging it up. "Would you like to have a seat?"

"Sure," Britt hesitated before he started to move, that was when the darkness must have dawned on her. "Oh, the lights."

He heard her gasp.

"I'm sorry. They're not still on, are they?"

"No."

"I have some on a timer, but they must have turned off already." She turned on the switch giving light to the room.

Britt wasn't sure what he expected but was a little surprised by the warm, pleasing feel of the room. It was neat, tidy and free from clutter. It wasn't even a quarter size of his apartment but didn't feel cramped. One thing that drew his attention was a group of pictures on the wall. Several portrayed a lively, smiling Rachelle in various locations with people that he guessed were her family and some friends. One in particular almost took his breath away. She was sitting on a rock in front of a lake. It was obvious she'd been hiking. A smile lit her face, and her head was tilted slightly to the side. He was certain it had been taken when she was unaware of it, but whoever took the picture had caught the true natural beauty of her.

"Can I get you something? I don't have any alcohol because it dulls the senses, though I wasn't much of a drinker before."

"I'm not much of a drinker myself." He caught the sight of her hiding a yawn. "Actually, I probably ought to go. It's getting pretty late."

"Sorry," her hand still covered her mouth. "I usually go to bed quite early so I don't have to get ready in a hurry to make it to the office. And I haven't been sleeping very well lately."

"This time, I think it's my turn to say I'm sorry, for getting you caught up in all this." He stepped closer to her.

"It wasn't your fault. Things just happen. You're not responsible for what other people do, no matter how they affect us," she said with more conviction than he'd ever heard from her.

"Sounds like good advice."

She blushed, "I spent a lot of time thinking about it after … my accident. Wondering what I had done to deserve what happened."

"Mind if I ask what did happen?"

"Car accident, I got hit in the front driver's side. A drunk driver. It was weird. I only suffered a few bruises, no broken bones. Not even much swelling from a concussion. They thought that I'd be fine, I was just knocked out, until finally I woke up and couldn't see."

"And what happened to the person who hit you?"

"He took off. He'd already had his license revoked for DUI. The police were able to track him down from witnesses. When they went to arrest him, he tried to run and rolled his car. He died, but luckily, he didn't hurt anyone else."

"He shouldn't have been on the streets in the first place."

"No, he shouldn't have, but it's still sad he died."

"You seem to have taken it in stride." He was surprised at her attitude.

"No. For the first month I was in denial. The next month I was a mess. Then I got mad, after that I came to face it. I realized I was letting what happened to me destroy my life and started to fight back. It took a couple months to really get used to living and truly functioning. Going back to work was terrifying. The first couple days, I was afraid that I would make a mistake. I even had a dream I ran into you in the hall one day. I mean literally ran into you."

"Too bad you didn't then I'd have met you sooner and under more pleasant circumstances."

"Not in my dream it wasn't." She shook her head.

"Was I that much of an ogre?"

She felt him move closer to her. "No, but you were a lot different then you are."

"Really, how am I different?"

"You're kinder, easier to talk to. I was tongue tied before. Well, I don't think I ever pictured you in my apartment, or that I'd feel comfortable with you."

"And do you feel comfortable?" he pressed, stepping closer.

"Yes, yes I do," she said more firmly, with a smile.

"I'm glad."

He was right in front of her now. Her face tilted up to him. In the soft light, he could see her trying to see him through the darkness. She was so inviting, so beautiful. He raised his hand and reached unconsciously to touch her, to run his fingers over the tender skin of her cheek. He wondered if it was as soft as it looked but stopped his hand just short. Rachelle wasn't his to touch, no matter how much he was beginning to wish it was so. No matter how easy it would be to lower his head and take those unprepared lips by the storm that was beginning to rage within him, he couldn't.

Britt forced himself to step back. "Good night, Rachelle." He crossed the room, pausing to look at the picture of the smiling woman on the lakeshore. Behind him, he heard her say a soft good-bye, that seemed to call him back, but he urged himself on.

"Don't forget to lock up after me." He was out the door. Britt stopped in the hallway trying to get his runaway thoughts in line. Whatever draw Rachelle Harris had over him, it was getting out of control. Maybe he'd been working too hard lately, maybe he needed a vacation or at least to get out more. When was the last time he dated someone? He'd gone to the charity fundraiser last month, but it had been almost a year since he had been seeing anyone regularly. Even then, he always knew something was missing in his relationship with Laura, though everyone said she was perfect for him. She was beautiful, intelligent, good bloodlines, and from a well-moneyed family. Everything proper and perfect for him, but nothing about her held his interest.

He heard the lock click on the door behind him. No, Laura didn't hold his interest, not like the woman on the other side of the door did. On the street below, he stopped and turned, looking up to her apartment. He wondered if she would remember to turn off the light. Almost as soon as the thought crossed his mind, the lights went out.

CROSO

Rachelle stood in the middle of the room after she heard the door close. She felt rooted in spot, her heart pounded. What was wrong with her? For a minute there she thought Britton Clairbourne was going to kiss her.

She was really getting delusional. He was being kind,

and she was blowing it all out of proportion. Her imagination was filling in the blanks that she couldn't see. Whatever it was, she was going to have to keep better taps on her runaway thoughts or she'd be setting herself up for a lot of hurt and embarrassment.

Funny, she had always been quite practical in her relationships. She had dated Richard for almost a year before she really considered they were serious, and then it still was hard to consider marrying him, though everyone talked like it was a done deal.

Maybe that was why his deserting her after the accident hadn't been so hard. At the time, it felt devastating. Then again, at the time, opening a can of soup was devastating. But when she made the turn to take her life back, she found she didn't miss him at all.

Britton Clairbourne had only walked out the door a couple minutes earlier, and she already missed him. No. She would not think like that.

ᏣᏅ

Rachelle just finished washing the plate and glass she used for lunch when there was a knock at her door. Feeling to make sure the chain was latched, she opened it. "Who is it?"

"Police, Detective Todd, are you Rachelle Harris?"

"Will you hold your badge to the door opening, please?"

She heard something brush the door and reached out, first bumping the leather before feeling the engraving.

"This is Dr. Lewis, she's a police psychologist."

"Hello, Miss Harris." The female voice came from the side.

"Just a moment, please." She closed the door and removed the chain, opening it back up. "Come in, please." She moved to the side, motioning them to be seated and followed them over.

"Were you notified of our coming?"

"Yes."

"Then you agreed to talk to us?"

"Yes, but I don't know what help I can be. I put everything he said to me in the transcript."

"Yes, we have a copy of that," Dr. Lewis said. "What we'd like to do is have you try to tell us how it was said to you the best you can. Roll playing it, if you will. Give us your feelings and impressions. Do you think you can do that?"

"Yes, I think so, if you read the transcript to me, I'll try to repeat it as close as I can to how he said it. Do you really think it will help?"

"It may help me get a feel for what we're dealing with," the psychologist answered.

"He's serious. He really wants to hurt Mr. Clairbourne."

"I agree, and we're taking the threats seriously, but we've got to find some clues to figure out who it is," the detective said.

Rachelle nodded. "Would you like anything or we can start now?"

"Let's start."

They were just finishing the transcript when there was another knock on the door. "Would you like me to get that?" Todd asked.

"Please," Rachelle answered.

She was surprised when she heard Britt's voice at the door.

ೞಬ

Britt was surprised when a man opened the door until he looked up and recognized Detective Todd. "Detective," he greeted the man.

"Mr. Clairbourne, this is a surprise."

"I wanted to be here while you talked to Miss Harris. I

just got caught up. How is it going?" He walked into the room.

"We're just finishing the transcript. Mr. Clairbourne, this is Dr. Lewis."

"Doctor," he greeted then turned to Rachelle, who was sitting on the couch. He moved forward, taking in her too pale face. "Rachelle, how are you?"

"Fine, thank you."

"Are you comfortable with Mr. Clairbourne here, or does he make you nervous?" Dr. Lewis asked.

Britt looked at Rachelle for signs that he might make her feel nervous, wondering if the psychologist picked up something. He didn't want to think that Rachelle might feel uncomfortable around him. What he saw was color warming her cheeks, and her face turned shyly to the side.

"It's fine. He doesn't make me nervous."

"Well, we're almost finished here."

Britt listened as they went over a few more lines then waited while the doctor wrote down the observations in her notebook.

It was the detective that broke the silence. "Well?" he asked the doctor.

"The man will not stop. He's filled with jealousy and wants revenge. He believes Mr. Clairbourne has done or is responsible for something done to him. So he has heaped every bad thing onto him. For him to win or to prove his importance, Mr. Clairbourne must 'pay.'" She made the motion of quote with her fingers.

"Who have you dated recently?" Todd turned to him.

"No one really. The last woman I dated even semi-seriously was a year ago, and our parting was mutual. How do we stop him?" Britt asked the doctor.

"Actually, he may have already given us the key."

The detective slid forward in his seat. "What?"

"Miss Harris," Dr. Lewis said simply. "I think that it's possible he blames Mr. Clairbourne for the loss of a woman he was obsessed with. I think he has shifted that obsession to Miss Harris."

Britt felt as if he had been punched.

"But I'd recognize the voice if I had met him," Rachelle objected.

"I doubt you have met him. It's your voice, or maybe that you were just pleasant when you first answered. And then, when he realized he frightened you, it brought out the protective instincts in him. It could be your voice reminds him of the woman he loved. Whatever it is, he has focused on you, and I think we can use it."

"How?" Todd asked.

"When he calls, and he will call again, Rachelle, you will need to keep him talking. Try to get him to give information about himself, maybe even set up a meeting."

"No," Britt cut her off. "No way, I don't want Rachelle, Miss Harris, anywhere near this guy."

"Don't worry," Todd came back. "We'd have it covered."

"No, I don't want her exposed to him. I don't even like the idea of her talking to him."

"I don't think we have a choice," Dr. Lewis spoke up, shifting toward him. "He has chosen her."

"I still don't want Rachelle put in contact with him. We can have someone else answering the phones."

"No," Rachelle exclaimed. "I can do this."

"It's not that I think you can't do it. I don't want you in danger from this psycho." Britt took a step toward her.

"He won't know who I am."

"Miss Harris," Todd interrupted. "I must point out, this man has been able to get into a couple of places in the company with very high security, plus gain access to specialized instruments. It's not unlikely he could find out who you are."

"Well, if he is obsessed with me, and has access, then it's more than likely he already knows who I am."

Britt didn't like what she said, but looking at the officer, it was obvious Todd agreed.

"I'll have a tap put on your phone immediately, if that's all right with you?" Todd asked.

"I'll move you to a hotel," Britt said at the same time.

It was Britt she chose to answer. "No, I'm not moving. This is my home."

"I won't have your safety jeopardized," he said it so forceful it made her jump.

"I'm not helpless."

"I don't think you are, but we know this man is dangerous. He's going to hurt someone, and I don't want it to be you."

"I don't want it to be me either, but if you read what he says, he wants to protect me, not hurt me."

Britt got her point, but it didn't change how he felt. "What if that changes? You could become a target."

"Mr. Clairbourne is right," Dr. Lewis agreed coming back into the conversation. "He could change in a minute, and it might not take much to agitate the change. You never know."

"Then we handle that when it comes, but as Mr. Clairbourne also said, someone is going to get hurt. So the sooner we catch this man the better."

"Someone else can do it." Britt didn't like being so stubborn with her, but unfortunately she could be just as stubborn.

She turned to the doctor. "Do you honestly think he will talk to another person and open up?"

They all waited for the doctor to answer. It was slow in coming, but after a moment she did. "No, no I don't." It was said softly. "But I must concur with Mr. Clairbourne. It could be dangerous. This man is highly volatile."

"But, if she's our only way to get him to talk." Todd joined Rachelle's side on the argument.

"First, we try it without her," Britt said firmly.

"Monday we'll have someone else screening executive calls."

"But," Rachelle started to object, he cut her off. "We'll trade you to take the other messages."

"What about Lois, if he comes after her?"

"I don't think that will happen, but if I have to, I'll assign security to watch over you both." There was finality in his voice.

Chapter Four

He had done it. She was so mad. She would have kicked him in the shins if she could've found them. When she got to work, Lois was assigned to accept the executive lines and she was to monitor the others.

Actually, she didn't mind monitoring the other calls, but she did mind Britton Clairbourne's high-handedness. Rachelle steamed again. One of the things she liked about him was the fact that he treated her like a competent person, not an invalid. It was amazing some of the stupid things people did when you couldn't see. One of the secretaries still hadn't gotten over talking loudly to her. Usually the thought made her smile, but not right now. Not today, she sat and stewed about the change in assignment.

"Rachelle," Lois' voice pulled her out of her thoughts. "I need to go to the ladies room. Can you cover me?"

"Sure."

"You okay?" Lois had already heard about it several times, and tried to point out Mr. Clairbourne was being wise and protective, and she thought it was kind of sweet.

"I'm fine."

"All right, I'll be right back." Lois stepped out the door while Rachelle turned to field a call for Mr. Douglas' office. Five minutes and three calls had passed when the next call came in.

"Clairbourne executive answering. May I help you?"

There was a pause on the line, she was about to repeat when the low voice came. "Angel Voice, I've been trying to call, but you haven't answered." Anxiety was heavy in the tone.

"I'm sorry. I've been handling other calls." Her heart pounded. It was him. "Have you called often?"

"Several times, I wanted to talk to you."

"I'm sorry I didn't answer." Rachelle did what Dr. Lewis suggested, giving sympathy, and trying to get him to talk. "What did you want to talk to me about?"

There was a pause. Her fingers waited over the keyboard. She quickly checked for her home position, and then almost lost it when he finally spoke.

"I saw you Friday night. You're so beautiful, innocent, and helpless. I want to take care of you."

"Where did you see me?" She fought to keep down the stab of fear she felt coming through in her voice.

"I watched you waiting at the bus stop. I drove around the block. I was going to offer you a ride. But, when I got back, you were already gone. Your bus must have come."

Not her bus. Britton had. If he hadn't, Rachelle shivered. "I'm sorry. I probably wouldn't have gotten in with you. I don't take rides from strangers. Do I know you? Have we met?" She tried to think of questions that would help her identify him.

"No. I want to meet you, but I can't right now." The voice seemed to drift.

"Why not?" she pressed, her fingers trembled slightly on the keys.

"I have to get Clairbourne first."

"Why?"

"Because he has to pay."

"For what? What did he do?"

"Only I can make him pay."

Rachelle knew she was losing him to his ramblings.

"He thinks he's so powerful. Mr. Almighty, in control, everything he touches comes out good. He doesn't care what he leaves, who he walks over."

"No, I don't believe that's true. Please listen." She tried but the voice kept coming.

"I'm going to take it all. Then he'll die."

"Please don't do this." Rachelle pleaded into the phone. "Someone might get hurt."

"Yes, they will, but don't worry, Angel Voice, you'll be safe." His tone dropped reverently.

"But what about other people? You just can't hurt innocent people?" She fought to keep her voice smooth, so she could reason with him.

"They're not innocent if they're around him. They deserve to be hurt."

"Why, why do they deserve to be hurt? I don't understand."

There was silence on the line. She waited for almost a full minute, knowing he was there. "Please, talk to me," she said softly.

"No one will get hurt today, but everyone will know I'm in control. I'm more powerful than Clairbourne."

This time the line went dead.

Rachelle slumped in her chair. She felt an arm slide around her and the familiar scent of Britton Clairbourne reached her as she was pressed into his shoulder. "It's all right." His words were low and rumbling. She didn't realize she was crying until she felt the roughened tips of his fingers tenderly brush the moisture from her cheeks.

A shaky sigh escaped her as she relaxed back against his shoulder. "How?" she managed to get out.

"Lois called when she got back and realized who you were talking to."

She nodded, straightening up slightly. "He's been calling all day but wouldn't talk to her."

"Shh." One hand ran comfortingly up and down her

arm. "Just a minute, wait until you feel better."

"I'm fine. He's going to do something again."

"Did he say what?" The gruff voice of Laslow startled her. She hadn't realized he was in the room.

"No." She pulled back, straightening her shoulders. "He said it would be noticeable." Rachelle forced herself back to the computer, typing to call back the recording and trace. As soon as the now familiar mechanical hum sounded, she requested the printed transcript. She sent it to the printer then to the file Britton had set up for them. By the time she'd finished, she had herself more in control.

❧

Britton watched Rachelle pull back, conscious of the older woman's eyes on him. He hadn't meant to take Rachelle in his arms. But from the moment he'd received the call then ran into the room and saw her at the terminal, he'd felt the need to hold her. When she slumped in the chair, it was instinct to reach for her.

It was also instinct to lift her into his arms, and carry her out of there, away from the world. Like a caveman back to his den. He wondered if Rachelle would be impressed if he did a little chest beating. He felt like beating something.

With calmness he didn't feel, he reached over taking the first page from the printer. His stomach tightened. The psycho knew who Rachelle was. He had watched her and would have approached her and picked Rachelle up Friday night if she hadn't gone with him. Now he really wanted to snatch Rachelle up and hide her away in his cave, where the psycho would never get near her.

"I'm sorry I couldn't get any more information." Rachelle called his attention back.

"You did wonderfully, but I thought it was agreed you weren't going to be answering the executive lines today."

"Lois needed a break," she said simply with a shrug.

Britton knew glaring at her wasn't doing any good,

though he suspected she knew he was doing it. "It looks like it was necessary, but we have a new problem."

"What's that?" Rachelle turned to him.

"He knows who you are. That might mean he might know where you live."

"I'm not going to leave my home," she said, knowing where he was going.

"I'll pay for everything."

"No, I'm not being chased out of my home. If I wouldn't allow blindness to do it, I'm not going to let phone calls do it."

"It's not just phone calls, and it's only for a couple days."

"If we're lucky and get some clues. But what if it turns into a week or two, or longer?"

"I'll cover it."

"No, I want my own home. I'm comfortable there. I know my way around."

"You could learn someplace else. It wouldn't take long."

"You're right I could, but I don't want to. At least not now, besides you read the message. He doesn't want to hurt me. He wants to save me from you."

Britt was torn between wanting to grab her and shake some sense into her or grab her and kiss her senseless. He knew which idea had the most appeal. "I'm not going to win on this, am I?" For the first time since he entered the room, a smile brightened her face.

"No."

He wasn't used to losing, but maybe it wouldn't be so bad losing to Rachelle. Glancing over at the other woman, she gave him a knowing smile that added to the feeling it wasn't so terrible losing this round. "I'll talk to you later. I left a meeting I need to get back to."

CREAD

Rachelle let out another sigh when Britt and the security chief left. Trembles from the delayed shock ran through her body.

"Are you all right?" She felt Lois' hand on her arm.

"Yes, of course. It's just a little scary. What do you think he'll do?"

"He won't let it interfere. He's not the type of man to run scared or back down," Lois said confidently. "Even if he let you have your way."

"I didn't mean Mr. Clairbourne. The caller, I need to come up with something to call him. Just 'the man' sounds too eerie." She shivered.

"I don't know what he'll do. He's crazy, if you ask me. You know, if you're frightened, you can stay with me," she volunteered, giving her arm a squeeze.

"Thanks, but you have a houseful with Jody's family staying with you while their house is under construction. Besides, like I told Mr. Clairbourne, I refuse to be run out of my home. And I would probably kill myself tripping over one of the grandkid's toys or at least take out a couple of lamps. I still have to be careful of them, I'm at three and holding."

"Well, if you change your mind, we'll make room for you. You're always welcome. I can't promise about the toys, but I can put the lamps away."

Rachelle gave a small laugh. "Thanks, I appreciate that, but I'm okay."

"Miss Independent," the woman muttered. "I wonder if you've met your match."

"What do you mean?"

"Oh, come on. I know you can feel it. Britton Clairbourne."

"Am I that transparent?" Rachelle groaned.

"A little, but I was talking about him. He likes you."

"It's a good thing it's about time to go home because you're losing it. Mr. Clairbourne interested in me."

Rachelle shook her head in disbelief.

"You might not be able to see how he looks at you, but that man has a thing for you."

"That man could have any woman he wants."

"And if he wants you?"

"Come on, Lois, that isn't even funny. I used to see pictures of the women he took out in the society pages, and believe me, there wasn't a blind virgin among them." She didn't bother to keep the sarcasm from her voice.

"Don't sell yourself short."

"I'm not, I'm realistic. Even my fiancé, who was supposed to love me, and thought I would be the perfect proper wife before I had my accident, didn't think so after."

"Richard was a jerk and not good enough for you."

"Yeah, well I didn't get him."

"Aren't you lucky?"

"Sure, I got a psycho who likes my voice," she sighed. "I'm sorry. I know you're trying to lighten my mood, but teasing me about Britton Clairbourne isn't the way. Right now it would be better for me to stick to reality."

⋘⋙

Reality slipped a little when she got home and tripped over a package as she walked into her apartment. She wasn't sure what was so ominous about the shoe box sized package, but she was reluctant to pick it up. Shutting the door, she fingered it a minute longer before pulling loose the tape. With shaky fingers, she pushed the packing out of the way until she touched the piece of satin, running her fingertip over it to the delicate porcelain face. Silky hair clung to her finger as she lifted the figure from the box. When she felt the wings of the angel, she almost dropped it.

Her breath caught. Panic hit her senses. He'd been there, at her apartment. Had he been there in the hall watching her arrive? Was he still out there watching? Leaving the package on the table, she made her way to the window, stumbling in her haste. She hit the end table. Rachelle reached for the lamp but was too late. It crashed to the floor. "Four lamps," she groaned. At least this one was brass, so the breaking glass would only be the light bulb. It took her a second to close the curtain. Ignoring the package, she cleaned up the glass, replaced the bulb, then righted the lamp.

Rachelle longed to call the number Britt had her memorize and place on her speed dial, but she refused, knowing he himself would pack her up and move her to a hotel, no matter what she said. Instead, she called the other number she had added to her speed dial, the police station.

"Detective Todd, please," she asked when an officer came on line.

"He's not in right now. Can I take a message?"

"Yes, please. This is Rachelle Harris. I'm involved with the problems at Clairbourne Industries. Detective Todd talked to me on Saturday." Great, rambling again. "Anyway I received a package from the guy doing it."

"A package? What kind of a package?"

"A box with an angel in it."

"Are you certain it's from our perpetrator?" She could hear the interest in the officer.

"Yes."

"Where was it delivered from?"

"It was waiting outside my door."

"You're certain it's from our guy?"

"Yes, when I felt the angel I knew."

"Felt, you touched it?" He snapped.

"Yes, I'm blind, but it's what he calls me, Angel Voice."

"All right, ma'am, I'm sending someone right over to pick it up. Please don't handle it further."

"I won't." It was said with easy certainty. Rachelle put the phone down and stood a moment trying to still her breathing. Deciding some music would help calm her, she put on the CD her sister gave her for her birthday and went to fix dinner. She was interrupted by the arrival of the officer, who took her statement and the package.

After dinner she called her sister Joann, who she had missed talking to the day before. They went through the normal things; family, work. She didn't mention the calls and attacks. Though her family had heard of the bombing on the news, she didn't want them to know she had any involvement, and assured her sister she hadn't been anywhere near it.

"So have you met any new and exciting men lately?" Joann teased.

"As a matter of a fact, yes, I have." Rachelle couldn't resist answering.

"You have! Tell!"

"Well, he's tall, dark and handsome," Rachelle started.

"Oh, come on, don't tease. I want to know." Joann almost pleaded.

"He is. He's also very nice, though he does have quite a domineering side."

"Where'd you meet him? Is he safe?"

Safe wasn't a word she'd use to describe Britton Clairbourne, but he did make her feel that way. "He's a very good man, hard working. I met him at work. He came to my office because of some problems with a message."

"You're dating?"

"No, but we did go out to dinner."

"You went out. This man must be something."

"It's really nothing." Rachelle was beginning to feel uncomfortable. "He wanted to ask me some questions and offered me a ride home and we stopped for pizza."

"That's all?"

"Yes."

"You sure you won't be seeing him again?" Joann sounded so disappointed, Rachelle almost felt like crying herself. Especially after what Lois said, about Britt liking her. He probably did as an employee.

"He's my boss."

"Mr. Matthews, he's not tall."

"No, Mr. Clairbourne."

"You had dinner with Britton Clairbourne?" The air of shock hung heavy.

"Yes."

"That man is a serious hunk. Wow!"

"What would Robert say to you talking like that?"

"I'm married, not dead. Besides Robert knows I think he's the only hunk for me. But wow, you had dinner with one of the most eligible bachelors in the state."

"It was nothing. He was being nice," Rachelle insisted feeling a flush of warmth on her face.

೧౩೮౦

Britt shoved a hand back through his hair. He wondered what Rachelle would say if he stopped by this late at night. Glancing at his watch, he realized she was probably asleep, snug in bed. He wished he was. He'd been so busy fighting damage control he had yet to eat.

Their guy had made his statement. This time the bomb was set on the sculpture in the quad. But the psycho had been wrong, someone had gotten hurt. A custodian coming across had got hit by a piece of flying cement. It was minor, six stitches, but the first blood was drawn.

Britt proceeded across the quad glancing toward what was left of the statue.

"We're done here for now." Detective Todd came toward him.

"Thanks," he glanced at the group of reporters waiting on the other side of the police tape.

"Do you want an escort to your car?" Todd asked, following his gaze.

"No, I'll hold them off with a promised press conference in the morning. Hopefully they'll accept that and give us some time to think how to handle this."

"That would be good. I'd like to go over details with you before you talk to them. I really don't want a copycat."

"I'll second that," Britt agreed. With a heavy sigh, he headed toward the group, blinking as camera flashes blinded him.

Chapter Five

Rachelle stepped off the bus feeling a heavy sense of anxiety. She was late for the first time since she returned to work. Her night had been plagued with nightmares; from someone watching her, followed by going out with Britt and making a fool of herself, bumping into things and knocking them over while all around people laughed, and Britt turned away to a group of gorgeous women. Finally, she got to a sound sleep only to sleep through her alarm, so she missed her bus.

She felt awkward on the unfamiliar bus, especially when she almost sat in someone's lap when the person didn't answer her. Then, to top it off, the bus started before she was seated and she fell, snagging her nylons.

She hoped, as she pushed through the revolving door into the lobby, that the whole day wasn't set to go that way. The loud hum of voices and confusion greeted her. She was tempted to follow the door around and back out, but forced herself to step out onto the marble floor only to lose her sense of direction when someone bumped into her. Several more people brushed against her, and she became completely lost. A wave of panic hit her, but she pushed it down. Forced to resort to groping, and having to make several apologies, she made it to the wall.

Frustration mounted as she moved, clinging to the wall. Thankfully she didn't run into any more people. When she made contact with the drinking fountain, she stood for a moment thankful to know where she was. Taking a deep steadying breath, she turned her attention to the buzz of voices around her.

Someone yelled out a question about the latest bombing affecting business. While another asked about security at the same time. The voice that answered had her turning in that direction. Britton Clairbourne's voice carried through the lobby.

"As I've said, we'll be continuing business as usual, just with extra security. We're cooperating totally with the police and government officials. They are doing everything they can. I have great faith in them. We'll figure out who's doing this. I want this company to be a safe and comfortable place to work."

Work, she was late for work. Rachelle tried to move forward to the elevator, only to be pushed aside again as people suddenly shifted. She lost contact with the wall, then her sense of direction, as she once more was bumped and pushed around. She wanted to scream at everyone to stop. She wanted to drop to the ground and cry, to be out away from all the people. She wanted Britt to come take her into his arms as he did a few nights earlier and make everything all right.

She turned and a woman yelled, "Mr. Clairbourne, Detective Todd," right in her ear. She heard the bell of the elevator not far away and tried to head toward it, only to come up against the brick wall of a man's chest.

"Excuse me." She tried to shift around him unsuccessfully. Frustration changed to fear in two words she heard uttered.

"Clairbourne will …" That was all she caught as she was either pushed away or the man walked off, but it was enough to know the man who was after Britt was there.

Right there in the lobby with her, security, the police, and Britt.

"Britt." She turned in the direction she heard him talking to reporters. This time it was her doing the pushing. She forced her way through the crowd, trying to reach his voice while not panicking. She tripped over a foot, but didn't fall because the people were packed too tight. Her ankle twisted enough to bring tears to her eyes, but she didn't stop.

"That will be all for now." Britt was saying. "We'll keep you abreast of any developments." His voice was moving. She was losing him.

"Britt," she yelled, pushing her way through.

osso

Britt heard his name called and turned in time to see Rachelle push her way toward him. Panic showed on her face, she turned her head frantically as if looking for him. One reporter bumped her, and she stumbled barely keeping her balance.

"Rachelle," he said, and she turned his way, reaching out. The crowd parted, letting him through. Ignoring all the other people, he caught her, pulling her close while wrapping his other arm protectively around her.

For a moment, she sagged against him, as if soaking up his strength. "We need to keep you out of crowds, then again," he felt the pressure of her against him, "maybe not."

Unfortunately she didn't stay close long. Pushing back, she tilted her head up. "He's here. He's here in the lobby."

"What?" It took a second to shift his thoughts from her pressed against him.

"He's here, in the lobby. I heard his voice." Panic filled her voice.

"You're certain?" His head shot up, looking over the crowd of people.

"Yes."

"Todd," he drew the detective's attention, bringing him close.

"He's here, Rachelle heard his voice."

"Is she certain?" The detective started scanning the lobby. "Where?"

"I was over by the elevators. I'm not certain where. People kept bumping into me."

"There must be a hundred men in here." Todd didn't hold back his frustration.

"Yeah, but that's a lot less than we had earlier."

"Right, I want you to walk around and try to talk to everyone, and have Rachelle see if she can identify the voice again."

"Can't you just have everyone held here?" Rachelle asked.

"Too many people, too many places he could duck out before we could get it closed off, and about half the crowd has thinned out already. Odds are he left already but it's worth a try. We also don't want to tip our hand. You might get lucky and find him," Todd answered.

"But if we can get him." Rachelle tried to protest.

"Then we will but I'm not sure I can arrest him just on the sound of his voice through a telephone. I'll need more proof, solid evidence that will hold up in court."

"But it was him, I know it."

"All right, I believe you. Let's cover the lobby the best we can." The detective patted her hand.

Fifteen minutes later most of the people had left, and Britt had talked with all that remained.

"Well, that's it," the detective said.

"None of them were him," Rachelle said dejectedly. "But I know he was here."

"It's all right, Rachelle." Britt tightened the hold he had on her hand. "It's not over. We can get copies of all the film then identify all the men here."

"Then I can talk to them all," Rachelle agreed.

"Well, in time we'll work it out so you can hear them all, but I don't want it to be face to face." Britt tried to add.

"But then … I can help. I know I can identify him."

"I know you can," Britt assured her, "but for now why don't I walk you upstairs?"

She was quiet a second. "It's not necessary to see me up. If you just show me to the elevator I'll be fine, and you can see about the video. I'm sorry I can't give you a description."

"Now, don't do that. You've given us the only leads we have." Britt knew he sounded stern, but he didn't want Rachelle feeling inadequate. Most people in her position wouldn't want to get involved, even if they weren't blind.

"You know, we could have you go around and talk to all your employees, on the pretext of reassuring them, and take Rachelle to see if she can find the person," Todd suggested.

"No," Britt said quickly.

"You think it's an employee?" Rachelle asked.

"It's a possibility. Whoever it is seems to know his way all over Clairbourne. It's easy to blend in when people aren't expecting someone not out of place."

"I could talk to people."

"No," Britt repeated.

"Maybe spend time in the cafeteria?"

"No!" This time his voice was sharper.

"But why?" Rachelle was becoming frustrated.

"What I said before, I don't want you near him. I don't want you to become a target."

"But what difference would it make? He already knows who I am." Rachelle tried to point out. The man could be so stubborn.

"I don't want to give him any reason to come after you."

"But."

"That's final, why don't I escort you upstairs now."

"Don't bother, just show me to the elevator. I'm quite capable of getting myself there." Her steely tone said as much as her words.

As soon as the elevator doors closed behind her, Todd turned to him. "I think you made someone angry at you."

"Yeah, well, it's for her own good." Though he tried not to let it show, it bothered him. Britt was unable to take his eyes off the elevator doors. He didn't want Rachelle upset with him. He just hoped he would be able to fix it in the future, because he was certain now, he wanted a future with her.

"Most people would welcome all the help and support they could get at a time like this, especially wrapped in such a nice package."

"With what that guy said, people around me could get hurt." Britt turned with a shake of his head.

"Bad timing." There was sympathy in the detective's voice. "That's quite a lady."

"Tell me about it." Britt looked back at the elevator Rachelle had just stepped into. "Real lousy timing."

ଔଛ

Rachelle was fuming as the elevator rose. Britton Clairbourne was impossible. She could find the man's voice, she knew she could. It made sense for her to talk with everyone she could. The elevator arrived at her floor. She got off and made it through the main area, still abuzz with talk of the press conference. Rachelle followed the hall on the right. The farther from the secretarial pool she got, the quieter it became.

Rachelle welcomed the calm. Her insides felt anything but. Turning down the last hall she heard someone say 'good morning Rachelle' and automatically returned the greeting as she passed the doorway. Five more steps down the hall, she bumped into someone.

"Excuse me," she apologized, her thoughts not leaving the man downstairs that infuriated and attracted her.

The man she bumped into said nothing, stepping aside to let her past.

"Sorry," she looked back reflexively but couldn't see the arm that came around her. One hand clamped over her month holding back her scream, as his other arm locked over her arms pinning them to her body. Taken totally by surprise, she was dragged across the hall before she could begin to struggle. Rachelle heard the door close behind them and began to fight. Kicking out, she twisted her head from side to side trying to dislodge the hand which tightened, pulling her head back. His fingers bit into her mouth.

"No talking, Angel Voice."

The voice sent fear straight through her. He lifted her off the ground and gave her a shake that would have rattled her teeth if his hand wasn't there.

Stay calm, she said over and over again in her mind and forced herself to relax.

"You were very foolish. I warned you, and you went to Clairbourne. I saw you go to him. You have to stay away from him." He gave her another shake. "I can't protect you if you don't stay away from him."

Rachelle tried to hold back a whimper as the hand squeezed down. The arm on her waist was hard muscle and felt like it would snap her in half. "You have to stay away from Clairbourne!" The voice growled in her ear then the arm was gone. With all the air squeezed out of her and the support gone, Rachelle went down. Her arms went out to catch her but it was her head that connected with something. A sharp pain knifed through her head, then faded as she dropped into nothingness.

Chapter Six

"If you're done with me, I think I'm going upstairs," Britt said, as they ended their discussion on what to do next.

"We're done. I'll let you know when I get copies of all the reporters' photos and stills from the video." Todd held up the surveillance tape they'd just picked up. "Are you going to stop and see someone on your way upstairs?"

Britt looked to the elevator one more time. "I think I might."

"Good idea," the man said.

"Match making, detective?"

"Just a man who's learned not to let a good thing slip away."

"Sounds like experience." Britt looked to the lawman.

"You could say. I met the right woman, but I pulled back. I was worried about dangers of my job, worried about leaving a widow."

"I have a feeling there's more to this."

"Yeah, she was killed when she stopped to get gas and walked into a robbery. The kid was so strung out he didn't even know he shot her."

"Man, I'm sorry."

The detective nodded. "Just be careful what you let slip away."

Britt entered the elevator with the thought going over again in his mind. Stopping on the fourth floor, he greeted several people as he passed.

"Good morning, Lois." He stepped in the office, glancing to Rachelle's empty desk. "Where's Rachelle."

"I'm not sure, and I'm worried. She's never been late before. I've called her home but there's no answer."

"She was downstairs and got on the elevator a good fifteen minutes ago."

"But," Lois stood, "let me try the ladies room."

Britt followed her out of the room. He stopped at a room with an open door down the hall. "Have you seen Rachelle Harris this morning?"

"She passed here at least fifteen minutes ago."

"Thank you." He turned back as Lois came toward him.

"She's not there."

"She passed here but didn't make it," he paused in the middle of his sentence. There were only two doors between where they stood and her office. Lois moved to the closest to check while Britt stepped across the hall.

He pushed open the door to the supply room but wasn't ready for the sight of Rachelle lying motionless on the floor. Fear like he had never experienced hit him. "Rachelle." He dropped beside her, feeling a burst of elation as she stirred slightly. "Rachelle," he brushed back her hair, stoking a finger over her silky cheek. He heard Lois gasp behind him, and figured the woman would call for help.

Rachelle stirred again, her eyes fluttered open. She blinked as if to focus them, confused. With a groan, she lifted her hand to her forehead.

"Lay still." He caught her hand. "I'll get the paramedics."

"Britt," she tried to push up.

"Don't try to move."

She ignored him, pushing her way into a sitting position. "I'm okay," she said, but reached for him for balance. Britt slid his arm around her, urging her body against his.

"It's my head."

"Let me see." Placing a hand under her chin, he tilted it up, gently sliding his hand into her hair. When he touched a bump, she flinched.

"You have quite a bump. Lois has someone on the way." He was certain that was where the woman had disappeared to after he heard her at the door.

"I'm okay, if you'll just help me up." She started to rise.

"You should stay still," he objected, but again it didn't stop her.

"I'm fine." She kept a hold of his arm to steady herself. "Where am I?"

"In the supply room just down the hall from your office, you don't remember where you were?" he asked concerned.

"I wasn't sure where he dragged me, though it didn't seem far."

"He?" Britt asked, feeling his stomach muscles tightening again.

"He was here. The caller. I was coming down the hall and bumped into someone, when I moved to pass, he grabbed me. He put his hand over my mouth so I couldn't scream, and pulled me in here."

"Are you all right?"

"Yes, I bumped my head when I fell trying to get away from him."

"Come on. Let's get you out of here, so I can call security." He lifted her into his arms, bringing a squeal and her arms around his neck. He went down the hall to her office, settling her into her chair next to the astonished Lois.

"Medics and security are on their way."

"Thank you." Britt sat on the corner of Rachelle's desk.

"Just rest a minute then you can tell me what happened. I'll get you a drink." He left the room.

"Rachelle," Lois started, but her phone cut her off. "Just a minute." Lois answered the phone. A few seconds later Rachelle's phone rang too. She automatically reached for the headphones, sliding them into place.

"Clairbourne Industries, executive answering. May I help you?"

"You're all right. I was afraid I hurt you."

Rachelle flinched at the voice. "You did."

"I didn't mean to. I just wanted you to understand that you have to stay away from Clairbourne."

"But you were the one that hurt me, and you hurt the gardener too after you said no one would get hurt."

"He was in the wrong place and I said I was sorry. I didn't mean to."

"But people are getting hurt. You have to stop this."

"No! Clairbourne's got to pay."

"Why? What does he have to pay for? What did he do to you?" Rachelle pressed then paused when he didn't answer. "If you want me to stay away from him you have to give me a reason."

"He took her away." The voice yelled in the phone.

"Who? Who did he take away?"

"I loved her but she couldn't see me because of him." The voice quieted. "She was so beautiful. You're beautiful. You have a beautiful voice. She had a beautiful voice too. I used to listen to her sing when she was in the shower. Do you sing?"

"Yes, at my piano. I like to sing. What was her name?" She tried again, desperately searching for words to keep him talking.

"Will you sing for me? I promise not to hurt you

again."

"I don't want you to hurt anyone. If you promise not to hurt anybody, I'll sing for you."

"Do you know the song Aubrey. That was her song. I memorized it."

"I know the song. I'll sing it to you if you promise not to hurt anyone."

"I have to. Clairbourne's got to die. Then she can rest and not feel bad. He has to die."

"No!" Rachelle cried out, but he was already gone.

"It was him." Britt's voice sounded behind her.

Rachelle nodded, too choked up to talk.

"You shouldn't have answered the phone."

"I didn't expect it to be him."

"You should've been resting. I'll take you home."

"That's not necessary."

"You were attacked."

"I'm trying not to think about that. Do you want me to go home and keep thinking about it over and over all day?"

"No, I don't want anything happening to you at all." He took her hand, running his thumb over her knuckles.

"Well, it did, so face it," she said bluntly, pulling back. The next instant she felt his arms around her and tears slipped free.

"I'm not going to cry. I'm not going to let him beat me." Still, she pressed her face into Britt's shoulder, unable to let go. It felt too good to be in his arms.

"Mr. Clairbourne, the medics would like to check her over now." Lois's words reminded Rachelle where she was and she pulled back, embarrassed.

"I'll make ... you a copy of the last conversation." She turned to the keyboard before he could stop her. It only took seconds to call up the print, and transfer it to his file to get herself back under control.

The medics then checked her out and pronounce that she should be okay, but she should take it easy. With advice that if she felt any dizziness or nausea to see her doctor they left.

"You sure you wouldn't like me to take you home?"

"No, I think I'll just go to the ladies room to freshen up." She ruined her self-composed image by wobbling a little as she stood.

"I'll go with her," Lois volunteered, moving beside her.

Britt tried to focus on the paper he'd just taken from the printer, but his thoughts were on Rachelle. The caller had attacked her, ten feet from her office, in the middle of his building, and no one had seen anything.

"Come on," he said to his security chief, who had come in a minute earlier. "I want to check with everyone on the floor to see if anyone was hanging around who wasn't normally supposed to be here."

Five minutes later they were back in the still empty office. No one had seen anything.

"This guy is like a ghost who comes and goes as he wants," Britt exclaimed in frustration.

"Or a figment," Laslow said.

"What do you mean?"

"No one else has talked to this guy. No one's heard him and he has attacked only Miss Harris."

"What are you saying?" Britt got his drift but didn't like it at all.

"Maybe she's making it all up." The security man waved the paper he was holding.

"Why?"

"A number of reasons. Attention. She gained a lot of attention, from you especially." His voice was full of scorn.

"And I suppose she made the bombs."

"Maybe they're a coincidence, or maybe she has someone helping her. She's pretty enough to lead some poor sap astray. A lot of men would do anything for what she has to offer, and when the lights go out, it doesn't matter if she can't see."

The gasp at the door jerked Britt's attention that way. He could tell by the expression on Rachelle and Lois' face that both women had heard everything that was said. And while Lois looked angry enough to take both men apart, Rachelle looker paler, more broken than when he found her on the floor of the supply room.

Britt straightened from where he leaned on the desk as she started talking.

"Why would I do this?" Her words were muted and rough. As if they had to be forced out.

"Rachelle." Her name was drowned out by Laslow's answer.

"Revenge, maybe you blame Clairbourne for your accident. It happened on your way home after you had stayed late working."

"It had nothing to do with work. It was an accident. Clairbourne was the only one who'd take a chance to hire me back," she defended.

"But they wouldn't cover the operation."

"It's not their choice. It's the insurance company's."

"Still," Laslow started again.

"Enough," Britt cut him off. "Leave her alone. I don't believe Rachelle has anything to do with this, except our guy's fascination with her." He sent his security chief a threatening look when it looked like the man would argue further. "Rachelle, why don't you come in and sit down and tell us what happened when he was here?"

Her head shook. "I think I'll take you up on the offer to go home. I don't feel very well after all."

"Rachelle."

She stepped back further in the hall. "Nothing happened. I got lost. I fell and bumped my head. What do you expect out of a blind woman?"

Britt wasn't letting it end. "Stop it."

"No," she said defiantly. "Lois will you get me my

purse? I don't know where it is." She held out her hand while the other secretary moved past the men to get her bag.

"I'll take you home," Britt said, figuring it was best to let her cool off with having her own way.

"No, thank you. I think I'll take his advice and stay away from you."

He knew she was referring to the attacker but she was so curt about it the words ripped through him. He felt an incredible loss. In fifteen minutes, he had gone from her wanting to help and support him, to not wanting to be around him. It was tearing him up.

The moment the purse touched her hand, Rachelle turned to Lois. "I'll call you later." She turned away and walked off, head held high.

The older secretary gave enough time for Rachelle to move down the hall before turning on them. "You have some serious problems," she said to the security chief in a very disparaging way, then turning to Britt. "And you, for a smart man are incredibly stupid. I don't care if you fire me. That is the sweetest, kindest woman there ever was. Even before the accident, she would never hurt anyone." Turning back on Laslow, she jabbed her finger at his chest. "As to your crude comment, you couldn't be farther off. Not that it's your business, Rachelle doesn't sleep around. She didn't even sleep with her jerk fiancé."

Britt's mind dropped everything but fiancé. "She has a fiancé?"

"Had. The jerk couldn't handle the fact she might be blind. That didn't fit his image of perfect show piece and hostess. He ended their engagement about her second week out of the hospital, as if she didn't have enough to handle at the time."

Britt had mixed reactions of wanting to plant his fist in the man's face, and happy there was no one in her life.

"Now, if you'll excuse me, I have some work to do

before I decide to take the day off also."

ఆౙౚ

Rachelle was trying to keep the tears in check all the way down the elevator and through the lobby. At the door she paused, slipping her hand in her purse to pull out the little sonar type instrument the size of a cell phone. It was an experimental devise made by Clairbourne for going into areas where night vision goggles were not helpful. Her former boss had arranged for her to try out the sonar to see if it was practical for sight limited people.

In areas where everything was familiar like home and the office building she didn't use it, but outside, it helped her to move around without having to grope or use a stick. Rachelle used it to follow the sidewalk. Picking up the cars in parking lot, she turned and headed for the street toward the bus stop.

"Rachelle."

She heard Britt's voice behind her. Not wanting to stop, she kept going. The sounds of his footsteps on the cement were gaining on her rapidly. "Rachelle," he said again, reaching her arm. Startled, Rachelle jerked and dropped the sonar.

"No!" Rachelle cried out as she heard it hit the ground. Dropping down, she moved her hands around searching for it.

"Rachelle, I have it." Britt caught her arms pulling her up.

"Is it broken?"

"The case is cracked, but it looks to be operating all right."

"No, I was given it with special permission for a trial." The tears she had been fighting for the last fifteen minutes slid free.

"It's all right," he took her into his arms. "I'll fix it. I happen to have an in with the designer." He held her to him a minute. "You know, I was asked about giving the sonar to an employee to try about six months ago. I don't know why it didn't register earlier it was you. I guess because I hadn't seen you use it."

"When I'm in a familiar place, I've tried to train myself to move with my senses, but when I'm outside or in an unfamiliar place, it's amazing."

Britt realized that she was focused on the instrument and not what had happened inside and decided to use it to keep her talking to him. "I've got the report you gave on it. Two months ago we placed fifty units at a blind school. I expect the report back in a month. If it's favorable, and the other tests go well, I hope to have them available to anyone who is blind. It wasn't what it was invented for, but it should have been. It's so simple. When it was developed and working successfully, I saw the possibility. That's why when Ralph said he had someone to test it. I agreed immediately."

"Why are you telling me this?"

"Because I'm hoping it will soften your heart enough to let me drive you home. I don't believe a single word Laslow said about you. I never did. I know you wouldn't do that, and I especially know you wouldn't hurt anyone. Please accept my apology. Let me take you home."

"If you'd like, I could come back into work." Rachelle couldn't keep her anger up.

"No, I think you should go home." Taking her arm, he led her to his car. He opened the door and helped her in. They had only gone a block when he asked, "Are you feeling a little more forgiving?"

"Yes, I'm not good at staying mad."

"A peacekeeper."

"Yes."

"Good. Then maybe you'll be willing to give in on a couple other requests."

"What did you have in mind?"

"I'd like to stop and have a doctor look at you."

"I'm fine."

"Yes, but you were unconscious for around ten minutes. I'd feel much better if you were checked out."

Rachelle was about to object when he added. "Consider it insurance for the company liability. I'd hate to have you come back and sue me."

"I would never do that," she protested. "It wasn't your fault."

"Well, that's debatable. Will you go?"

"Yes," she sighed. "If it will make you feel better."

"It will."

"What's the second thing?"

"Will you go with me to talk to Detective Todd? I want to report the attack on you and give him the latest transcript."

"Yes, of course."

"Thank you. Do you have a certain doctor you'd like to see?"

"Not really, I usually just go to the clinic and see whoever's available. I hadn't needed a doctor much before my accident and then they just assigned me to someone."

"All right, we'll go to my doctor if you don't mind."

"That's fine." Rachelle settled back in the comfortable seat. The car had the new car smell to it, but it was Britt's scent that filled her senses. He had a fresh, clean scent that was musky male but not heavy cologne. It was distinctively him. She liked it. She knew she would always be able to pick him out in a crowd.

"Are you sure you're all right? You were awfully agreeable and now you're very quiet."

Rachelle felt the soft touch of his finger on her cheek. "It's just," she paused to formulate her thoughts. "I didn't like being angry with you." When his finger gently traced her cheek again, she continued turning like a flower to the sun, to his touch. "It felt wrong and … it hurt." She dropped her chin, embarrassed by what she'd said.

She heard the turn signal then felt the car pull off the road and stop. This time when he touched her it was his whole hand that cradled her chin, tilting it up.

"You're right."

She felt his breath on her face, as he leaned closer.

"It did feel wrong, but this feels right." His words dropped low just before she felt his lips brush across hers lightly then again, giving her a chance to become accustomed to him before he settled in. His fingers slid into her hair, tilting her to him as his lips did their magic. Rachelle got lost in the sensation so different from any other she'd ever had before. She wondered if it was because it had been so long since she had been kissed, or that she couldn't see, only feel, but the kiss was heightened with electricity.

A little "umm" that came from deep inside Britt suggested it was the same for him, as did the words that followed. "Now that was right." He pulled back only to brush his lips against hers again, snagging one more taste of her still sensitive lips, before settling back in his seat. "We'd better get going before we draw a crowd."

Rachelle blushed, realizing it was broad daylight, and they were sitting in a parking lot somewhere. There was no regretting the kiss though, never in her life had anything felt so perfect.

She was surprised when she felt his hand rest over hers. "Do you mind?"

"No." She opened her fingers letting them interlock with his. He brought her hand to his lips before releasing her.

A few minutes later, they turned into another parking lot.

When Britt came around to get her out, Rachelle let her hand stay in his as they made their way into the building.

"This way." He led her down the hall. "You'll like Dr.

Christensen. He's a little older, kind, with gray hair that circles his head. He's kind of like the old fashioned TV doctor."

"Have you known him long?"

"About ten years." They stepped into the office, going to the check in desk.

"Mr. Clairbourne, is your shoulder still bothering you?" The woman at the desk greeted him.

"No, it's doing fine, but can you fit us in to be seen?"

"Sure, in fact, you lucked out. We had a cancellation."

"Perfect."

"You'll need my insurance card," Rachelle said next to him. "What did you do to your shoulder?"

"Last month I was on vacation and went white water rafting on the Colorado River. We took a spill, and I strained it. I had it checked out when it was still bothering me, because I was headed overseas on business."

"Mr. Clairbourne, you can come back now." The nurse stood at the open door.

"Do you mind if I come back with you?" Britt was hoping she'd let him stay with her.

"That's fine, I guess. They're only going to be looking at my head."

In the room, the nurse took her vitals and asked a couple of questions about what happened to her then left them alone to finish filling out the paperwork. They'd just finished when the doctor entered.

Britt held out his hand. "James, how are you?"

"Fine and who is this?"

"Rachelle Harris. Rachelle, this is Dr. James Christensen."

"Hello." Rachelle held out her hand.

"Hello." He took it. "Now what seems to be the problem here?"

"Rachelle took a fall and hit her head. She was unconscious for at least ten minutes."

"All right, let's have a look." He approached her. "I'm going to feel your skull." He slid his fingers into her hair, coming into contact with the bump. "That's good sized. Do you have any nausea?"

"No."

"Dizziness?"

"No."

"Sleepy?"

"A little, but I didn't sleep well last night."

"Are you having nightmares?" Britt asked, before the doctor could comment.

"No, I just had trouble going to sleep."

"Let me look at your ear and eyes." The doctor fell silent.

"How long have you been blind?"

"Just over nine months."

"What happened?" He continued to study her eyes.

"A car accident. It caused swelling and a blockage."

"So there's nothing wrong with your eyes. They look healthy and are beautiful besides."

"It's in the passages back to the brain."

"I read not long ago about a doctor having some success with laser for that. Have you checked out if you would be a good candidate?"

"My doctor said it was a possibility, but it's still too new of a surgery that the insurance company won't cover it."

"What do you mean?" Britt interrupted. "Is there a possibility you can see? That was what Laslow was talking about."

"It's a slim chance, less than fifteen percent. And there are some risks."

"The risks aren't any higher than any surgery, and they have raised the success rate to close to thirty percent," Dr. Christensen added, "from the article I read."

"Even so," Rachelle looked taken back. "The insurance

still will not cover it. It's too new, and there are only about a half dozen surgeons doing it. You have to have all the money up front and I don't have that kind of money."

"Couldn't you get it?" Britt asked, unable to believe she hadn't given it a chance.

Rachelle shook her head. "It will be around three-hundred thousand dollars. The banks won't loan on anything like that. My parents just helped my sisters out buying their houses so they are tapped." She shrugged her shoulders. "I couldn't ask them that anyway, not when there's only a one in seven chance that it would be successful. They need to think about retirement at their age. The odds are they would just be throwing their money away."

"What about the guy who hit you?" Britt tried a new route.

"I told you he was driving after his license had been taken away. He had no insurance. His wife had left him. He was in debt. He had no one."

"Wouldn't your uninsured motorist pay?" Britt's muscles tightened with anger.

"They paid some, but I was out of work for over a half a year. There were medical bills, therapy, being taught just how to live on my own. I could have stayed on disability, but it only goes so far."

Besides, Britt thought, she isn't the type to be taken care of. She was the type who takes care of others. Rachelle should be a mother. He pictured her with her arms around a little girl with light-brown hair and a little boy that looked like him, and her beautiful body swelled with another child. He was almost shocked at the clarity of the image until he realized that was where his thoughts had been headed from the moment he had met Rachelle. He wanted a family with Rachelle, and he wanted it to be forever.

"James, can you arrange for her to be seen by the specialist that you were talking about?" Britt turned his attention to the doctor who had been following their conversation.

"Probably, if he thinks that she's a candidate. I'll need her file from the accident. If you'll sign a release, they can fax it over to me and then I can make arrangements for the tests he wants. We can start with a blood test today. That's pretty standard."

"You're forgetting one thing. The insurance won't cover it, and I still don't have the money," she pointed out.

"Don't worry about it. I'll talk to the insurance company. I pay enough for all the employees. They'd better listen," Britt said firmly.

"And if not, you'll pay for it," she made the prediction.

He shrugged. "If that's what it takes, yes. I won't have you denied the possibility of your sight when there is a chance, just because of money."

"But …"

"No buts," Britt countered. "We'll wait until we see what the doctor says first before we argue about this."

"Shall I have my nurse come in and draw some blood then?"

"Yes, thank you," Rachelle said, after a slight hesitation.

"You're welcome, but I haven't done anything yet." The doctor reached out and squeezed her hand in reply.

"You've been very kind. I appreciate what you're doing."

"Well, let's see what happens for now. I want you to take it easy today. No bending, lifting, or climbing on things. If you start to feel nauseated or dizzy, I want to know."

"I'll be careful," she promised.

"Good, if there's nothing else, I'll have my nurse call you when I hear something. She'll be back in a moment to do the blood. I'll see you later, Britt."

"James."

The two shook hands.

When Rachelle remained quiet after the doctor left, Britt stepped to her. "Are you upset that I pressed for an appointment with the specialist?"

"No," she shook her head. "I was thinking about maybe I had let things go too easy before. At first I was overwhelmed and didn't know who to go to, to fight. So much was happening, I was just trying to survive and keep my sanity."

He reached out and lifted her hand in his. "I'm going to talk to my Human Relations people, and make sure there aren't any more of my people left in similar situations like this."

"You're a good man, Britton Clairbourne."

"It's the company I'm keeping." Britt rubbed his thumb over her knuckles.

They were still holding hands when the nurse came in.

Chapter Seven

"Mr. Clairbourne, Miss Harris. I was going to call you both later," Detective Todd greeted them as they entered his office. "Miss Harris, this is Agent Stevens. He's working with us."

"Hello, sir."

"Miss Harris." The agent took her extended hand, giving it a firm shake.

"Is it normal to have an agent?"

"A bomb was used, which makes it federal and also Clairbourne Industries handles some government contacts, sophisticated equipment, like the scrambling device that is being used," the agent replied.

"Won't you have a seat?" Todd suggested, moving back to his own chair. "We haven't made much progress yet. The media people have agreed to give me copies of their photos. I only told them we wanted to check just in case, like in some arsonist cases, the person likes to watch. So they know nothing of Miss Harris, and that she might be able to identify the man."

"Thank you," Britt answered. "But we have another problem. He attacked Rachelle."

"What? When?" the men asked together.

"Right after she left us, in the hall outside her office.

He pulled her into a closet, and threatened her about coming near me. He'd seen her at the news conference. She was knocked out."

"I hit my head. I fell when he released me," Rachelle clarified, and then repeated everything that happened for the two detectives, who then went over the transcript.

"All right," Todd said finally. "We'll have a team go check for any evidence, but a storage closet that is used by the whole floor will probably not give us anything useful in the way of prints."

"Harlan has the room sealed up for you."

"Thank you, I appreciate that. While we're talking prints, there was none on the angel except yours. We're still trying to track down where it was purchased. No one saw anyone near your apartment or in your building that stuck out, but we're still looking."

"What are you talking about?" Britt interrupted, looking at the two detectives then to Rachelle.

The men looked at each other then Stevens answered. "Our man left a package outside Miss Harris' apartment last night with a porcelain angel in it."

Britt's attention shifted to Rachelle in time to see her shift uneasily in her seat. *She'd better be uneasy.* "You didn't tell me?"

"It was nothing. I called the police, and they came and got it."

"That's why you didn't sleep well last night. You should have called me."

"And you would have acted like you are now. I can hear the tightness in your voice. You would have come over and packed me up and moved me out."

"That's right."

"No, it's not. I told you before. I won't let him run me out of my own home."

"He knows where you live. It's not safe."

"He probably knows where you live and that's not safe

either. You haven't moved yet, have you? And don't tell me that's different."

"It is. I don't want you hurt."

"I don't want you hurt either. But he doesn't want to hurt me. He does want to hurt you though."

Britt wanted to continue the argument, but it wasn't getting them anywhere. He fell silent for a moment. "He hurt you today."

"I don't think he meant to. He was warning me away from you."

"Well, maybe you'd better listen. From now on, I'll stay away from you. That way you'll be safe. Can you take her home?" He turned to Todd, not waiting for the man to answer. "I better get back." He started out of the room, leaving Rachelle behind.

"I'm sorry," Rachelle said after him. "I promise next time to tell you immediately if something happens."

Britt paused in the doorway. "Hopefully, there won't be a next time if I stay away from you." He walked out.

Rachelle didn't know what to do. She felt an immense sense of loss. She tried to tell herself it was foolish because Britt was never hers, but for one incredible kiss. After all, she only met him a week earlier. The only meal they shared was not really a date, no matter how nice it had been. And his kiss, she felt tears rise.

"Miss Harris, we'll give you a ride home now."

"Thank you." She hoped she could make it home before the tears came.

CRBO

Britt sat at his desk, but the chair was turned toward the window, away from the work that required his full attention. Never in his life had he thought the word 'jerk' would apply to him, but it did now. He couldn't believe he had walked out on Rachelle that way. Even if he knew she was safe with the police, safer than with him, he'd been wrong.

He knew he had to stay away from her for her own sake, so the psycho didn't come after her again. But he could have handled it better. His male ego had gotten in the way though when she hadn't come running to him after receiving the package. Rachelle was right. He would have packed her out of there. She was his to protect. That kiss had proved it to him, if not to her. Now if she'd just talk to him ever again. That was, if they caught the guy, and if he didn't get killed first. If, if, if, well he had too many plans for the future to give in without a fight.

Turning back to his desk, he pulled the phone book from the bottom door and thumbed to florists, dialing the number.

"Flower Basket."

"This is Britt Clairbourne. I'd like to request a delivery to go out as soon as possible. Can you do it within an hour?"

"It depends on what you'd like, sir."

"Something fragrant." He thought about what Rachelle said, but roses were too normal. "Pansies don't smell much, do they?"

"No, sir."

"What about sweet peas?" He was not even sure what they were.

"They have a very nice smell."

"I'd like them then."

"Let me check if they're available."

He was put on hold for a moment then the woman was back on the line. "We can do that, but it will be about two hours."

"That will be fine."

"Are mixed colors all right or do you want a certain color?"

"Mixed would be fine."

She gave him a price. "Make it two bouquets." He

gave her the address and his credit card number.

"What would you like the card to say?"

"No card, but add an extra five dollars to the tip for the delivery person to give her a message. Just say, "I'd like to apologize for losing my temper, but it is for the best right now that I don't see you. I won't have you put in danger because of me. That will be all, thank you.""

Britt hung up as the intercom sounded.

"Mr. Clairbourne, Mr. Laslow and his security people are here."

"Send them in."

Four men walked into the office. Britt remained seated motioning them to chairs.

"Laslow, Dickerson," he greeted the two older men, turning to the younger men that settled on the couch. "Warren, isn't it?"

"Yes sir, Dustin Warren." The tall, brown-haired man who looked like he spent all his free time in the gym spoke up.

"And," he couldn't come up with the name, though he had seen the stocky man often.

"Jordan, Mike Jordan."

Britt nodded, turning back to Laslow. "What did you find out?"

"No usable prints. There must be a hundred people in and out of that supply closet. No other evidence."

Britt nodded. He was afraid that was how it was going to be.

"We figured out where the scrambler disappeared from, but it's hard to say how long ago it was taken. It could have been a month or more."

"I can't believe someone could just walk in and take one and walk out and no one notice," Britt exclaimed.

"It wouldn't have been that easy. But we're still checking on how it was managed. Who would have had access and who knew it was there."

"I want to see the list when it's available."

"Of course."

"Ryan, who isn't here right now, along with Dickerson, Warren, and Jordan, are going over the security groups. Ryan and Jordan are night shifts. Have you considered a personal guard yet?" The security chief asked, not for the first time.

"No," Britt said firmly. "But I'd like someone assigned to Miss Harris. I don't want that guy hurting her again."

"Is Miss Harris all right?" Dickerson asked.

"Yes."

"Where is she? She wasn't at her desk when I stopped to ask her some questions," Dickerson asked.

"She should be home now. A doctor checked her out and suggested she should rest today."

"I still think you should consider having security with you," Laslow urged.

"No, I like my freedom too much to have someone always watching me."

"You're an open target," the security chief countered.

"He doesn't want me yet. He wants some blood and pain first, but I want him before it gets to that. So let's find him."

⊂⊃⊅⊃

The nap Rachelle had didn't help much, nor did the two pain relievers or the music as she cuddled on the couch, hugging a pillow to her. Tears had started almost as soon as she had closed the door behind the officers that escorted her home, and showed no sign of stopping. If this is what it was like when you truly loved a man, she didn't want it and didn't want anything to do with Britton Clairbourne.

The thought was punctuated by the doorbell. Wiping the tears away, she went to the door. "Who is it?" she asked, through the chained door.

"Delivery for Rachelle Harris," the voice of a young man came through the door.

"What is it?"

"Roses," he said, as if she were a little short on brains.

"Let me guess, red."

"Yeah." The kid definitely thought she was nuts.

"Is there a card?"

"No."

"Who are they from?"

"They were billed to Britt Clairbourne."

Rachelle felt her heart skip a beat.

"Ma'am?" the voice said from the hallway.

"Just leave them outside. I'll get them." Rachelle closed the door, debating whether or not she was going to bring them in. After his attitude and actions for him to think that he could make amends with a dozen roses. She wondered how many women he'd sent roses to. It was probably nothing to him.

Well, she wasn't that easy. Opening the door, she let her nose guide her to the flowers. She picked them up, and then moved down the hall to where two elderly, widowed sisters lived. Rachelle knocked on the door then waited for it to open.

"Rachelle, this is a surprise. Do you have the day off?"

"Yes."

"Come in, oh, what beautiful roses. You have an admirer." Mabel gave a girlish laugh.

"Actually, I thought that maybe you and Ruth would enjoy them."

"Oh, dear, how sweet. Ruth you have to come see what Rachelle has given us."

"Roses."

Rachelle heard another voice that had the same warm cadence as her sister's, but was a little higher pitched.

"We haven't had roses for so long. Thank you." The woman came over and gave Rachelle a hug.

"Won't you stay and have a cup of tea with us?" Ruth invited.

"I can't stay today. I just came to drop these off."

"At least take a piece of cake with you. I just finished it," Mabel insisted.

"That would be wonderful. Thank you." Rachelle talked to Ruth a minute while waiting for Mabel to get the cake before returning to her apartment. She was at the door when someone approached her.

"Are you Rachelle Harris?" the female voice asked.

"Yes." Rachelle turned to the woman.

"These flowers are for you."

"Flowers?"

"Yes, Mr. Clairbourne didn't send a card, but asked to have the message delivered personally. He said to say, 'he was sorry for losing his temper. But that it was best for right now that he doesn't see you.' That must be about what I saw on the news. Wow."

Rachelle caught the fragrant scent and was having trouble fighting back the tears. "Sweet peas."

"Yes, he was quite insistent on them. I have to admit we don't do many bouquets with them."

Rachelle reached for the vase bringing the blossoms to her face.

"Would you like me to carry the other one in for you?"

"The other?"

"Yes, both vases are for you."

"Oh," Rachelle unlocked the door. "Please come in." She moved the entertainment table, after taking in one more deep breath of the sweet fragrance she placed the flowers in the middle. "Would you put the other flowers on the kitchen table?"

"Of course."

Rachelle found her purse to get out a tip.

"Mr. Clairbourne already took care of that," the woman said, moving back to the door.

"Thank you." Rachelle showed her out. With the door locked, she headed to the kitchen and the other bouquet. Cupping the soft petals, she inhaled deeply. He remembered. She couldn't believe it. He actually remembered what she'd said, what she liked. Her first instinct was to reach for the phone to thank him but remembered what he said. He didn't want her near him now. That probably went for calling him, too. Though she thought he was wrong, she would respect it and wait for him to call her. That is, if he ever did. Refusing to dwell on that thought, she made her way to the piano and started to play.

She was deep in her music when the phone rang. She picked it up on the forth ring hoping to hear Britt's voice on the line.

"Were you resting?"

She recognized the voice immediately though it was muffled. She sank to the couch, then remembering the recorder the police had put on her phone and searched for the button to turn it on.

"No, I was playing the piano."

"You're feeling better."

"Yes."

"You went to the doctor."

"Yes, how did you know?" She was taken back.

"I know everything."

A chill of fear raced through her.

"Did you like my flowers?"

"Your flowers?" She stammered, turning toward the table.

"The roses, didn't you get them? They were long stemmed red roses," he said, with unmistakable pride.

"I didn't know they were from you. There was no card, and the delivery person said that Mr. Clairbourne's name was on the receipt."

"Yes, I told you I know everything. He paid for them.

Though, he doesn't know it yet." The voice changed to a laugh. "I put them on his credit card. I told you he would pay." The laughter was harder this time. It stopped abruptly and the voice drop to what almost sounded like a low purr. "Did you like the flowers?"

"They, they smelled beautiful." Her voice squeaked.

"That's not an answer. You didn't like them." There was no missing the anger.

"I d-didn't know they were from you." She stammered over the words. "The delivery boy said they were from Mr. Clairbourne. I took them to a couple of older widow ladies."

There was a pause. "You gave them away?"

"I didn't know," Rachelle said back, now very frightened.

"You thought they were from Clairbourne." The voice was back to its eerie calm. "You gave them away. That's good. That's so good. Too bad you didn't throw them away. I can't wait to tell him you threw away the flowers you thought were from him. That's good, so good."

"You're going to talk with him? When?" Rachelle felt a stronger burst of fear.

"Soon, but first we're not done playing. He hasn't begun to hurt. I want him to hurt. I want him to be alone." The haunting voice caressed each word.

"You still haven't told me about her. Why don't you tell me now? I'm not at work so I have time to listen." Rachelle forced herself to be calm and think. "What was her name? Tell me about her?"

"She was so beautiful. She smelled so nice, like roses. That's how I knew you'd like roses. She liked them. She got them all the time."

"Did Mr. Clairbourne give her roses?"

"No, but she wanted him to. She pretended he would. She would sit and have conversations with him as she stroked her long hair. Like yours. She would wear these soft little things with these bows on. Do you wear those?"

Rachelle felt a wave of sickness. "No, I don't."

"Of course not, you're an angel. Angels don't wear red or black. They wear white. They're innocent − sweet and innocent. I will protect you my angel."

He was gone.

Rachelle's hand trembled as she put down the phone and turned off the recorder. She had to fight to control her breathing to keep from crying. Forcing herself to stand, she walked back to Ruth and Mabel's apartment on shaky legs.

It was Ruth who opened the door.

"Rachelle, back so soon."

"May I use your phone, please?"

"Yes, of course dear. Are you all right? You look terribly pale."

"I'll be fine, if I can use your phone."

"Of course, of course." The woman took her hand leading her to it. "Would you like me to dial?"

"Yes, please." She gave her the number then accepted the phone with still trembling fingers. "Is Detective Todd there?" she asked, when a voice came on the phone.

"Not at this time."

"Is there someone I can talk to about a case he's working on?"

"Detective Adams is. He's Todd's partner."

"That would be fine. Thank you." And the call was transferred.

"Adams," a deep masculine voice answered.

"This is Rachelle Harris."

"Yes, Miss Harris."

"He called again, this time at my apartment. I did like Detective Todd said and recorded it, and then went to neighbors to call."

"I'm on my way right now. Why don't you wait at your neighbors, and I'll be there in ten minutes."

"All right, I'm in 3D." She put down the phone. "Is it

all right if I wait here?" she asked, feeling Ruth's presence hovering near her.

"Certainly, is someone threatening you?"

"No, he's threatening someone I know. He just likes to call me and talk."

"Heavens, is this the guy doing the bombing at your work?" the woman gasped.

"Yes, but you can't tell anyone except Mabel."

"I'm here, dear." A similar sounding voice came from a few feet away.

Rachelle nodded. "The police are trying to keep it secret, so he doesn't quit calling."

"They're hoping he'll tell you something that will help them?" Mabel surmised.

"Yes."

"We'll keep it secret, but how frightening for you. No wonder you're so pale. Why don't you sit down, and I'll make you a nice soothing cup of tea?"

"No, thank you. But I would like to sit down and relax. The officer will be here soon."

"If you're certain, it's no trouble."

"Yes." She was feeling a little steadier.

Having him call her at home was more unsettling for some reason. Thankfully, Detective Adams knocked on the door in under ten minutes. After Mabel checked his ID, Rachelle accompanied him back to her apartment. First, he tried the call back and was surprised when it went through. It was a pay phone number. The other surprise was that the recording had both sides of the conversation.

"Our guy is getting sloppy in his need to brag to you. We'll get him."

"I wasn't able to get any information out of him."

"You did well. Besides, every bit of information helps. We just have to figure out how."

"Like her favorite song, he wanted me to sing," she exclaimed. "That was the most personal information I've gotten so far."

"Yes, it all ties in," the detective said.

"I don't think I've the patience to be a detective."

"A lot of people don't. It's been glamorized on TV for too long, making it look exciting, but in actuality, it can be quite a long tedious process, putting together bits and pieces. Like the song, it was done by David Gates and Bread. That gives us a possible idea of age," Adams pointed out.

"Unless they liked oldies or soft rock."

"Still, it's information," he returned.

"Maybe they just like the name Aubrey. You know the song, and Aubrey was her name ..." Rachelle sang the words, "I loved her ..." she petered out. "That's it." Rachelle rose with excitement. "Aubrey is her name, the name of the woman."

Detective Adams stopped, going over it in his mind. "Yes, you could be right."

"I know I'm right. It's like he said about the roses. She always got them from men. Like she was selfish, self-centered may be a better word for it. She didn't care if it hurt him that she had flowers from other men. So it makes sense her favorite song had her name."

"All right, you convinced me. We'll check on it. See if Mr. Clairbourne knows any Aubreys, or if there have been any employees by that name. It sounds as if she's dead. So we'll even check deaths in the past year or two."

Rachelle nodded. "You might want to tell Mr. Clairbourne the guy has his credit card number. He charged the roses to him. Who knows what else?"

"I'll let him know immediately," the detective agreed. "You might want to consider spending the night with a friend or a neighbor."

"I'll be fine," Rachelle said, though inside she felt a quiver of fear. She walked him to the door, closing it behind him. It seemed eerily quiet in the apartment.

Stopping to turn on one of her CDs, she went to the couch, sitting back so she could take in the comforting smell of the sweet peas.

◌ঙ৪০

Britt had only been in his apartment a few minutes when the doorbell rang. "Detective Adams," he greeted the detective who had more gray in his hair then its natural dark brown. "Don't tell me there are any more problems tonight."

"Yes and no. Nothing bad to do with your company has happened, but there are some things you'll need to take care of, and I have some questions for you."

"Can I get you something?" Britt asked, leading him into the living room.

"No, thanks. Do you know or have you dated any women with the name of Aubrey?"

"Aubrey," he paused to think. "There's an Aubrey in the cafeteria. That's the only Aubrey I can place."

"You've never dated one?"

"No, I'm certain of that. What is it? Do you have a lead?"

"Just a hypothesis, but we might have a little more to go on. Our guy called again. This time at Miss Harris' apartment, and though he muffled his voice, he didn't use the scrambler. We were able to trace the call to a phone booth. We have a crew going over it as we speak."

"Is Rachelle all right?" The need for the answer burned in him.

"Yes, it was a call to brag. He sent her a bouquet of roses. Two dozen, long-stemmed, red, impressive."

Britt felt ill. The man had sent two dozen roses to his little sweet peas. Then next words hit him hard.

"He charged them to your credit card. So you'll want to call right now and cancel that."

He nodded. "Well, at least I hope Rachelle enjoys the

roses."

"Actually, she gave them to a couple of older widow women that are her neighbors."

"She did?"

"Yeah, she had these two big bouquets of bright colored flowers. The way she fidgeted with them, I'd say she preferred them."

Britt felt like letting out a whoop. She kept his flowers. Instead, he calmly said, "If you'll give me a minute, I'll call and cancel the card that was used and put a password on the other."

"Good, the question remains how he got it. If you'll check when he used it, it might tell us about when he got it."

"I'll get that."

A few minutes later he turned back to the detective giving him the information. "Was Rachelle able to record all the conversation?"

"Yes."

"Can you get me a copy?"

"Sure, I'll stop by your office tomorrow about nine."

"That'll be good. Are you certain Miss Harris was all right?"

"She seemed so, though it upset her a little. She was quite concerned about you," the detective added.

Britt ignored the words. "She doesn't need to worry. I'll have a security guard outside her building and one in her hall."

"You should tell her. It might make her feel better."

∞

The phone rang six times, and he was about convinced she wasn't going to answer when she picked it up. Her voice was strained with obvious tension when she said, "hello."

"Are you all right?"

"Mr. Clairbourne." Her formal address caught him off guard.

"Britt," he said firmly. "Now answer me."

"I'm just fine. His voice can't hurt me. He wasn't here."

"Well, you don't have to worry about him. There are two security guards at your place. So don't panic. You'll probably never know they're there."

"But," she started to object.

He cut her off. "It's that or a hotel room." He left no leeway in his voice.

"All right, as long as they stay back."

"They will," he promised.

"I thought you weren't going to have any contact with me. It's too dangerous."

"This phone can't be tapped or traced. I'm using my own technology back against him, but I'll keep this short. I just wanted to check on you."

"I'm fine."

"I don't want you to worry, but if you need anything, call."

"I'm fine."

"Yeah, well, good night."

"Thank you for the sweet peas."

"You're welcome. Rachelle, I'm trying to do what's best."

"I know. Goodnight."

"Goodnight." He heard the line cut off.

ೞ৪ঝ

Rachelle picked up one of the bouquets and took it along with her to her bedroom, placing it on the nightstand. She readied for bed then laid back, letting the sweet, gentle smell comfort her as she drifted off to sleep.

ೞ৪ঝ

Britt sat at his desk with the two detectives and his

chief of security, staring at the small listening device they had located.

"I want this room, my outer office, and the executive answering checked twice a day. This guy has too much access. I can't believe it." He felt more frustrated than ever. "We have to tighten security."

"The guy is clever and he's smart," Todd put in. "He knows his devices. We're checking the ex-military records in the area. We're still running the name Aubrey. Personnel gave us three names that worked for the company in the last two years. Our psychologist figures it's not any further back than that. So far, the only weakness he's showing is Miss Harris."

"She seems to be our best connection, but Dr. Lewis is getting concerned this guy might swing. She thinks your decision to stay away from her is wise but also says it may not matter. If he takes it in his mind she's helping us, or you too much, he could flip."

"And then?" Britt was afraid he already knew the answer.

"Then, he'd want to punish her. Miss Harris would become a target with you. The only problem is she is still our best source of leads. I think it would be a good idea if she talked with as many people as possible, if not with you, on her own."

"No, I'm not giving him any reason to turn on her. Especially, if Dr. Lewis thinks he's getting volatile."

There was a knock on the door and it opened. "Mr. Clairbourne," his personal assistant stepped in. "I think you'd better see this? Darrell held out the morning newspaper, folded open to the society section. The set of photos caught Britt's attention before the caption. The first was in the lobby after the press conference when he had pulled Rachelle to him. The next was when he caught her at the bus stop. His hand cupped her face. Looking at the picture, it looked like he was about to kiss her. The last showed him helping Rachelle into his car, her hand in his. Again her face turned up to him. The picture was classically beautiful even in black and white.

His eyes shifted from the pictures to the caption. 'In Times of Trouble, Life is Going Good for Clairbourne.' The first line read, 'Who is the new woman in Britton Clairbourne's life? Could, in the midst of all the turmoil, one of the most eligible bachelors fallen? If it's true, Mr. Clairbourne looks to be a lucky man.'

"A lucky man," he repeated out loud. "Come on." He came out of the chair and around the desk with the newspaper still in hand, letting the men follow. He knew Rachelle was in. He had already checked with security. They had followed her from the bus to her office.

Not waiting for the elevator, he ran down the two flights. "A reporter put some pictures of Rachelle and me together in the paper," he said to the men behind him.

The noise in the large office room stopped as he came through the door, but several people had newspapers on their desk, and he knew he and Rachelle were the topic. Ignoring them, he headed down the hall.

Chapter Eight

"I told you, I wasn't seeing things," Lois said again. "It's right here in black and white. No one's going to doubt there's something going on between you two."

"He doesn't even want to see me." Rachelle couldn't keep some of the pain she was feeling from slipping out.

"It's not that he doesn't want to, he's protecting you."

"Part of me believes that, but part of me–" She let it hang, but Lois finished for her.

"Thinks, he can't possibly want you. That's the jerk you were engaged to talking."

"Maybe, but–" the phone rang halting her answer. "Clair–"

"You lied!" The words came sharp as daggers in her ear before she could finish the greeting. "You lied. You knew the flowers were from me. That's why you gave them away. You lied."

"No," Rachelle gasped, terror filling her, but he wasn't listening.

"You love him! You lied to me. Made me think you were innocent, but you're not. You're not an angel. You're with him. You love him," he yelled in the phone.

Rachelle couldn't deny what she knew was true. "Please, you have to stop this."

"I've just begun," the man growled out cruelly, and

then slammed down the phone in her ear.

"Rachelle."

Rachelle jumped when Britt called her name from behind, and she turned reaching for him. She was caught, lifted out of the chair and into his arms. Shudders swept through her as she clung to him. "He saw the picture in the newspaper," she mumbled against his neck.

"It's okay," Britt soothed, and she felt his lips brush her cheek.

"No, he's crazy," she cried, pressing tighter to him. "I think he's going to do something. He didn't say it, but I know he is."

"Shhh." Britt rubbed his hands over her back. "We'll face that when it happens."

"Where's the transcript?" Laslow barked out, making her jerk. Britt sent him a glare over her shoulder, but she still pulled back.

"I'm sorry, I didn't. When he yelled, I … I."

"It's all right." Britt pulled her back to him. "Just tell us what he said."

"He kept saying I lied. That I knew the roses were from him. And that was why I gave them away. That I was helping you, that I loved you, and that I wasn't his angel. He said that he had just begun. I know he's going to do something."

"Don't worry, we'll stop him. From now on you stay with me and we'll try to find his voice, if you think that you're up to it."

"Yes." There was a quiver in her voice but no doubt in her resolve.

"Then let's give you a tour of Clairbourne Industries."

"I thought that you didn't want me with you."

"I want you with me. I just didn't want you in danger. Now, I'm afraid you're not safe no matter what. My first instinct is to send you away."

"I won't go."

"I know, so I would rather keep you close, so I can look after you. I know that sounds egotistical and domineering, but it's how it is."

"All right," Rachelle said simply, laying her head back down on his chest, while Britt continued to coordinate with the officers and security chief standing at the edge of the room.

Britt turned to the officers. "Where do you think we should start, here at the main office or where the first explosion was?"

"I'd say here. First, print a list out of all the male employees then mark them off as you eliminate them," Todd suggested.

"With your permission," Adams cut in, "We'd like to bring the dogs into check this building. I think Miss Harris is right. He's going to do something, and he's moving closer toward you."

"Should we evacuate the building?" Britt asked, almost losing his train of thought when the hand that Rachelle had resting on his chest, slid down and around his waist.

"No, let us check it out first. If there's something to worry about, we'll let you know."

"All right, Harlan can take you around."

The security chief nodded and all three men left the room.

"I think I'll get some fresh air," Lois said, following the men out, leaving Rachelle and Britt alone.

"That woman deserves a bonus." Britt's voice dropped low, with a husky tone.

"What?" Rachelle tilted her head back.

"You didn't even know what you did." Seeing her confusion, he continued. "Maybe I can show you." He moved one hand from her back to place it on her rib cage. He could feel her breathing pick up and it excited him. Letting his hand slide down, he let his hand linger there. Her breath caught as he slid it around her waist. A small gasp escaped her, and she trembled.

"Yes," Britt tightened his hold.

"I'm sorry," she said breathless. Her head rested back down. "I just wanted to feel ..." She broke off as his other hand came up to cup her face. Tilting it up, he lightly kissed her lips.

"You don't have to ever apologize for that. There's this connection between us. It's special."

"Do you believe that?"

"Yes, I do." He kissed her again. "We'd better stop this. We have people to talk to."

Rachelle knew they caused a stir when they came into the cafeteria together. Most everyone had seen or knew about the newspaper, but obviously no one ever really put them together seriously. Now there was no way to miss how Britt kept in constant contact with her, either holding her hand, elbow, or his hand on her waist.

Britt stopped at each table greeting people and talking casually. Rachelle thought of what a diplomat he made. Unfortunately, none of the voices were the one they wanted to hear. After eating, they started going through the rest of the floors again. Rachelle was surprised how easily Britt talked to his employees and how many people he knew by name.

As the afternoon wore on, frustration set in a little. "I really thought this would work," Rachelle said to him.

"Give it time."

"I guess I just didn't realize how many employees work here."

"In this building, we have approximately seven-hundred and eighty people, but in the whole company, at this location there's approximately two-thousand."

"You know, I think I knew that, but it just didn't seem like that many until I was trying to listen for one voice."

"Do you still think you can pick out his voice?"

"Yes, but so far no one is even close."

"Well, we're done with the first and second floor. Do you want to head to the third floor or are you ready for a break?" His cell phone rang before she could answer.

"It sounds like you're needed elsewhere," she said, waiting while he answered the phone.

"I'll be right there," he said, a second later. "I've got to go upstairs." He took her hand. "I'd like you to go downstairs and wait by the security desk in the lobby for me."

"What is it?" She held him back as he started to go. "Britt?"

"The police found a bomb upstairs."

"You can't go up there." She clutched at him, fear coursing up her spine.

"It's all right. I won't be near it. They've started evacuating the building. I want you downstairs before there's too much confusion."

"But?"

"Don't worry." He kissed her cheek. "I'll be down for you in a few minutes. Just wait there at the security desk." He saw her to the elevator and then headed up as she headed down.

"Miss Harris," Rachelle heard her name as the elevator doors opened.

"Yes," she answered it hesitantly.

"I'm Dustin Warren from security. I'm supposed to see you to the security desk and wait with you until it's safe."

"Oh, that's not necessary," she tried to decline as people began to flow from the stairs.

"Mr. Clairbourne called down and insisted. If you'll come this way." He led her out of the crowd.

"That's some cold you have," she commented for something to say.

"Not a cold, allergies."

"Sounds bad."

"I've had them about two weeks. The medicine the

doctor gave me makes me drowsy so I can't take it while I'm on duty. Why don't you have a seat here?"

"Thank you. Do you know what's happening upstairs?"

"No, but there shouldn't be anything to worry about, you're safe down here."

Rachelle felt a shiver ripple through her. "I don't feel safe. I wish this would end."

"I'm sure it will soon."

"I hope so." Rachelle fell silent, waiting anxiously as the minutes ticked by. She was so locked in her thoughts she jumped out of her seat when she finally heard Britt say her name.

"It's all right," he murmured into her ear as his arms encompassed her. "The bomb squad has removed the bomb safely. They're checking the building over again, but it looks like it's over. I'm sending everyone home. I just have to talk to the detectives a minute then I'll take you home." He let his hand slide down her arm, taking her hand.

"May I stay with you?" She held tightly.

After a second, he pressed his lips to her cheek. "Right by my side?"

"Yes."

His lips slid over her mouth. "Let's go."

It felt good to be back in familiar territory when Britt walked her down the hall toward her apartment.

"Looks like you have a delivery," Britt said, as they approached her door. "Are you expecting something?"

"No, who's it from?"

"Matthew Harris."

"Oh, that's my dad." She reached for the package.

"I have it."

Inside the apartment, Rachelle turned on the light for him then followed him into the kitchen. "I wonder what it could be. My parents just left to go to a cousin's wedding."

Britt slit the tough tape and watched as Rachelle pulled

back the packing. She started to reach inside, when he caught her fingers, pulling them back.

"Britt?"

"Don't touch it, Rachelle."

"What's wrong? What is it?"

"It's just broken and I don't want you to get cut on the sharp edges."

"What is it? Britt!" She stressed when he didn't answer.

"I don't think it's from your parents."

"What is it?" she repeated.

"A figurine." He paused then sighed. "It's broken."

"You don't think it was broken by accident?" Waiting for the answer, Rachelle got a sinking feeling.

"It's a porcelain angel."

"Oh, I'll call the police station and see about getting it picked up." There was a slight tremor in her voice, but it was nothing compared to the trembling that ran through Britt as he looked down at the broken angel, smeared with red stuff that he sincerely hoped was not blood. The message was clear. Rachelle was on his marked list.

Thirty minutes later, the package had been sent to the lab. Detective Adams reentered the apartment after questioning people in the building that might have seen something. "No luck."

Rachelle sat on the couch holding a flower stem with three bright pink blossoms on it. Britt's arm encircled her.

"We know the package was placed there before noon. One of your neighbors noticed it there then," the detective continued.

"So not long after the newspaper came out and the phone call."

"No, if he does work at Clairbourne Industries, he probably did it on his lunch break. It would only take him about twenty-five to thirty minutes to get here and back."

"He knows her address and her father's name," Britt

said.

"He possibly has access to her file. It may help cut down the suspects, but if he's good enough with computers, he could access it from anywhere."

Britt nodded, "I still don't like it."

"We'll have extra watches in the neighborhood tonight," the detective assured.

"Good idea. I don't like that the guy's anger is focused on her."

"I agree. We'll do all we can to keep her safe." With that he said good-bye. Britt saw him out. He returned to find Rachelle in the kitchen with a frown on her face.

"What's wrong?" He came up, sliding his arm around her.

"I was trying to decide what to fix for supper. With everything happening, I forgot to call in a grocery order."

"It's all right. I was planning on taking you out." He pressed his lips to her temple. "I think we need an evening out."

"But–"

He cut her off, placing a finger over her lips. "You're not going to say you can't go. We've already proved your fine by going out with pizza and lunch today."

She still looked like she would object, and then smiled brightly. "Do I need to change?"

"Well, I think you look gorgeous, but if you have some sexy evening gown you want to put on for me, I won't object."

"I don't know about sexy but …"

"If it's on you, it will be sexy." He didn't hold back the wicked tone from his voice.

C**80

A few minutes later, when Rachelle stepped shyly back into the room she did feel sexy like she never had before. She heard Britt's intake of air.

"Beautiful."

The word made her shiver.

The black dress with metallic thread was a simple trim cut. It belled three quarters of the way to her ankle. Her shoes were higher than anything she'd worn since the accident, afraid of catching a heel in some unseen crack and falling, but she trusted Britt to watch out for her.

"You look so beautiful I hate to take you out where I have to share you with other people."

"We can just stay here."

His chuckle sounded a bit forced, and his breath seemed to be coming too fast. "No, you don't, you're not getting out of this. We're going out." She heard him walk toward her. There were only a couple inches between them when he stopped. She could feel his presence surround her, and when she tilted her face to him, one hand came up to cradle her face.

"You are so beautiful." His voice almost growled, but she felt no fear. Her heart leapt with pleasure when she heard the truth in his words. He found her beautiful and desirable. Then she lost all thought as his lips settled on hers. She leaned into the kiss just as he pulled back.

"We'd better get going." His lips grazed her cheek, before he took her hand to lead her out the door.

Her nerves almost got the better of her when they came to a stop and the valet opened the door welcoming her to one of the most expensive restaurants in the city.

"Britt," she let out in panic.

"I'm here," he said, taking her hand.

"I don't know about this," she whispered.

"I do." He came back with no uncertainty.

"What if I knock something over or spill something?"

"I'm sure it won't be the first time it's happened here."

"Yes, but I probably have a better track record than most people. A couple months ago I couldn't eat anything without spilling," she confessed.

"You've come a long way. I'm not concerned."

"I am," she came back. "Do I look all right?"

"You look incredible."

"I don't wear makeup anymore. Not being able to see what I'm doing, I'm afraid I'd end up looking like a clown."

"You don't need makeup. You have wonderful skin." His finger brushed her cheek, "and the most beautiful eyes." He pressed his lips above them.

He flinched as a camera flash blinded him.

"Britt?" she said as he pulled back.

"Let's go inside." He placed her arm on his, tucking her to his side.

"Mr. Clairbourne, your table is ready." The maitre d' greeted them making Rachelle realize Britt had planned to bring her here all along.

This time, when she moved to shift behind him, he stopped her motion, keeping her to his side. "It'll be okay, trust me," he said, moving her with him.

Rachelle forced herself to relax and move with him. She found it was becoming easier to put her faith in him.

"Here you are," the maitre d' again spoke. Britt moved her in to position to be seated so fluidly that Rachelle figured no one probably noticed she was blind.

"You know we should go dancing sometime. We move pretty well together."

"I like to dance. When I was in college, I took a couple of classes." Rachelle smiled.

"We definitely need to do some dancing then."

The conversation turned to other things after Britt ordered for them. Time, with the dinner, disappeared. Side by side again, they made their way out when someone called Britt's name.

"Darrell," he greeted his executive assistant at the top of the cement steps. "Having a night out?"

"Yes, I treat myself here at least once a month. And

with all that was happening, I thought tonight was a good time."

"We thought the same thing," Britt agreed.

"Did you enjoy yourself, Miss Harris?"

"Yes, I did. Thank you." Rachelle had met the man on several occasions and could remember what he looked like from before her accident. Darrell Mason was equal to Britt in height, but rail thin, with black rim glasses that looked good on him, instead of nerdy. He was an extremely competent man, with outstanding people and organizational skills. He was who she was used to dealing with when there was need of contact with Britt's office. "Still having problems with your allergies?" she asked the man.

"Yes. Mr. Reese and I are both having bouts with allergies."

"I didn't know Carlton had allergies," Britt commented, referring to his brother-in-law.

"Yeah, he came in yesterday all stuffed up, blaming it on the ventilation system, wanting you to do something about it."

"Figures," Britt said. He didn't think much of his brother-in-law but had been pretty much forced into hiring him. At least he did a passable job most of the time.

"Right," the man agreed. "I left the list the police asked for on your desk before we evacuated the building."

"Thanks."

The man nodded as his car stopped in front and the valet got out. "Well, have a good night."

"You too," Britt returned.

"Goodnight," Rachelle added.

"Still in the mood for dancing?" Britt asked, turning his attention back to her.

"Would you mind if I asked for a rain check?"

"Not at all. I wanted to ask you about attending a party with me this weekend." He didn't get a chance to hear her answer. Distracted with the roar of an engine, Britt looked down the street in time to see the headlights come on the car racing down the road. The high beams flooded the street, spotlighting Darrell as he came around his car.

Britt called a warning, alerting the man, but Darrell wasn't quite able to get out of the way before the car clipped him, sending him flying.

"Britt what?" Rachelle cried as people screamed and tires squealed.

"Stay right here. I'll be back. Darrell just got hit by a car."

"No." She dug her fingers into Britt's arm.

"Stay here," he repeated, then was gone.

Britt reached his assistant the same time the valet did.

"Robbie went to call an ambulance," the young man said.

"Darrell, can you hear me?" Britt leaned over him, checking for bleeding but careful not to move him.

"My leg," the man groaned.

"Lay still. Looks like you have a broken leg."

The man groaned again. Britt slid off his suit coat, putting it over him. He started to ask about other pains, trying to keep him alert. He paused only long enough to glance up to make sure Rachelle was fine.

A minute later both the ambulance and the police arrived. "I'll follow you to the hospital." Britt patted his shoulder.

"That's not necessary." Darrell protested, his pain lessening now that he was given a pain killer. "You need to take Miss Harris home."

Britt glanced again up at Rachelle. She was still by the doorway, one hand rested on the granite wall. She looked frightened and confused. "I'll check with the hospital and get there as soon as I can. You know my number, so use it if you need anything."

"Yes, sir."

Britt left him to return to Rachelle. She jerked when he

said her name.

"Is Darrell all right?" she asked anxiously.

"He has a broken leg, luckily that appears to be it. It could have been much worse. They're taking him to the hospital now."

"Did you want to go to the hospital with him? I could get a cab home or go to the hospital with you."

"You wouldn't mind if we swing by the hospital? I'd really like to see him settled."

"Not at all."

His hands framed her face. "Have I told you how terrific you are?" He pressed a kiss on her nose, then her lips, leaving her too breathless to answer.

ଔଓ

Britt nodded to the security guard as they passed him in the hall outside Rachelle's apartment. It seemed like an eternity ago they left, and their mood had altered completely. Rachelle was quiet, fear showed on her face, as she clung to him. He could feel a tremor run through her body though she fought to hide it. He didn't feel much calmer. Neither said anything, but both suspected the incident was no accident.

Once inside the apartment, he turned on the light and left her at the door to check the apartment. "It's clear," he said, returning to her. "But I don't like leaving you here alone."

"I'll be fine." Her smile was forced.

"I could still get a room for you at The Towers."

"No, I'd rather stay here. This is where I feel comfortable."

He wanted to object, but was learning he needed to respect her wishes, no matter how his protective instincts wanted to over-rule. "If you need me, call." He reached up cupping her face.

"You're not going to try to change my mind about

staying?"

"No, I don't want to start a fight with you. Just call."

"I will," her promise was whispered.

"Goodnight." He tilted her chin up to align their lips. Kissing her was becoming an addiction. He couldn't get enough of her and doubted he could if he had a lifetime. He was willing to see, and wondered what Rachelle would do if he asked her to marry him right then. No, not tonight, not after everything bad that had happened that day.

He broke the kiss. "I'll see you in the morning." He almost groaned when her tongue came out to lick her lips.

"I'll be ready anytime around seven. If you'd like breakfast, that's about six-thirty."

"I may take you up on that. What are you serving?"

"Cereal and orange juice or, if you're really nice and ask, I might be talked into making my special waffles."

"Waffles, I'll see you at six-thirty." Unable to stop himself, he dipped his head, to sneak one more kiss. "Sleep well." He forced himself out the door.

He waited in the hall until he heard the lock on her door click. He turned to the guard. "Warren, you on guard tonight?"

"Yes, sir, until two."

Britt nodded. "Thanks, I hope you have a nice night."

"You too, sir," the man returned.

Britt was almost to his car when he realized he never got to finish asking her about attending the party this weekend at his family's estate. He knew it could wait until morning, but he wanted to give her more time to think, so he would have more time to argue her objections and talk her in to it.

He headed back upstairs, hurrying down the hall, missing the security guard. When he reached Rachelle's door she answered within a few seconds of his knock.

"Who is it?"

When he answered, the door opened immediately.

"What's wrong?" she asked anxiously.

"Nothing, I just never got a chance to finish asking you to a party this weekend. It's a charity social at my family's estate. It's a yearly event my grandmother started. Anyway, I have to be there, and I was wondering if you'd be willing to accompany me?"

"A charity," she sounded stunned. "It sounds big."

"It's kind of, but you have nothing to fear. Everyone will adore you, and after tonight you proved you can handle yourself beautifully."

"Tonight was a test?" She sounded hurt.

"No, I just wanted to prove to you your first objection was ungrounded."

"What if I had spilled everything on the table?" Her face tilted to the ground.

"I'd still want you with me. Nothing is going to change that. I know it's too soon to say this, but I think I'm in love with you."

Her head shot up, her eyes searching as if trying to see him. "Britt."

"It's all right. We'll talk about that another time. I guess that wasn't fair of me to throw that at you right now, so back to the party. I'll be at your side. It will be fine. Just trust me."

"You're right, it's not fair to say something like you love me and then make me decide," she groaned, overwhelmed.

"Is that a yes?"

"It's a … I will think about it."

"Thank you. That's all I ask."

"I don't think you know what you're asking. I've never been to anything like that. I don't know what to expect or how to act."

"Just be yourself. People will love you."

"They'll love watching me bump into things."

"That's not going to happen. I'll be there." He realized

she was talking as if she had already accepted.

"What do I wear?"

"What you have on is perfect." He felt exuberance at winning.

"It's the only real formal, nice thing I have. I need to have it dry-cleaned."

"We'll drop it off at the drycleaners in the morning. My mother always has her hair and make-up done before. I can see if the same person can do yours if you wish, though I'll admit I like you just how you are, soft, touchable." As if to prove it, he reached up and ran his fingers over her hair. "And you certainly don't need make-up. You have beautiful eyes. They might not see me, but they're so beautiful to look into."

"I always worry that they look funny, staring off into blank space."

"No, in fact, I think most people don't even realize you don't see. Most of the time, I forget it when you turn to me. It's like you see into my soul like no one ever has."

He caught the O her mouth made.

"Why is it too soon?" she whispered.

His heart rejoiced at her question, thinking that it might mean she was in love with him also. Unfortunately, the phone rang before he could ask.

"Sorry, it's probably one of my family members. They take turns checking on me." She slipped from his arms. "They're all overprotective of me. I have to answer it before they panic. Hello?"

It was a familiar voice that answered after a long pause, but it wasn't warm or friendly. "Broken angels don't go to heaven. They can't fly. Mason flew, but he had help and he still didn't land in heaven, just like you won't land in heaven and neither will Clairbourne. You shouldn't have lied. I could almost forgive you, if you hadn't lied."

"You hurt Darrell Mason," she cried.

"He shouldn't be helping Clairbourne. I warned

everyone, but he didn't listen. No one listened. Well now, they'll listen to me. Now they know I can destroy Clairbourne. I can destroy him anytime I want."

"Please, don't do this. Would Aubrey do this? Would she hurt people?"

"Aubrey wanted Clairbourne like I wanted her. He just toyed with her, and she toyed with me. She died, now I will toy with him. He'll die and I'll be left with everything. I'll win, and then Aubrey will want me again."

The phone went dead in her ear and Rachelle slump back into Britt's arms, which had encircled her sometime during the conversation. She felt too drained to make any response, though Britt didn't ask for any, as if he understood.

He lifted her up and carried her to the couch, cradling her in his lap, as he punched the police number on his cell phone and notified them of the new call. Since there was a car in the neighborhood, they would pick up the recording in a couple of minutes.

They sat in silence until the knock came. Britt settled Rachelle on the couch. "I'll be right back." He went to the door.

"I'm Detective Salmon." The man showed his ID.

"Sorry to drag you over so late."

"No problem. I'm on late shift. I was just coming back from the accident site where your assistant was hurt. Since your name was mentioned, I wanted to check it out."

"It was no accident." The words came from the couch. "It was him. He admitted it to me."

"We were working under that assumption." The detective moved into the room toward Rachelle. "We were able to get a good description of the car and a couple numbers off the plate. Hopefully that might give us a good lead to the identity. We'll get him."

"I know you're trying. I just hope it will be soon." Rachelle said solemnly, the events of the night seemed to wear down on her,

Britt moved behind the couch, laying his hand on her shoulder.

"We'll do our best." The detective hit redial on the phone, which no one answered, then exchanged the memory stick with a new one. "Why don't you contact Todd or Adams in the morning? They might have something for you."

"I will. Thank you." Britt showed him to the door. Rachelle remained quiet as he came back to sit by her.

"It was such a lovely evening," she said sadly, as she leaned against him.

"It was. Why don't you head to bed?" He placed a kiss on the top of her head.

"I am tired." She raised her head. "I just don't want you to leave yet."

"I'm not. Go on, I'll lock up."

"It's a deadbolt and I need to do the chain."

"I'll get them. Just tell me where to find a pillow and a blanket."

"A blanket? You can't sleep here. We're not married."

"That's why I'll be sleeping on the couch."

"Are you sure you'll be comfortable on the couch?"

"No, so I'll expect those waffles you promised me earlier." He was expecting more of an argument. When it didn't come he figured it proved how shaken she was.

While he locked the door, she disappeared into her room, returning with a pillow and two blankets and a sheet. "Will this be enough?"

"That will be fine." He took them from her before she knocked over the lamp she was beside.

"I don't have anything for you to wear." She caught her bottom lip, as if she could pull the words back.

"It's all right. I can sleep in my shorts if you promise not to peek," he teased.

"I'll try." Her return was heavy with false lightness.

"Thank you for staying." She turned serious. "I'm trying to be strong, independent and brave. But I really don't want to be alone tonight."

"I could drive you to your family."

"No, they all left with my parents for my cousin's wedding two days ago. They'll be gone for a week. They decided to turn it into a vacation. My parents are going to take everyone to Disneyland."

"Why didn't you go?"

"I just didn't feel quite ready for traveling yet."

"You would've been fine, but I'm glad you didn't go. I'm glad to be with you."

"Me too, even if they were here, I wouldn't want to bring trouble to them. I need to learn to stand on my own."

Britt lowered the bedding to the couch before turning back to her. He knew by the way her head tilted up, she knew he was in front of her. "Do I get to stand with you?" He slid his arms around her waist.

"Are you sure you want to?"

"I'm sure." He kissed her lightly then stepped back when yearning threatened to overpower him. "Have a good night. And remember, I'm right here. You're safe. I won't let anything happen to you."

"I know."

He helped her adjust her course when she almost turned into the table.

It was the first time he'd ever seen her lose her location in her apartment. He wondered if it was fatigue, nerves or what he'd like to think, that she was distracted from his kiss. He wished he could truly believe the latter.

Chapter Nine

The cry jolted Britt from his sleep. He shot from under the blankets, bumping his shin on the coffee table. Stumbling toward the closed door, he didn't pause before opening it, but as the moon filled the room with light, he froze.

Rachelle lay in the queen size sleigh bed. Even from ten feet away, he could hear her rugged breathing which was joined by an agonizing whimper.

"Rachelle." He crossed the room, settling on the edge of the bed. "Rachelle." He reached out, stroking her cheek with his fingertip. At first, she turned from it, but when he continued the caress and repeated her name, she relaxed and turned to his hand. "That's it sweetheart. It's all right. I'm here."

"Britt," her voice quivered out of the dark.

"Yes, love. You were having a nightmare."

"The car, it came out of nowhere, the lights flooding through my window. I knew it was going to hit me. I couldn't even scream."

Britt wondered if she had the dream often, or if Darrell getting hit set it off. He hated the thought of her facing nightmares alone.

"I'm sorry, sweetheart." He reached for her, pulling her up to his bare chest. He felt her heart racing like a hummingbird. He wrapped his arms around her, and after a moment, she relaxed. The position gave him the feel of her curvy woman's body and almost ripped a groan from him when her fingers splayed over his chest. When her fingers slid into the mat of hair there, the groan slipped free, but she didn't seem to notice.

"It was dark when I woke up. At first I didn't understand. I just thought it was night. I was never afraid of the dark, but now sometimes …" the words hung unsaid. She pressed her face against his chest. "Now what frightens me the most is forgetting what things look like, no longer being able to picture the blue sky, flowers, waterfalls, people. I have several nieces and nephews. I miss seeing them change. I can feel them, but I wish … I wish I could see you and know that you're real and that you're here with me, that I'm not making you up."

"I am here and real." He laid her back to the pillow, careful to keep the sheet between them. He stretched out behind her, wrapping his arms around her. "I'm here, just relax."

"Christmas was the hardest. I love Christmas, the lights, decorations, and the shopping. But it was horrid. People everywhere confused me. I couldn't see what to buy. I tried to say it was all right because the sounds and smells were there, but," She turned in his arms pressing a tear dampened cheek to his chest.

More than anything he wanted to promise she would see next Christmas, but he couldn't. It wasn't within his power, but he would do anything to make it possible. He ran his hands over her back. The thin sheet and silky nightgown did nothing to hide the feel of her from him. The desire he felt for her blossomed, but he pushed it down. He knew he could bring a respite of forgetfulness to her with his body, but that wasn't what Rachelle needed. She needed his love and comfort. When the time came for them to be together, it would be a joyful celebration of a union meant to be forever. Not an act to chase away the darkness.

He felt the heavy sigh leave her then one hand slid over his shoulder and down his arm, drawing with it another groan. His stomach muscles tightened as her hand slid around his waist. With another sigh, her cheek did a couple, cuddling kitten rubs against his chest as she settled into place. Her heart beat slowed and steadied into sleep.

〇〇〇

Rachelle woke feeling more warm and content than she ever had. Maybe dreaming of being cuddled against Britt had something to do with it. As the fog of her dream lifted, she realized two things. Her pillow was hard, and it carried the distinctive scent of Britt.

"Britt," she whispered, running her hand over the heated skin under it. A large hand covered hers.

"Easy, sweetheart, I'm here." She felt a slight shifting and his lips brushed her head.

"I was dreaming." She stopped, embarrassed.

Britt watched the color pinking her cheeks and thought if her dream was anything like his, the color was well deserved.

"You held me when I had the nightmare."

"You needed to be held." He wondered if she was going to apologize.

"It's been a long while since," she stopped.

"Since you turned to someone," he said for her.

"I've tried to be strong."

"It's all right to need someone. I'm just finding that out." He cupped her chin in one hand, tilting it up. The kiss was warm and sweet. Breaking the kiss, he brushed his fingers back through her hair. "Do I deserve waffles?"

A smile blossomed from deep within her. "I think so, if you don't mind letting me take the first shower."

"Let me see, lay around in bed for an additional twenty minutes so a beautiful woman can fix me breakfast. I don't know."

"I'll make it fifteen," she returned playfully and slid out of bed.

Britt had to hold back a moan as she crossed the room. Closing his eyes did nothing to block the vision already imprinted on his mind. Once he heard the door close, he sank back into the pillow.

Her innocence was killing him. Likely the nightgown she was wearing would be considered modest, but after holding her shapely body all night, he knew the figure under it too well. He yearned to go after her and bring her back to bed. The deep steadying breath he took backfired on him when it filled his senses with the fragrance of her. He never should have come into her bedroom. He shouldn't have held her. And he certainly should not have fallen asleep in her bed. But he didn't regret falling in love with her, even if his timing was a little off.

He glanced at the delicate, brightly colored blossoms in the vase beside her bed. A few of the blossoms were beginning to fade. He reached out and picked off the fading blossoms, keeping it pretty, though she couldn't see them. He liked the smell of them. They reminded him of Rachelle. They were perfect for her.

CXBO

Rachelle let the water run over her body, trying to cool it, but it burned from within. She wondered what Britt would say if he knew her thoughts. He would probably think she was foolish, or naive. And he'd be right. She had never awakened next to a man before, and though they hadn't done anything, it didn't change the feeling of desire she felt.

She wondered what she would have done if Britt wanted to make love to her, always before it had been relatively easy to say no, even with her ex-fiancé. When Richard had pressed, she had told him she wanted to wait until their wedding night. What would Richard say if he ever found out that her reason for not sleeping with him was – it never felt right? He'd readily agreed when she deny him, then he turned around and told their friends, gloating like it was a great boon. Rachelle remembered how it hurt.

She knew Britt would never do that. He would keep their relationship between them. He would never pressure or put demands on her. Maybe that was why their relationship was more confusing for her. For once, she truly longed to belong to a man, to have him tell her he loved her, ask her to marry him and be his. And Britt was so worried about her safety and taking care of her, he didn't seem to see it. Or maybe he just didn't truly care for her that way and didn't want to hurt her feelings. Turning the water a touch cooler, she rinsed off.

CRBD

Britt stood in the doorway to the kitchen watching Rachelle make waffles. As she poured the batter in the iron, he was afraid she was going to burn herself, but with amazing skill, she completed it. "It smells good in here," he stepped into the room, "looks good, too."

"The sweet peas aren't fading?"

He glanced at the table. "No, they're still pretty."

"They smell nice."

"They do. You know, I didn't even know what they were until I saw them. I thought sweet pea was a character in Popeye."

"A Popeye fan, huh."

"Actually, I was more of an adventure fan like, Flash and the Fantastic Four.

"Green Lantern and Spiderman?"

"Yeah, but don't tell my mother. She thought that they were a complete waste of time." He reached over and picked off a blossom.

"I used to read them."

"Hmmm, something in common."

"Yeah, along with how many other thousands of people."

"You're the only one that counts."

"You must really want those waffles. Sit down and they'll be right up."

He settled at the table, watching her. "How can you tell when they're done?"

She removed a perfectly golden waffle from the iron. "Smell for one thing, but the secret is actually," she leaned forward and lowered her voice. "They don't stick when you try to raise the lid." She joined him at the table.

03&0

"Where are we going?" Rachelle asked as the elevator rose past her floor.

"My office," he said simply.

"I really should get to work. I was gone almost all day yesterday."

"I thought I'd keep you with me to listen for our guy."

She was doubtful it was the real reason, but let him lead her out of the elevator into his office. "Are you sure you don't have ulterior motives."

"Actually I do. I like having you with me." He closed the door.

"That's not fair," she said, knowing she couldn't argue against that.

She felt and heard him laugh lightly. "You could say you like being with me too." He tightened the arm he had around her waist.

She surprised him when she turned to him. His other arm came around her instinctively when she placed hers around him.

"I do like being around you." The words were said so softly that, if her face hadn't been tipped toward him, he might not have heard her.

Her face, as always, didn't hide much, and what was there took his breath away. Drawn to the image of love, like a man dying of thirst, he took her mouth. He savored her to his soul, knowing he could never live without her. He wanted to declare his love but swallowed the words when the doors burst open.

If Carlton Reese even noticed that he was disturbing anything, it didn't stop him. "Britt, you have to do something about the air circulation," he wheezed. "It's doing nothing for my allergies."

"Carlton," Britt snapped, as Rachelle jerked away from him. "Did you not notice my door was closed?"

"Yes, well, I wanted to talk to you. You're late and Darrell hasn't been at his desk all morning."

"Darrell is in the hospital. I just stopped to see him. If you're concerned at all, he's doing well," Britt said annoyed not only at the disruption, but the man's thoughtlessness. "He'll be going home in a day or two. And I was just about to call the secretarial pool to have them send someone up."

"That's not what it looked like you were doing." The look his brother-in-law gave Rachelle was enough to make Britt clench his fist. The man tried his patience. If it wasn't for his stepmother and sister, he would have fired him long ago. Then again if it weren't for their insistence, he would never have hired him. He knew Carlton had aspiration of moving up into the top leadership, but it would never happen. The man was unwilling to do things he thought were unworthy of him, and tended to blame others when his work was not done or done right. Two things that Britt could not tolerate, besides, the man just grated on his nerves.

"I suggest you go back to your office and try to do some of your work," Britt said pointedly.

"But, what about the air? How am I supposed to

breathe?" the man whined.

The look Britt gave him had shaken many men, turned quite a few deals, and was enough to send Carlton Reese scurrying from his office.

"Britt, is there anything I can do to help?" Rachelle stood holding onto the back of the leather wingback chair in front of his desk.

His first thought was to say no, then he realized like him, she needed to keep busy and more so, for her to be helpful and productive while he was keeping her from her job. "Can you call down and get someone to cover for Darrell?"

"Of course." She let her fingers guide her around the chair. His heart constricted as he watched her reach for his desk, but when she touched it, she moved around it quite confidently until she came to his chair.

"The phone is on the right." He came over, picking up a file. "Why don't you take a seat?"

She settled and moved her hand cautiously up, once she found the phone, her fingers moved with more sure actions. Britt opened the file but his attention remained focused on Rachelle. She was so beautiful and amazing. After everything, she was still ready to help him. There didn't seem be anything she couldn't meet straight on.

"Is there anything else I can do?" she asked, putting the phone down after the call.

Love me. Was his first thought, instead his mind raced for something that would keep her satisfied and safely ensconced in his office.

"Actually there is. I have some dictation Darrell hasn't had time to type up and add to their folders. Would you mind typing them up, so he won't be so far behind when he gets back?"

"Not at all."

"There are over half a dozen of them."

"That's all right."

"If you just want to get as far as you can, you can work here. I have a teleconference in about fifteen minutes. It'll take at least an hour, then we can have lunch. I have a one o'clock appointment, another teleconference and then another appointment, so I'm going to be pretty busy most of the afternoon, but I want to wrap up everything that I can today."

"That's no problem. Just tell me where to put the files." Rachelle was ready to get to work.

"A printed copy goes in the top drawer, and you can just mark the computer file, dictation and the date."

"All right."

Britt opened the drawer reaching for the recorder. He noticed the small sonar device to replace the one that had gotten broken. "I forgot to give you this," he said, placing it in her hand.

"Oh, thank you." She beamed up.

"You're welcome." He handed the recorder to her. "Will you be all right here?"

"Of course, don't worry about me."

"I'm afraid that's impossible. I find I can't help thinking about you, so I worry about you." His kiss was quick and hard.

CR&O

Rachelle finished the dictation about three o'clock. She knew Britt had figured they would take her all day. She also knew they were mostly busy work, but they did need to be done, so she didn't mind. Now that she was finished, she wondered what she should do next. Britt would be tied up in his meeting for another hour.

It didn't take long to make up her mind and leave a message for Britt. She headed down to her office. The trip was slow until she made it to her floor, but once she was in familiar surroundings, she moved along with ease, feeling more confident than she had the entire day.

She could hear Lois as she approached the room. Since no other voice sounded, she knew the older woman must be on the phone. She slid into her chair to wait.

"Rachelle, I thought you were working upstairs today."

"I finished and thought I'd come see if you could use a hand." She smiled.

"What I could use is a break. How about we go downstairs and grab something fattening."

Rachelle laughed. "Sounds good to me."

"I'll ask Sara to cover for me."

Rachelle stood, following Lois out of the room. At the doorway, the direct line to the office began to ring.

"I'll get it," Rachelle said, turning back.

"It's probably the man upstairs checking on you."

Rachelle figured the same. Coming back into the room, she picked up the phone. "Executive answering, may I help you?" There was no answer, and the line went dead. Shrugging her shoulders, she put down the phone and headed out the door around the corner and down the hall.

The explosion behind her was deafening. Rachelle slammed into the wall before sliding down to the floor. She felt boneless. Her ears rang, drowning out all other noise around her. Rachelle coughed as dust and smoke filled the hall. Fear of fire sifted its way into her mind. She tried to get to her feet, but her legs didn't want to hold her. Clinging to the wall, she made it up, stumbling over something on the floor and went back down.

"Rachelle," Lois yelled, reaching her side. "Stay down."

CB&O

Confusion filled the floor as Britt pushed his way through the people crowded around to see into the hall. Dust still hazed the air, but there was no sign of damage. The only thing truly amiss was the two women on the floor.

"Rachelle," he called her name, fear filling his soul as

he ran to the woman who was becoming everything to him.

"Britt," she tried to move, but Lois kept her down.

"You shouldn't move until the paramedics check you out," Lois counseled.

Rachelle didn't seem to listen to her, reaching for him. "Britt."

"I'm right here." He dropped down beside her, catching her in his arms. He tilted her head up so he could look her over.

"I'm not hurt," she assured. "I'm just a little shaken. Was anyone else hurt?"

"No, everyone's fine." He tightened his hold on her. He felt her take a deep breath and sigh in relief. Britt edged back enough to catch her chin, tilt her face up to study her. Wisps of hair she had placed up that morning in a comb had come free. There was a smudge on one cheek. Shock and fear widened the eyes that wouldn't let her see him. He used his hand to stoke her cheek to reassure her.

"I fell into the wall. My ears were ringing a little after the explosion, and everything was confusing, but I'm okay now."

"Yeah, well, I want you checked out to be sure," Britt said firmly as the people from security arrived.

"Please keep everyone back," Britt directed.

The security man nodded back, but when he wasn't having much success, Britt released Rachelle and stood. "Ladies and gentlemen, please calm down. I would like you to evacuate the building. Those of you from this floor please stay in a group, so the police can talk to you. We're going to be sending everyone home early again, but I would like you to check in so we have a list, and can make sure everyone is accounted for. Warren, can you handle that?" He turned to the other security guard there. The man nodded his head and moved off toward the stairs.

With everyone settled and the security handling the crowd Britt turned his complete attention back to Rachelle.

Holding her was short lived because both the police and paramedics arrived. Rachelle was checked out and pronounced to be fine.

With the all clear given for the executive floor, he moved her upstairs, where he made her lie down while the police went over what happened on the floor below. His office was where Detective Todd found them. After the greeting, he took the notes from the officer who had questioned Rachelle and then motioned for Britt to follow him out of the room.

"Miss Harris was definitely the target. It was a relatively small amount of explosive designed to take out one person. It was placed under her desk. When it went off, if she would have had been sitting there, it would have likely killed her. This one was also different because it was set off by a trigger. Since she was with you all day," the detective stopped but Britt finished the sentence.

"He knew when she went down."

"She said the phone rang, and no one was there. I imagine it was him, making sure she was there. It is just luck that she and Mrs. Raymond stepped out when they did."

"Luck," Britt felt it burn cold within him. He had not been able to protect her. It was just luck she was alive, and if she would have died, it would be because of him. His interest in her drew the killer. His love marked her for death. The psycho had it right, a week ago to hurt him, the company was a good way, but now, the way to hurt him, to destroy him, was through Rachelle. In just a few short days, she had become his life.

Funny, for most of his life he knew he had so much, it almost seemed selfish to wish for love. So he accepted the comfortable, cool relationships with glamorous women that were fortunate like him. He'd accepted that until a sweet, gentle woman showed him what it was like to be blessed with her love. Even though she hadn't said the words yet, he knew she loved him. Just as he knew she would always be the most precious thing to him.

Straightening himself, he looked to Todd. "Are there any clues?"

"Not yet, but the crime team is just beginning to collect and go over the pieces."

Britt nodded, "I'm moving Rachelle to a hotel."

"I think that would be an excellent idea, but she won't like it."

Britt was shocked at the detective's comment, he knew Todd was right, Rachelle wouldn't like it. "She doesn't have a choice." She also didn't have a choice about the ending of their relationship, which he was going to do. He knew that would make her mad because she was too bright not to figure out why he was doing it. It would hurt her too, but it was better having her hurt than having her killed for him.

The detective must have been as observant as his job would dictate. "You might want to rethink what you're going to do."

"I will keep her safe."

"But will the cost be worth it?"

"Anything is worth it."

"Even if it hurts her, like this will?"

Britt flinched at his thoughts being said out loud. "It's for the best."

The detective didn't look convinced but said nothing.

"Do you need me for anything?"

When the detective shook his head, Britt turned away. He knew what the man was saying was true. It would hurt Rachelle, but that wouldn't stop him. Rachelle would be safe even if it meant losing her forever.

Rachelle jumped when he entered the office. "Britt?" The tremor in her voice called to him.

"Come on, let's go." He kept his voice controlled as he came and took her arm. Though awareness shot through him, he pushed it away. He had become good at pushing emotions away over the years. That was what made him so successful at business. He just didn't know how well until Rachelle turned to him.

"Britt?" Again she said his name, but this time the question was laced with confusion. She stepped toward him.

He took a step back. "We're going to your apartment so you can pack a bag." He took her elbow but kept his distance. "I'm moving you to a hotel. This time there will be no argument." He snapped the words, making them hard and cold.

Pain then anger flashed over her face, but she stiffened her shoulders and started to walk.

Good, he thought as he directed her to the elevator. She'd better stand on her own.

ᘓ৪০

Rachelle pushed the tears back again as she laid a pair of jeans in her suitcase. She didn't understand what happened to the man she was beginning to know and love. The man that held and comforted her the night before had now shut her out. She was afraid he was gone from her forever. During the car ride to her apartment, he had remained silent. He released her arm once they reached her building. Going up, he was aloof, frozen from her. He took her arm briefly when her thoughts distracted her and she lost her position, but he released her again the moment they reached her apartment.

"I'll wait here," he said from by the door. "Pack enough for the weekend at least."

Not knowing where they were headed, she put in her nicer casual clothes and, at the last minute, added her swimsuit, though she figured it wasn't going to be like a vacation. Deciding she was ready for anything but a formal occasion, she closed the bag.

"Do you have everything?" The coldness in his voice startled her as she stepped into her living room.

"I think so. Where are we going?"

"I have a room reserved for you at The Towers." He stepped forward and took her bag.

"What am I to do there?"

"Stay hidden."

"For how long?"

"As long as it takes." His voice came back hard, and she flinched.

"Then I'd like to take my flowers."

"Leave them." He cut her off sharply.

"No," she said just as strong. "Why are you being like this? What's wrong?" She stepped toward him reaching out, but he must have moved.

"Nothing." His voice came from several feet away. "Get your flowers then, if you have to, so we can leave."

ᏟᏮᎨᎧ

Britt looked at Rachelle. She held the two bouquets to her. "I didn't get a suite as you insisted. The room is small enough you should be able to memorize it easily. The bed is a queen. There are nightstands on either side."

"You might want to remove the lamps, I tend to break them." She tried for a joke, but he ignored it.

"There's a small table by the window with two chairs. A dresser on the opposite wall and the bathroom is by the door. The closet is across from that. Pretty standard."

"Thank you." The words sounded choked, drawing him near, but he stopped himself and pulled back.

"There's a security guard next door and another that will be patrolling the hall. So that should be it. You can order anything you want from room service."

She nodded.

"Good-bye."

"Good-bye," she whispered softly.

For a second, he stood unable to move, not wanting to leave. Britt resisted the urge to take her in his arms, and wipe away the pain he saw on her face. Instead, he turned abruptly, forcing himself out the door.

ᘓᘔ

Rachelle heard the door lock and felt the pain rise. He was gone. He hadn't hugged her. He hadn't kissed her. He hadn't even said when he would be back, but then again, she knew he wouldn't be. What she didn't know was why. What had she done to bring about the change?

Well, it wasn't like she hadn't been left before. She stiffened her shoulders, moving carefully to the dresser, she put down one of the vases, and then made her way to the table, to place the other in the center of it.

That accomplished, she turned and collapsed on the bed in tears. Never had she hurt so much.

ᘓᘔ

Britt slammed down the folder. Trying to concentrate on it was useless. All he could think of was Rachelle. Sweet, loving Rachelle, hurt, bewildered Rachelle. Her pain was so plain to see. And knowing he was the one to put it there was tearing him apart.

He stretched his hand out to the phone, but he pulled it back. He yearned to go to her. It was too late though. He had cut her off and she knew it. It was better this way, he said in his mind for the thousandth time. But, if that were true why did it feel so wrong?

The chimes of the clock rang three times in the dark night. It was a mournful sound matching how he felt. He wanted Rachelle. He reached for the file once again, and then pushed it away just like he did her. Agony raged through him. Slamming his hand down on the desk, the sound echoed into the ring of the phone.

"Rachelle," he said as he snatched it up.

The voice on the phone laughed. "Wrong! You sent

her away, such a noble gesture to keep her safe. Did you really think it would stop me? I thought you should know she cried herself to sleep. I think that it's really rather fitting that she dies like Aubrey, broken-hearted because of you. Yes, you can think of it while you're waiting for your turn to join her in death. Think of the last thing she did before she died was cry because of you." The phone went dead in his ear.

Chapter Ten

Britt dropped the phone not caring where it landed as he ran for the door. Not waiting for the elevator he took the stairs two at a time. His car tore out of the parking lot, skidding into the street. It wasn't until he had the car straightened out that he found his cell phone that he left in the car had been smashed and knew it was by the caller. The man had everything planned.

He was five minutes from The Towers. Britt decided he couldn't risk the time to stop and find a phone to call the police. Maybe if he was lucky an officer would try to pull him over for speeding. He would pay any ticket. He just prayed he was in time. If he could get to Rachelle in time, he would never make her cry again.

೮೩୫

Rachelle came wide awake wondering what time it was. Her body still claimed exhaustion, but between her restlessness and finally crying herself to sleep, it was not surprising. Reaching for the nightstand, it took her several seconds to find the watch her sister gave her on the unfamiliar surface. She fumbled and pressed the button. "Three-o-eight," the cartoon voice said.

Three, Rachelle groaned, wishing she could believe it was in the afternoon. Before she had time to think anything else, she heard the faint sound of a foot pressing down into the carpet.

"Wh ... ho's there?" She knew the words were stupid. If there was someone in the room, they wouldn't be answering. *This is foolish, I'm scaring myself.* It was just the sounds of the unfamiliar hotel. She waited, listening. When no sound came, she relaxed and her thoughts went to Britt.

The thought was hardly through her when she heard another sound. This one was closer, more distinct. Someone was in her room. She started to move when she felt something wet seep through the blanket. Rachelle rolled away but got tangled in the sheets. Fear filled her. She kicked and tried to scramble free, but a hand caught her hip and pulled her back. Her scream was cut off as her face was shoved into the mattress. In terror, she kicked her legs, but the blankets impeded her motion. A hand came down on the back of her neck with brutal force pushing her face deeper, cutting off more air. She fought to push back and gained an inch, enabling her to gulp in a lungful of air before a knee was rammed into her back. She went down.

Swinging her arms out did nothing, she couldn't reach her attacker. She tried to shift under him but only got the knee ground harder into her back. It wasn't until lights began to flash in her mind that she realized she was suffocating. With renewed effort, she fought back. Frantically, she grabbed the edge of the bed, then the desk and tried to pull herself forward.

A hand gripped her arm pulling it back, while the other hand kept the pressure on her neck. Feebly, Rachelle clawed at the desk in desperation, her hand bumped into the base of the lamp. She locked on it, pulling back with what strength she had left.

The lamp crashed down. A muttered curse sounded through the ringing in her ears. Then her own cry as the heavy brass lamp clipped her shoulder before it came to rest on the bed.

She was too stunned to realize the pressure was gone from her neck and back. She gulped air and jerked as there was another slam against her door.

⊂ℜℬↄ

Britt kicked the door again, and finally felt it budge. He wished he had the master key, but as startled as the night clerk was when he burst through the lobby door and yelled for security and the police to go to Rachelle's room, he knew the man couldn't produce it. He just hoped the man would get the police.

One more kick and the door gave way, banging back against the wall. He pushed it back open. The room was flooded with light. Britt caught the motion of someone on the balcony, but he couldn't force himself past the woman on the bed. Rachelle lay unmoving across it. A lamp lay broken by her shoulder. The flowers she loved were mashed around her. Anguish as he never knew hit him. He was too late. He stumbled forward reaching for her, needing to hold her. He had been a fool to push her away.

She jerked when he touched her hair. "Rachelle," he gasped, trying to catch hold of her as she started to struggle. Britt called her name again as he turned her over. She groaned and her body began to tremble. He pulled her to him.

"Britt."

His name was barely a whisper, but it never sounded so good to him. "I'm here sweetheart, I'm here. Don't worry. I'll never leave you again," he promised, pressing kisses to her temple. "Careful, you're hurt," he gasped, when she flinched.

Rachelle made a slight shake of her head grimacing. His hands were already sliding over her. "Where?"

"My neck, shoulders and back."

Britt held her against him and lifted her hair. Her

137

reddened skin showed where fingers had been. "I'm sorry, love." Gently, he ran his fingers over her abused flesh, bringing a whimper.

"Freeze!" the command came from the doorway. Britt looked up at the two officers standing there with guns drawn. "Let the lady go and back off the bed, real slow." One of the officers motioned with his head, his gun never moving.

"Wait a minute. I'm not your man. He went over the balcony." Britt knew it was too late to catch him. The man was long gone.

"Hands up," the officer returned, not slackening his stance.

Slowly, Britt raised his hands. Rachelle remained clinging to him.

"Just call Detectives Todd or Adams. I'm Britton Clairbourne. This is Rachelle Harris. They can explain everything."

"Like you breaking into the lady's room in the middle of the night." The other officer finally spoke.

"I didn't." Britt stopped. "Well, I did break in and I will pay for the damages, but I had to get to her." Britt realized that didn't sound any better. "Before he killed her," he added, wishing Rachelle would come out of the stupor she seemed to have fallen into.

"Move off the bed." He was ordered again.

At his shift away from her, Rachelle became alert. "Britt," her voice wobbled.

"Rachelle, sweetheart, I need you to look over at the doorway and tell the officers there who I am, and that you're in no danger from me."

"Danger?"

"Yes, there are two police officers with guns pointed at me."

Again she flattened herself to him, wrapping her arms around his neck. "Don't shoot him. Please, don't. He saved me. He's ... he's my boyfriend." She stumbled over the words making Britt laugh. After everything that happened, she sounded like a high school girl caught kissing a boy. Though considering what she was wearing and where they were, it would look like they got caught doing a little more than kissing.

As the guns slowly went away, he lowered his hands, sliding them back around Rachelle. The men looked back toward the broken door then back to him. "What happened here?"

After Britt started to talk, one of the officers went to find out what happened to the security men next door. He came back a minute later, saying he'd called an ambulance. One of the security men was just regaining consciousness, and the other was still out. The officer then disappeared back into the room.

A few minutes later the floor was filled with people. Rachelle finished describing what happened after the ambulance took away the unconscious guard. Britt insisted the paramedic check her out while he went to listen to what the other security guard told the police.

"I was doing my rounds in the hall, stopped to get a cola for us. I knocked on the door. As Jase opened it, I was hit from behind."

"Jase is the other guard?" Detective Adams, who had shown up a couple minutes earlier, asked.

"Yes, Jase Gordon. I didn't see anything until the officer found me."

The officer nodded taking notes.

"Warren, you better have the medic check you out before you go," Britt suggested to the man before he turned to go back to Rachelle's room.

She huddled in a chair, trying to follow all that was going on around her, when he stepped through the broken doorway. She looked overwhelmed and exhausted. Forcing his eyes from her to the manager, who hovered just outside the room, Britt motioned the man over.

"Is the suite reserved for Clairbourne Industries available?"

"Yes, sir, it is."

"I'd like to move Miss Harris into it for the rest of the night."

"I'll get the key card immediately."

Britt moved to the officer in charge of the scene. "Are you done with us?"

The man looked over at Rachelle sitting in a chair, wrapped in a blanket, and nodded. "We know where to reach you."

"We'll be out of town for the next couple of days. I have to attend a fundraiser and I want to get Rachelle away from all of this for a while, but Detective Adams has my number where I can always be reached."

"I'm sure you know this, but if you think of anything to add, let us know."

"Of course." He went to Rachelle and knelt down in front of her. "Rachelle," he said softly to let her know who was there before he placed a hand on her arm. "Let's gather your belongings. We're leaving."

"Home?" she asked hopefully.

"No, just upstairs to a different suite but don't worry, I'm going to stay with you."

"I thought you didn't want me anymore." Her voice cracked and chin dropped to cover its trembling.

The whole picture she presented made him ache. "Please, listen to me." He reached out tilting her chin up. "I want you with me, I promise. But I was afraid that having you near me was putting you in more danger. I couldn't let that happen."

"But it makes no difference. He's still going to come after me."

"I realize that now. All I succeeded in doing was hurting you, and leaving you alone and vulnerable, while making myself miserable. I plan to stay closer now, though. That is, if you'll let me. He's going to have to go through me to get to you. Will you trust me again?"

She caught her bottom lip between her teeth. Tears glistened in her eyes. "Yes." It was a soft, but sure answer. His heart soared. He felt as if he'd received the greatest honor in his life.

"Let's go." He helped her up. There was not much to gather up because she hadn't unpacked anything. The instant the manager appeared with the keycard, they headed up stairs. It only took a few minutes to have Rachelle tucked in bed. "I'm going to leave the door open. If you need me, just call." He caught the motion of her lip being caught in her teeth again.

"Tell me?" he urged her to say what she was holding back.

"Will you stay here until I go to sleep?"

"My pleasure." He lay out on the top of the covers, beside her. Stretching an arm over her, he pulled her tight. With a sigh, she cuddled into him and in just a few breaths was asleep.

Britt knew he should move to his own bed but he couldn't tear himself from her yet. He had almost lost her. He would never forget the sight of her still body on the bed. He pulled her closer, turning his face into the silky stands of her hair, taking the scent of her into him. He could smell sweat-peas and wondered if they were from her lotion or the flowers crushed around her on the bed.

He pressed his lips against her temple and vowed again to keep her safe. This time though he would see to it personally. If anyone wanted to get to her, they'd have to go through him. He kissed her again, relaxed, and was asleep.

CRBD

Rachelle relaxed back into the comfortable leather

seat. The sun was coming in through the window, warming her body. The soft hum of the powerful engine and the gentle music on the radio added to the conditions drawing her from sleep. Britt's hand brushed back a lock of her hair then stroked her cheek. Since waking up beside him this morning, Britt seemed to have an incessant need to touch her — a hand on her arm, around her waist, stroking her cheek, or just holding her hand. Rachelle didn't mind. She liked the physical contact with him.

Waking up beside him again felt like the most natural thing. She wished he would have done more than one brief kiss before he bolted from the bed to his room for a shower. But then again, if he was feeling anything like she was feeling, the brief kiss was for the best.

Never had she been plagued with such strong feelings and desires. The same feelings that felt as if they'd crush and destroy her the evening before when he sent her away, now lifted her up in joy. The only difference being, Britt wanted her. She didn't doubt it. Rachelle drifted in the pleasure of it.

⋘⋙

Britt let his fingers slide over her cheek, down her arm to her hand, taking it in his. Her fingers curled around his. He knew by her breathing she was asleep. It was another twenty minutes before he turned off the main road onto his family estate. The Clairbourne Estate had been in his family for over a century. Though he was rarely there, it belonged to him. His stepmother spent more time living there than anyone, but even Tiffany, his stepsister and her husband, Carlton, spent more time there than he did. There just seemed no reason to drive the almost a half hour there, when his apartment was less than five minutes from work. And if he admitted the real reason, it was because there was no one special waiting for him there.

Until the last few days around Rachelle, he hadn't

realized how much of life he was missing. He'd become a workaholic. It had happened so gradually. At first, he had been working hard to get the company on even ground. Then it was to get it the way he wanted it. Soon, it had just become the norm to spend all his time at work. He never thought about life much outside work except on the rare occasions he got together with friends for trips they took. And, since they started getting married and having families, those had become less frequent, down to just once or twice a year.

Glancing over at the woman beside him, he realized he'd found an important piece of what was missing in his life. It was time he did some serious courting of Rachelle. He wanted her to know how well they were suited.

Britt pulled up to the main drive, circling around to the front door instead of going back to the garage. He stopped the car and turned to her. She was so peaceful he hated to wake her. Leaning over, he brushed her hair back from her face. When she let out a soft sigh, he could resist no longer. He brushed his lips over hers. He kissed his way across her cheek to her neck and felt her react. Her hand came up to caress the side of his face. He went back to her lips for a full passionate kiss. Her fingers burrowed into his hair, holding him there, not that he had any intention of ending the kiss yet.

He let her learn the taste of him, as he reveled in her. She followed his movements. A groan escaped her, when he finally managed to pull back.

"Umm," she purred. "That's a nice way to wake up." Her voice was velvet soft, and it was all he could do to resist going back for more of her.

"How did you know it was me?"

"I know." There was an intriguing blush on her face.

"You sound certain."

"Well, let's see. I fell asleep in your car, with you driving. Which I do apologize for, I've not been very good company."

"That's all right." He let the subject change for a minute. "You needed the rest. You didn't get much last night."

"Yes, and you should take that as a compliment. I don't trust many people's driving enough anymore to fall asleep."

Britt knew she was serious, but that she was also keeping the subject from the one they started. "Thank you. Now, how did you know it was me?"

She hesitated, "Your scent for one thing."

"Is that bad?"

"No, not at all," she hurried to pacify him. "I like it. It's fresh, clean, masculine, but not overpowering at all. It's nice." She stopped and blushed.

"Thank you, I won't change then. What else?"

Her lip caught in between her teeth, in that way he was beginning to love. He wondered what she would say if he told her it made him want to go for the lip, claim it between his teeth for himself. She spoke before he could do it, and her words about sunk him. "The feel of you, no one else makes me feel the way you do when you touch me." The words were whispered, but they echoed in his mind.

"Yes," he said, coming into kiss her again. This time, it was him that groaned. "We'd better go in before we get caught making out in the car. And that hasn't happened to me for nearly two decades." That brought a laugh from her.

He got out of the car and came around to get her.

"Oh, smell the fresh air and flowers," she exclaimed. "Tell me what your house is like?"

He described the flowers running up on either side of the walk, paying attention to them for the first time since he couldn't remember when.

"We have six steps here." He warned her and let her feel her way to get the foot spacing on them. He drew her to the side, where there was a foot-wide stone railing. She paused to finger it then turned to him. "Britt, how big is this house?"

He knew this question was coming and sighed. "Three stories about twenty-two thousand square feet."

She stopped. "That's not a house. I'll never be able to find my way around."

"You'll do it easily." He drew her up the steps.

"Easy for you."

"For you too, I've seen you at work."

"I've been doing that for months, and I still get confused every once in a while."

"Well, if you get disoriented just yell and I'll come find you. I plan on staying very close."

"You better and it would be a good idea to put any valuable breakables away."

He laughed, though he knew she was serious. "Ming vases away."

"You have one?" she gasped.

"No, not my taste, but I don't want you to worry."

"Well, I will. I'm at five lamps now, and the only reason it isn't more, is that I changed to brass in my apartment. I haven't been counting light bulbs."

"Yes, but the last one was well spent. Feel free to break as many of my lamps over attackers as you need." He kissed her on the nose, pulling her toward the door like a reluctant child.

"Britt." An older woman's voice called him as they entered. "About time you got here. You haven't been home for too long."

"Been busy." He released Rachelle to give the plump older woman a kiss on the cheek.

"I know, I've heard all about those dreadful doings. Are you okay, my boy?"

"Fine. Mae, this is Rachelle. Rachelle." He caught her hand and brought it to the woman's. "This is Mae. She spent half her life chasing me out of her kitchen."

"Huh," the woman scoffed. "There's truth in that. I couldn't keep this boy full. He was always eating and growing. I couldn't keep up with him. Now I hardly see him." There was a genuine sadness in her voice at that, but she waved it off. "Mrs. Clairbourne's not here. She went to town."

"I'm going to take Rachelle on a tour of the house." He knew the woman was studying her. Mae had been like a second mother to him. He was happy when the woman smiled as if satisfied.

"I'll be in the kitchen if you need anything."

"We'll be there in a few minutes." He led Rachelle up the stairs, stopping first at the room that would be hers, letting her get used to it.

Thirty minutes later they came through the living room, toward the kitchen. Rachelle hung on to Britt's arm with one hand while trailing her other hand along the wall.

"I'll never find my room again."

"That's all right as long as you get the right wing, on the right side of the house, if you miss your room, you'll end up in the bathroom or my room. So it won't be too bad."

"As long as I get the right wing and the right side of the house," she repeated sourly.

"Nothing to worry about, I'll watch out for you." He slid his arm around her so they were walking arm in arm. He warned her about the double swinging doors to the kitchen before leading her through them.

"All settled Miss Harris?" Mae's mellow voice greeted her.

"Yes, thank you, and call me Rachelle, please." Rachelle missed Mae's glance to Britt and his nod.

"Can I fix you something to eat?"

"Actually, I was wondering if you'd mind fixing us a picnic lunch. Rachelle and I are going to take a walk around the grounds, and I thought we'd stop and enjoy ourselves. That is if you'd like?" He squeezed Rachelle's hand.

"That sounds wonderful."

"I'll have it ready in five minutes."

"Perfect," Britt said, "I'm going to run up and put on some jeans. Rachelle, would you like to wait outside?"

"No, I'll wait here. If that's okay?"

"Of course," he placed her hand on the counter and pressed a kiss to her cheek. "I'll be right back."

Rachelle edged to the side. When her hip bumped a chair fastened there, she settled into it. "Is there anything I can do to help?"

"No, I have all the fixin's ready. The day before an event I always keep a tray ready, because I never know who will be around and when."

"Do they hold these often?"

"Twice a year, the summer fundraiser and a Christmas social, it's a combined party and charity event for gathering gifts and toys. Mrs. Clairbourne does a real nice job with them. She raises a lot of money. People find it easier to give, just to be invited."

"You sound like you've been doing this awhile."

"I've been here twenty-eight years. I started out just a part time cook, but it grew over the years. Now I oversee the house. I have people that come in to help with the cleaning and caterers for the social events. It's a wonderful job, and I have a wonderful place to live. It would be nice if Britt was around more. He lets too much of life pass him by, though maybe that's changing. You're good for him. He looks happy."

"I wish that were true. I know with all that's happening he's under a lot of stress, and I'm afraid I'm just one more worry. My blindness is a complication for him."

"That's not what he feels for you. Take it from me. I've known him a long time. He cares for you."

Rachelle could feel the color rise in her cheeks and

was helpless to stop it.

"So you care for him, too. That's good. He was a good boy, a touch on the lonely side as his wealth cut him off from people at times. Still, he grew into a good man, though he's remained lonely because of his sense of responsibility and drive to build Clairbourne. It's time he found someone to make him happy, so he won't be alone anymore."

Rachelle was still at loss for words when she heard Britt walked back into the kitchen.

"Please, tell me you're not telling her secrets of my youth," he said with mock distress.

"Only the real juicy parts, someone has to warn her."

"Thanks a lot," he said with exaggerated dryness.

"You're welcome. Here's your lunch. You two enjoy yourselves."

"Thanks, Mae." He gave the woman a squeeze before helping Rachelle from the stool and snagging up the basket.

"The sun feels so nice," Rachelle exclaimed, stepping outside. Turning to the warmth, she tilted her face up.

"It's a beautiful day, clear blue sky."

"Describe it all to me. I want to picture it."

"Well." He put the basket down, stepped behind her and wrapped his arms around her shoulders. "The house sits on a small rise. Straight ahead and to the right, about three hundred feet away is a grove of trees that stretches out almost a mile. There are also a few scattered trees across the lawn and a small stream that trickles through it." Taking her hand he pointed out. "It comes from that direction. There's a foot bridge over there. Though, you can step over it almost anywhere. Up this way, where the stream starts, there are a couple small ponds with fish and water lilies and some plants, flowers and bushes around them. They continue over this way, where there's a swimming pool. It's behind the house on the right corner. Tan and reddish tile connects it to the house. There's stairs leading down to the pool from the upper floors to give easy access. So if you want to go down to the pool later."

"That would be nice. I haven't been swimming for a long time."

"We'll go." He kissed the side of her cheek. "Back to the yard, there's a rose garden stretching to the left. It was left over from my grandmother. My grounds keeper really lords over it. There are about thirty different varieties. It smells beautiful, you'll love it. Beyond there are the stables."

"You have horses?"

"Five. My sister keeps them exercised. I don't ride much anymore. Right now, I'm wondering why."

"Can we go see them?"

"Why not." He dropped his arm to her waist, snagging the basket back up, and headed her that direction.

"Oh, smell the roses."

"I told you."

"You said nice, this is much better. There must be a hundred bushes."

"Approximately, hold it a moment." He picked a flower. "For you."

"Oh," she touched the soft petal. "What color is it?"

"Pink and white with touches of yellow."

"A Peace Rose?"

"I don't know their names. I just like how it smells."

"Me, too." She laid her head on his shoulder as his arm came around her again. She held the rose so they both could smell it. Picking the flower was a sweet gesture but the sweetest was he removed all the thrones before handing it to her.

Rachelle lost track of where they were going. It wasn't much further before she caught the scent of the stables.

"We're here. Since the weather is nice, we keep the horses in the pasture instead of the stalls." He directed her to the fence.

Rachelle stretched her free hand out through the boards, keeping the one with the rose tight over her heart.

Britt made a clicking sound.

She shifted toward the horses when she heard the sound of approaching hooves. Britt slid his hand down her arm directing her to feel the velvet of the horse's nose.

"This sweet lady is Daisy Mae."

Rachelle laughed as another horse butted her arm. "Let me guess, Little Abner."

"Nope, Charlie."

"Charlie?" she asked, in disbelief.

"Actually, Sir Charles the third. He came with the name. I just shortened it to Charlie, besides, he's kind of a funny pest, but he's a good ride."

"And Daisy Mae?"

"I named her. I tease Mae I named her for her, but actually we have a patch in the pasture where these little daisies grow wild, and as a foal, she always used to lay in it to sleep. She's a good horse, nice, gentle. She just turned fourteen."

"Could I ride her?" Rachelle turned to him.

Britt only hesitated a second. "If you'd like. You don't have to for me. I can come down later."

"I'd like to. I haven't been on a horse since I was a kid. You'll have to guide her though."

"She'll follow Charlie. I'll get them saddled." He left her to get the tack.

"What's the name of your other horses?" She continued to pet any horse she could reach.

"Butterscotch," he said, coming up with a saddle. "I call her Scottie. It fits her personality better. A friend of mine got her for his daughter, but she couldn't handle her. So I helped him find a different horse and kept her." He told her about the other horses until he led Charlie and Daisy Mae from the pasture.

"Ready for a leg up?" He directed her to the mare,

helping her find the stirrup. Rachelle swung easily in the saddle. "Nice," he said, and got on Charlie.

"This is great. I can't believe it."

"Well, let's ride."

For forty-five minutes he led her through the trees until he reached the area he wanted. "Ready for lunch?"

"I'm starving. Being out in the fresh air has my appetite going."

Being with Rachelle had his appetite going too, but he was hungry for her, Britt thought as he came to help her down. Wrapping his hands around his waist, he wondered what she'd do if he took a bite out of her. "Good, let's eat."

He handed her the blanket he had brought, picked up the basket, and then caught her hand leading her a few feet away.

Later, Rachelle sighed after taking the last bite of her croissant sandwich. "This was perfect."

"I could use a nap." He shifted so he was lying stretched out with his head on her thigh. When she didn't move, he crossed his arms over his chest and closed his eyes. He opened them again when he felt her caress his cheeks. The smile she had for him was incredible. With a sigh he closed his eyes again and let her gentle strokes lull him to sleep.

ଦୃଷ୍ଠ

Rachelle couldn't believe the feel of the man leaning against her. There was something special about being able to just touch him. Careful not to disturb him she settled back into the thick grass and let her fingers study his face. He had such wonderful cheek bones. His was a strong face. It surprised her how easy it was to bring it up in her memory, but it was there in fine detail. His jaw was getting a touch rough with stubble. His lips were curved in a smile. He was happy, she thought just before following him into sleep.

Rachelle felt the velvet touch on her cheek. It glided over her lips then made its way over her chin in a tantalizing path down her neck. The weight on her stomach shifted, and the velvet stokes took up its trail again. This time she caught the fragrance of the rose.

"Waking up with you is getting to be a habit," she mumbled contently.

"A good habit I hope," Britt answered continuing the rose's trail.

"I think so."

"Good, because you make an excellent pillow and are much better than a teddy bear."

She smiled then it faded. "Britt."

"What is it, sweetheart?"

"I need to tell you something before you get the wrong impression especially after the last couple of nights. I ..." She found the words difficult to get out now that he was waiting. Taking a breath, she forced the words out. "I don't sleep around, just so you know. So you don't expect ..."

"I know, I could tell."

"Well, it's a little further than that. I've never. I mean ever."

She felt his hand cup the cheek the rose had just caressed. She shivered with awareness.

"It's okay Rachelle."

"I thought I should tell you, so you'd understand."

"I do understand." In his mind, he added that it was okay, because he planned to be the only man to ever make love to her. "Come on, we better get back."

Chapter Eleven

"Did you two have a nice picnic?" Mae greeted them as they entered the kitchen.

"Wonderful, Britt took me for a ride on the horses. It had been so long since I've ridden. I loved it."

"It's been awhile for him," the housekeeper commented. "Bet you enjoyed it too." She looked at him and grinned.

"So right you are."

"Melissa is back. She's glad you showed up. She was worried since you hadn't called."

Britt winced. "Things have been a little hectic, but I should have."

"You're right, you should have. You work too hard." The voice came from by the doorway. "It's good to see you take a day off finally."

"Melissa," he greeted his stepmother as she came forward to give him a kiss on the cheek. As usual Melissa looked as if she just stepped out of a fashion magazine. She wore a pair of basic black pants with a cream cashmere sweater. Her platinum hair barely touched her cheek, accentuating her high cheekbone and smoky eyes.

"I was beginning to wonder if you were going to show," she chided him. "But your tux is back from the cleaners and hanging in your closet."

"You didn't doubt I'd be here for a minute."

"You're right, I figured you would. You're like your father. He didn't like black tie affairs either, but he looked incredible in a tux."

Britt just laughed. Melissa Clairbourne had several faults. She was shallow, didn't know much about real life being born with a silver-spoon, but her love for his father wasn't one of her failings. Neither was her charity work. She cared about raising money for the children's hospital and could run a charity function like no other.

Britt took her hand leading her two steps to Rachelle. "I'd like you to meet Rachelle Harris." He caught Rachelle's hand bringing it up. "Rachelle, this is my stepmother, Melissa Clairbourne."

"It's a pleasure to meet you," Rachelle said, clasping the hand as it brushed hers.

Melissa looked perplexed at Britt for a moment. "It's nice to meet you. I saw your picture in the paper the other day, but I didn't know you were dating anyone."

"Oh, Britt and I—"

Britt cut her off. "Have only been seeing each other a short time."

"I should warn you, Tiffany invited Maureen to stay the night. She's coming out with them this evening."

Britt groaned inside. "I hope she doesn't think I'm going to be her escort."

"You know your sister," Melissa said.

"Yes, I know her." Britt wasn't happy at all. He knew his stepsister meant well, but the pushing her best friend at him continually was getting to be too much. Maureen might be eagerly willing, but he was not in the least interested. "I wish she'd listen to me."

"If you're concerned about me don't worry. I'll stay in my room out of the way," Rachelle put in softly.

"No, you won't. Whatever gave you that idea?" Britt

objected.

"I … I don't really fit in here. I don't know anyone." She tried to reason.

"You know me, and I want you by my side." He caught her arm, letting his hand slide down to hers.

"I didn't bring a dress appropriate for the evening."

"I know. I didn't give you the chance to stop by the dry cleaners or your apartment, so I figured I'd take you shopping."

"But I."

"I'm not letting you object. You are my choice. Melissa, don't you have someone coming to do your hair and make-up?"

"Of course, Laura's coming."

"Do you think she would have time to do Rachelle's, too?" It was hardly a question.

"I'm certain, but I'll call her immediately to let her know." She left the room leaving them alone.

"You're all set," he said in finality. "We'll go shopping, and then out to dinner."

"You really like to direct my life," she said with a sigh.

"Does it bother you?"

"A little, I'm used to fighting since my accident to prove I can take care of myself. But I will admit it has felt good having you taking care of me lately."

"I do care about you." He squeezed her hand.

"I know." She smiled.

"But you'd like me to ask instead of dictating."

"Yes."

"All right then, what would you like to do?"

"Well, I feel funny about having you take me shopping but I will need help, so I can accept that but … instead of going out to eat, could we come back here and eat like we did for lunch? Then maybe we could swim, listen to music or even watch a movie if you'd like."

"You like listening to movies still?"

"Yes, it's interesting what your mind comes up with for scenes and if the actors are familiar, it helps me picture them."

"There's a movie or two I wouldn't mind seeing. We could light a fire even though it's not going to be cold tonight."

"There's always air conditioning," she laughed.

"Right."

"You don't mind?"

"Let's see, sharing you with a crowded room of people, where you're slightly tense or having you relaxed back in my arms all to myself. Hard choice."

"Who said anything about in your arms?"

"A man can always hope."

"Well, maybe a little cuddling would be acceptable."

"Cuddling, I like the sound of that. How about it?" He lowered his lips to kiss her in way of finishing the question. Britt drew the kiss out until a moan escaped from her.

"What was that again?" she whispered when he drew back.

He slid his arms around her and kissed her again.

⊂ℬ⊃

Shopping with a man was a new experience for Rachelle. Just inside the door she stopped. The music that greeted her, suggested very high class. The feeling was backed up with the scented air. Rachelle got the feel the shop was far outside her means. "Britt, I don't know about this."

"Don't worry. This is where Melissa and Tiffany always shop for their gowns."

That confirmed it for her. She could handle buying a new gown but nothing in the price range that would be here. "I can't afford to shop here," she said firmly, not at all embarrassed.

"You're not, I'm buying," he answered back.

"But I can't let you pay that much for me."

"We've already had this discussion. I pick out the dress. You pick where we eat and what we do."

"But I can't allow you to do that."

He stopped her with a finger against her lips. "Stop saying that, just think of it as a bonus for all the stress you've been caused because of me."

When her lips started to move, he stopped her. "Agree."

"Mr. Clairbourne, how are you, sir?" The shopkeeper came up before Rachelle could object again.

"Fine, thank you." He removed his fingers from her lips.

"My name is Georgia. May I help you?" the woman asked anxiously.

"We need a dress for tomorrow night."

"Yes, yes."

Rachelle heard the woman's hands clasp together.

"What did you have in mind?"

Rachelle decided she had no choice, but she could lay down some guidelines. "Nothing flashy, I'd like it to be on the conservative side. Black is always practical."

"You already have a beautiful black gown. I was thinking something lighter. But you're definitely right, nothing too flashy, just classy."

"Why don't you come this way and we'll …"

Rachelle heard the catch in the woman's voice as she realized she was about to say see. "I'll show you where the selection is."

It was getting real easy to move with Britt.

"I'd say a size six."

"Usually," Rachelle said, feeling slightly embarrassed.

"Here we are then."

"Not the red one, and let's eliminate the orange also," Britt said beside her.

"Yes, please," Rachelle added.

"What about this lovely gold sequined?" the woman suggested.

"Is it yellow toned?" Rachelle asked. "I don't look very good in yellows." She was still while the dress was held up to her.

"Umm, you're right. The gold is not a great color on you," Britt rejected it also.

"There's this stunning aqua crepe. The color ought to be perfect."

"Color's nice," Britt said, "but I don't know if I like the cut."

"What's it like?" Rachelle asked and the woman answered.

"Stunning, trim fit. It cuts across the breast with a push up bra to give the best to your figure. It would look perfect on you."

"No, thank you, it doesn't sound like me. Do you have anything with shoulders?"

"Of course, I have this halter with the intricate bead work."

Immediately Rachelle thought of showy.

"Or I have this."

"Yes, that's more like it." Britt exclaimed and Rachelle turned to him.

"Britt?"

"It's a whitish material with a blue shimmer to it. I guess it's what you would say, slim cut, with a slit that would go to your thigh. I don't think it would be too high. Its sleeves . . . puff out kind of, and then narrows at the elbow. The neck doesn't look like it will be too low either. I'm not sure what you call it."

He helped Rachelle trace the lines of the dress. "Want to try it on?"

"I guess."

"This way," the woman led the way, carrying the dress.

Britt stayed as her guide until they reached the dressing room.

"Do you need a hand?" Georgia asked as he released her.

"I can manage," Rachelle assured her, stepping into the dressing room. She fumbled through removing her clothes and sliding the dress over her head. The material felt incredible as it slid over her body, smooth and silky. It hugged plenty but it wasn't tight except for the constrictive sleeve which made it so she couldn't reach around to get the zipper past halfway up. Standing there frustrated for a moment she finally steeled herself. "Umm, Britt."

"Yes," his voice came from just the other side of the door. Rachelle wasn't sure if she was relieved or more nervous.

"I need help with the zipper."

CBEO

Britt almost groaned aloud as the image came to his mind. His first instinct was to join her and take care of it, but with the heat rising in him, he thought better of it. He didn't want to raise any more speculations about him and Rachelle than him buying her a dress would cause. "I'll get the sales lady." It only took a motion for the woman to come.

"May I help you?"

"Yes, she needs help with the zipper."

The woman nodded, and after a light tap on the door, she stepped in. "Oh, spectacular," she gasped. "That's wonderful on you."

"Except that I need a little help with the zipper."

"Certainly," the woman lifted it the last six inches. "Mr. Clairbourne will love it."

"You don't think it's too much for me?" Rachelle ran her hands over her sides.

"Oh, no. It's perfect."

"I've never had a man pick out clothes for me before. My sister usually helps me and she knows my taste, but she's out of town."

"Well, Mr. Clairbourne has excellent taste. The gown is lovely on you. The coloring, as is the fit, is perfect. Let's show him."

Timidly Rachelle stepped from the room. "Britt."

She heard his footsteps approach. "Beautiful." His voice was a low growl full of appreciation.

"She has a wonderful figure to dress and very beautiful coloring."

"Very."

"You like it?" Rachelle asked, still self-conscious. Her hand fluttered up in front of her. Britt caught her fingers bringing them to his lips.

"You look lovely in it." He kissed the pulse point on her wrist making her heart race.

"It's ... it's not too bold ... or flashy?" She had trouble getting the words out after the feel of him on her skin.

"Not at all." Britt found it hard to take his eyes off of her. He knew Rachelle had a good shape and would draw attention, but oh wow. She was beautiful. He forced himself to swallow. "It is very elegant. Trust me. It's you."

"All right, if you think so."

"I do. Why don't you change, and we'll go find some shoes to match."

"I guess I can't get by with a simple pair of flats, can I?"

Britt laughed. "Don't worry. Remember. I already promised I'll be right by your side."

"So you can help me up when I fall on my face."

"I promise I won't let you fall." He took her hand, bringing it to her lips. "Unless it's for me," his voice was low so only she could hear it before brushing his lips over her knuckles.

Rachelle figured it was already too late for that. She

was in love with Britt Clairbourne. Wise or not, her heart was his forever.

Hours later, she couldn't have been happier, relaxing against him on the couch. They had spent about an hour in the pool, then going with the earlier thought, he built a fire, turning up the air conditioner wasn't necessary. They sat in the middle of the floor and ate the dinner Mae prepared for them before moving to the couch to watch the sequel to a movie that had been one of her favorites about two years before she lost her sight.

When Britt's arm came around her back, it had been the most natural thing to cuddle back into him.

"Comfortable?" His lips brushed her temple.

"Umm, very. This is nice." She turned into him, letting her head rest against his chest. His arm tightened.

"I wish it was going to be just us the rest of the weekend."

"You'd get bored," she countered.

"Not with you." He kissed her temple again. "When I'm with you, I find I don't need anyone else."

"That's such a nice thing to say." She tilted her head to give him a kiss, getting his cheek.

"It's the truth. We're going to have to work on your aim." He slid his fingers in her hair to hold her in position while he continued the kiss. The growl that escaped his throat was echoed by one from her. Her arms came up around his neck, aligning her body to his as his hands ran over her back, in long caressing movements that molded her to him.

When the kiss ended, she felt as if her very soul had been branded by the essence of him. He was in every one of her senses.

Britt felt like he couldn't get enough of her. It was like his soul thirsted for her, and the more he drank, the more he yearned. It had never been so for him. She was desire. She was passion, ambrosia just for him. He knew she could never be this way for another man, just as he knew there was not another woman for him. With this kiss, Rachelle was his and he was one more step to winning her forever.

"I think our movie ended," he whispered in her ear.

"Oh, I think I missed part of it."

"That's okay. We can listen to it again. I think it's becoming my favorite movie." The huskiness in his voice had her knowing what they were doing during the end of the movie was his favorite part.

"I think we'd better go to bed." It was after the words came out, and he groaned, she realized how it sounded. "I mean, I to, you to," she fumbled with the words.

He stopped her with a hand over her mouth. "I know what you mean and you're correct. We both should go to our separate beds. Though, I'm not likely to get much sleep." Even with a cold shower. He let the thought cross his mind.

He stood, pulling her up to him, his arm sliding naturally around her. "Let's go."

⋘⋙

Rachelle found it surprisingly easy to go to sleep, even as worked up as she had been. She could honestly say she slept fine. She just hoped no one asked about her dreams, they would make her blush. She definitely had to get her thoughts away from kissing Britt.

When she stepped from her room, she heard no noise to indicate that anyone was around. From the earlier chime of the grandfather clock at the bottom of the stairs, she knew it was a little after seven. From the time she had spent around Britt, she knew he was usually up and busy long before this. So instead of trying to make her way downstairs on her own and risk breakables on the way, she decided to knock on his door and hope he wasn't still asleep or just out of the shower.

"Britt," she called. When he still didn't answer, she

decided he must be downstairs already.

Maneuvering the stairs was easy, but once at the bottom, she was unsure which way to head to find Britt. The path toward the kitchen was the most familiar so she opted for that one. Rachelle moved forward counting the steps in her mind. She stopped two thirds of the way catching the sound of Britt's voice. She changed directions, unable to make out what he was saying, but as she drew closer, it became clear he was talking about security and the recent attacks.

Her foot caught a chair leg. She cried out, and almost went down. Only good balance and her quick grab on the chair saved her. Tears filled her eyes as she sank into the seat. She counted to ten, holding her breath waiting for the pain to stop. "One of these days I'm going to get steel-toed shoes then just you beware."

"Threatening my chairs are you?" She heard Britt just a couple feet away from her.

"They started it."

He laughed, "I knew you had to have a mean streak somewhere." His voice was directly in front of her, and Rachelle realized he had knelt down.

"You don't know how many times I've about broken a toe."

"Well, we can't have that."

A shiver ran through her when she felt his hand on her ankle. His fingers caressed their way over her arch as he slid off her shoe. "Ohhh," she gasped in pleasure.

"You like that?"

"Yes, I've never had anyone touch my feet like that. When I was little, my brother used to tickle them."

"Were you close?"

"Pretty much for a brother and sister, meaning we got on each other's nerves, but no one else better threaten us. That's the problem, now he's really overprotective. He's the worst of my family. That reminds me, I'll need to call them this morning."

"How about right after breakfast, then I thought that maybe we'd take another ride. We'll have to do it early because of the preparations for the party."

"I'd love to."

"Good, let's eat before I start nibbling on your toes."

"Yeah, right," she laughed not realizing how serious he was.

"How's Darrell?" She knew he would have already checked.

"He's doing fine. They're letting him go home this morning." He slipped her shoe back on her foot.

"That's wonderful."

They moved to the patio where breakfast was waiting. "Are you sure we'll have time to go for a ride?" she asked, spearing a piece of melon.

"Sure, we won't have to worry about getting ready until about five. This is one of those parties that all I have to do is show up. So, after the ride, I thought we could relax around the pool again for a while. I'll even rub plenty of sunscreen on you so you don't get sunburned."

"Oh, so sacrificing of you." She returned hearing the drudgery tone he put in his voice.

"What can I say, a man's got to do, what a man's got to do. We wouldn't want you looking like an overcooked lobster at the party."

"Perish the thought. Like, I'll be comfortable anyway," she added under her breath but he was close enough to hear.

"You're still not worried, are you?" He reached for her hand, interlocking her fingers, seeing the answer on her face, he leaned over and kissed her. "You have nothing to worry about. You're poised enough to handle yourself anywhere."

"I'm …" she tried to cut in but he wouldn't let her.

"Beautiful, so beautiful and sexy. You'll make both the

men and women jealous. The women will want to look like you and the men will want to have you on their arm, but they can't, because I won't give them a chance." This time when she started to shake her head, he stopped her by raising a hand to her chin, cupping it.

"Yes." His lips brushed hers. "Yes!" he said firmly. "Please, you can do this. Sometimes I have to attend things like this. It's not often, but I really would like you with me."

He waited but not long, the answer came after a shaky breath. "I'll be with you."

"Thank you." His answer was almost a whisper of relief. His mouth brushed hers again. "By the way, good morning."

"Good morning."

"Did you sleep well?"

"Yes, thank you. How about you?"

"I kept dreaming of a certain lady sleeping down the hall from me."

Her blush deepened and her lips formed a sweet little 'O', that he couldn't help taking one more time.

She was so sweet, so perfect for him that he couldn't believe he'd lived without her. It hit him that he couldn't live without her now that he had found her. With all the madness going on in his life, nothing was more important than the woman in his arms. The words of love were on his lips when he heard voices coming from the formal dining room. He barely pulled back from Rachelle before his stepsister, her husband and her best friend stepped out on the patio.

"Oh, Britt, there you are. We missed you last night."

"Hello, Tiffany, Carlton, Maureen. We hid out in the game room, ate and watched a movie."

"You watched a movie?" His stepsister's gaze went to Rachelle, and he knew Melissa had told them about her. He didn't like the look of amusement Carlton gave Rachelle.

"Yes, it's been a long time since I sat down and watched a movie. We watched one of Rachelle's favorites. Carlton, you've met Rachelle but Tiffany you haven't." He caught Rachelle's hand in his own. "Rachelle Harris, this is my sister, Tiffany." He waited for Tiffany to say hello, "and her best friend, Maureen."

"You're the woman he was with in the newspaper." The voice was sweet and harsh at the same time.

"Newspaper?"

"Surely someone told you, you were in the newspaper."

Rachelle shook her head and looked to Britt.

"Someone caught a picture of you getting into my car."

"Getting in." The woman laughed. "It looked more like Britton was going to devour you. Then again, he really is a very passionate kisser, so that makes sense."

Rachelle didn't need to see the catty gleam in the woman's eyes to know it was there. Maureen was used to getting what she wanted, and she wanted Britt. Rachelle felt Britt stiffen beside her and without thought raised her hand to his chest. "I would have to agree with that," she said, feeling the need to stand for herself. "If you'll excuse us, we're going to go out riding."

"You can ride a horse?" Maureen wasn't ready to back down her attack.

"Rachelle is an excellent rider. I'll talk to you later."

"I think excellent is stretching it," Rachelle commented as they walked away.

"Not much, you handled yourself brilliantly back there. I don't think you have anything to worry about at the party tonight. And, just so you know, I've never kissed Maureen, passionately or otherwise. I have no desire to kiss her in the future. In fact, I think all my kisses are going to be reserved for you."

A flush colored her face so fast, he chuckled, stopped, and pulled her to him. He kissed her temple. "Oh, Rachelle,

I can't believe how I love you."

She pulled back, looking up as if trying to see him. She raised her hand to cradle his cheek. Her finger brushed his lips feeling them for the truth. "Britt."

He kissed her palm.

"I can't believe you could really care for me."

"I don't only care for you. I love you."

"Britt," she gasped out again.

"I know it's sudden, but believe it. I've never felt the way I do about you."

"I thought it was only me."

"No, but I'm glad to know it's not one sided."

"It's not. I've been fighting it since I first touched you."

Chapter Twelve

"Britt. It looks like what I've been seeing in the papers is true. Since this is the lovely woman that was pictured with you. She must agree with you."

"She does. Rachelle, I'd like you to meet Judge Conrad Kincade. Judge, Rachelle Harris."

"Miss Harris," he took the hand she offered.

"Rachelle, please. It's a pleasure, your honor."

"Looks like you're making this man happy."

"Thank you. I hope I do."

"You do," Britt said beside her before pressing a kiss to her cheek, making her blush at the open show of affection.

The judge laughed heartily. "Good for you. Leave them no doubt she's yours."

"You make it sound like." She paused, searching for the word she wanted. But the judge didn't need it finished.

"It is," he laughed. "I'll talk to you later." He walked away.

"It's good I'm not the jealous type. I'm afraid what they'd give me for challenging a judge." Britt mumbled in her ear, tightening his hold.

It was Rachelle's turn to laugh not realizing how serious he was. She had made many conquests today, and she wasn't even aware of it. She was so beautiful with her hair styled up in an artful twist, he longed to rip out. Her make-up was kept light with just touches to accent her already fine features. She was gorgeous tonight, but that wasn't what won people. It was her inner-warmth. At first she had clung to his side, but once she relaxed, she had loosened her death grip. After that, the contact she kept was natural loving touches. She'd grown confident until she radiated pleasure at his side.

"Have I told you how beautiful you are?" The words came out and he meant every one of them.

"Thank you." She beamed up, her face tilted to his.

Desire rocketed through him, drawing him closer so that he forgot the two hundred people around him. Closing the space between them he knew Rachelle was aware of what was happening. She leaned into him.

"Britt, there you are?" The voice came from behind her.

Britt jerked up. "Tiffany." He greeted his step-sister and her best friend. "Where's Carlton?"

"Oh, around somewhere, he had people he wanted to talk to. We were looking for you. We thought that it was a shame you couldn't dance. So we came up with an idea. I can play hostess for Rachelle, so you and Maureen can dance."

"You were always so good," Maureen spoke up.

"Thanks, but I was just about to take Rachelle out dancing."

"Oh, I could go with you. I wouldn't want to see you embarrassed."

Britt felt his temper flare. "I'm never embarrassed around Rachelle. Rachelle, are you ready?"

Rachelle only nodded, too shocked to speak. She didn't need to see to know all eyes were on her as they moved out on the dance floor, but the moment Britt took her in his arms the whole world fell away and it was only them. No one else mattered.

By instinct, her body moved with his. Only Britt and the music existed in her magical world. She could see them in her mind. It was her little girl's dream, her woman's fantasy, and it was real. She felt his lips touch her temple, and she pressed closer to him. "Britt," she didn't mean to say his name aloud, but it came out a whisper only for him to hear.

"Yes, this is nice. We need to do this more often, but," he paused, "without the other people around. I want to be alone with you." There was no mistaking the huskiness in his voice or the pressure of his body against hers. They danced three more dances until they both couldn't stand the hum of desire any longer.

Britt played host with Rachelle on his arm the rest of the night. He introduced her to his friend, Steve, who remodeled the building where he lived, and his wife, Cassie. Rachelle started to get the feeling that Britt's friends accepted her as part of him. She'd never felt so happy. It was all so unreal, like a Cinderella fairy-tale that she was afraid would disappear at the stroke of midnight. It was the vibration of Britt's cell-phone that broke the spell.

"Sorry, it's my private line only for emergencies." He slid the phone from his pocket. "It's a security line." He guided her out of the crowd to where it was quieter before connecting the call. "Clairbourne."

"Do you feel safe? Tell Angel Voice I will see her. You can't be with her forever, except maybe in death." The muffled voice cut off.

Britt's body felt like he had turned to stone under her hand. The waves of silent tension buffed her, but instead of pulling back, she reached for him, tracing her fingertips along his cheek. He came alive at her touch, pulling her tight to him as if he was sheltering her with his body.

"Britt?"

"It was nothing," he said the words, but didn't relax his hold.

"It was him." It wasn't a question. She knew he wanted to deny, but he didn't.

"Yes, he just wanted to let me to know he hadn't forgotten me."

"Is he going to do something tonight?" Fear rang through her voice.

"I don't know, he didn't say." He brushed his hand over her cheek to calm her.

"He's building up to something big."

"Possibly, Rachelle, I want you to stay very close to me. I've tried keeping you away from me but that doesn't work." He dropped his hand sliding it around her to edge her closer.

"I think I can handle being around you." She forced lightness in her voice.

"I'm serious. I don't want anything happening to you. I couldn't live with it."

Rachelle wished she could see him then more than anything in her life. She also wished they were alone, so she could tell him how much she loved him. Unfortunately, there were too many people milling around for that kind of declaration. Then again, he probably knew because the way she felt surely must show.

⚇⚇

Britt sat back in the chair in his room and stared out at the dark night. It was a relief to have the party over, and all the guests home safely. Since the phone call he'd been worried. At least his concern hadn't been obvious, not like his feeling for Rachelle. He was certain there wasn't a person there that hadn't chatted or wagered about what was happening with his love life. Not that he minded. He wondered what the odds were for his getting married and how soon. If he had any say, the payout would be soon.

His thoughts drifted to the room just down the hall. Was Rachelle dreaming of him, or was she wide awake thinking of him? He wanted her to be thinking of him. She had been tired when he walked her to her door, and his desire for her was so strong he hadn't dared to give her more than a single kiss. Was it enough to leave her wanting him like he did her?

Tomorrow he would talk to her about a life together. Rising from the chair he moved to the bed and stretched out. Forgetting the madman after him, he contemplated a future with Rachelle and let the thoughts take him into sleep.

CR80

The morning air smelled heavenly as Rachelle stepped out on the balcony. The sun warmed her face. She couldn't help but smile. For the first time in a year, she felt like she was greeting the day full and content. Too happy to even let the loss of her sight shadow the day. She had learned to be happy, but this was a leap above.

Figuring Britt was already up, she followed the railing down the stairs having discovered that was the easiest way to make it to the patio where she guessed they'd meet for breakfast. She wondered what their plans were for the day and hoped they'd have time for another horse ride.

Rachelle knew she was getting close when she could hear the hum of voices, but it was another ten steps before she could make out the words.

"Britt, she's hardly suitable. What you're doing is kind. Showing her so much attention. But last night people thought you were actually serious about her. You wouldn't believe the speculation running around the room," his sister ranted. "Poor Maureen was mortified at the way you cast her aside. I don't know how you could treat her so after all this time."

"All this time. There's never been anything between Maureen and me. She's your friend and that is it." Britt's voice cut back. "And I happen to be very serious about

Rachelle."

"Heavens, Britt, really, you're a powerful, prominent man. You need a woman who will be a good hostess, an asset to you with the proper breeding."

"If I want breeding and bloodlines, I'll buy another horse. And I can hire someone to plan parties for me. What I want is a woman who loves me."

"Then have her."

Rachelle picked up the wheeze in his brother-in-law's voice.

"After all, I'm sure she's very good in the dark."

The wave of pain that ripped through Rachelle almost took her knees. She couldn't believe that anyone would talk like that.

"You better not finish that if you want to have any teeth left in your mouth." Britt's voice never sounded so icy. "And you will never talk about Rachelle like that again."

"Really, Carlton," Britt's stepmother gasped. "I must agree that was extremely crude. Rachelle is a very nice young woman. We all can agree on that. I like her very much. But Britt, Tiffany does have a point. She would hardly make a suitable wife for you. You need someone with grace and refinement. Last night people were kind to her, but you can't expect that all the time."

"She really doesn't fit here." Tiffany started up again. "You saw how uncomfortable everyone was around her, and it wasn't just her blindness."

"I saw nothing of the kind."

"They were embarrassed. They felt sorry for you. You can only expect their acceptance so far."

"Acceptance, Rachelle is charming, intelligent, and beautiful. She only sees the good in people."

"She doesn't see anything. That's the point, how will you feel when you're at a formal dinner, and she spills food all over herself or she walks into a display and destroys the thing. She's an accident waiting to happen, numerous accidents. If she pleases you, that's fine, enjoy her."

"Enough." Britt's voice raised in anger. "If you want to remain in this house you will stop this. Who I spend my time with is my business alone. And you will not refer to Rachelle as a plaything."

"That's all she's good for." Carlton's voice was cut off with the sound of flesh hitting flesh and Tiffany's scream.

"Britton!" Melissa yelled.

Rachelle didn't think to try to keep in her gasp.

"Rachelle."

She heard Britt say her name. He'd seen her on the edge of the patio, but it was too late. The dream she was living in popped. His family was being torn apart because of her. It was all make- believe and lies that she could fit in here.

She heard footsteps coming toward her and backed away.

"Rachelle," Britt said her name.

"No," she turned away. Losing her point of reference, she tripped over the railing, and tumbled down three steps to the grass.

"Rachelle," Britt called her name again. This time his voice was laced with something that might have been fear, but she didn't stop to think about it.

She had to get away. Stumbling to her feet, she ran, not caring the direction, just away. Tears burned her eyes. She heard footsteps closing in, could feel them pound the ground behind her and she pushed for more speed.

"Rachelle, stop. There's a tree." His words penetrated her pain, but she refused to stop, only changed directions to stay away from him. "Rachelle." He was gaining on her.

She had no idea where she was. She had to get away. She didn't belong here. The thought rang over and over again in her mind. She couldn't get between him and his family. She couldn't hurt him.

Tears streaked down her face. Her heart ripped apart. She ran deeper and deeper into the blackness hoping it would swallow her. She felt a stab of pain as her toe hit something then she was falling. The breath left her body as she hit the ground hard and rolled over and over. She finally came to a stop face down with no more strength to run. Britt yelled her name, but she was too dazed to answer as pain and tears washed over her.

∞

Pain knifed into Britt as he watched Rachelle go down. Her mad dash was terrifying to watch. Her head had missed the large tree branch by inches. She had been moving fairly close to the stream then with a scream she went down. He felt his world stop when she fell. *Please, let her be okay.*

He slid to the ground by her side, relieved when her shoulders shook with sobs. "Oh, sweetheart," he slid his hand up her back, over her shoulder.

A gasp burst from her, and she tried to pull away.

"Easy, are you all right?" He pulled her to him and thought he better rephrase that. She wasn't all right.

"Let me go." Pain filled her voice, but he didn't think it was physical.

"No. Quit fighting me."

She started to shake her head. Words tumble out amidst her sobs. "No, I want to leave. I want to go home."

"Shh, sweetheart, it'll be okay."

"No, I'm causing trouble ... hurting your family. I didn't mean to."

"You are not hurting my family. Tiffany's just mad because I didn't let her friend get her claws into me. Maureen's got her all stirred up. She does that. And as for Carlton, well, I've wanted to do that for a long time. The guy bugs me. I don't know how Tiffany ended up with him. But Rachelle, it doesn't matter, not a word they said. I love you. It's my choice. No one else's and you are my choice.

And as for the party, no one was uncomfortable around you, but it wouldn't have mattered. I love you."

"No." Great pain burned in her voice, she fought to push away.

"Yes, I love you." He stressed each syllable, pulling her back to him. "Rachelle, I love you. I want to marry you."

She went limp, tears streaming down her cheek. "I don't want to hurt your family."

"You won't, they'll accept you. Tiffany just got everyone thinking I'd marry Maureen. They'll come around, but even if they don't, having you in my life is what's important. You make me happy. I have felt more joy in the last couple days than I have my whole life. I want that. I want you forever."

Rachelle calmed and leaned lax against him. "How can you say that?" She took a deep breath. "We've only known each other a couple of weeks."

"And I could have said it a couple days ago, because it's true. I love you. And I know you love me. Will you deny it?"

She shook her head. "I can't. It hurt so much when I thought you didn't want me and now, when I thought I couldn't ever be with you." She tightened her hold on him.

For a full minute Britt held her to him, sitting in the grass, and then he pressed her back enough to frame her face with his hands. He tilted her face up as though she could see him. "Then say you'll marry me."

"Britt."

He watched her eyes try to move over him. Knowing she was trying to see the certainty in his face.

"Are you certain?" She was hesitant with the question, but there was such hope on her face he felt it to his soul.

"I'm certain. Will you marry me?"

Her countenance glowed with light. "Yes." She threw her arms around his neck. Her lips found his with ease, and

Britt found himself bursting with joy at the passionate woman who would be his wife. She tasted sweet and smelled like the little flowers he had given her. She was nectar to him, and he started to drink but only allowed himself a minute, knowing full well if he didn't, it would kill him to stop.

He held her tight trying to get himself under control. Her breathing was heavy. "Are you all right?" He pressed a kiss to her temple, feeling her nod slightly. "Let's go back and make the announcement."

"Britt, no, please, can we leave now?" She forced in a deep breath. "I know you probably think this is like riding a horse. That when you fall off you should get back on. But I think everyone needs some time to cool off, calm down and it will be better. As you said, Tiffany counted on you marrying Maureen. We have to give her time, give them all time to come to terms, or there's no telling what might be said and not meant, but can't be taken back. And I don't want you to hit Carlton again."

"How do you know it was me that hit him?" His lips twitched into a smile.

"Please, he doesn't strike me as the type that would strike someone head on. Like what he said in there, it was when he didn't know I could hear. He's been very charming toward me in person. Besides, he's forever whining to you, instead of taking care of things."

"Good points. I didn't hit him half as hard as I wanted to. It was just enough to get his attention and make him shut up."

"My protector," she leaned forward and kissed his cheek.

"You missed." He teased though he figured that was where she aimed.

She smiled. "I'll have to work on that. I'll get better with practice." She kissed him again.

"Oh, practice. We'll have to do that a lot."

"What if I'm a quick study?"

"No, I think we'll need to take our time to make sure you get it right."

"That sounds like a lot of practicing."

"All good things have their sacrifices. I'm willing to make this one."

Laughter bubbled out of her, and she leaned into him again.

附

Britt had been quiet since they left the house. Rachelle knew he was thinking of something. She hoped he didn't regret his proposal. Ten minutes later, she was relaxed back in the seat when he spoke. "What kind of wedding do you want?"

Surprised, she paused and thought. "I don't know. When I was little, I wanted the big wedding with all the fancy dresses, flowers, cake. You know – everything. That's what I was planning with Richard, and then the guest list started to sound like a client social for him. Everything was for show. When my accident happened and he broke off our engagement, I realized the big wedding wasn't necessary and that I'd forgotten what was important."

"What was that?"

"A man that loved me."

Britt dreaded to ask the question but couldn't stop himself. "Did you love him a lot?"

"At the time, I thought maybe I did, but then I realized I was in love with the idea of being in love. I wanted to have my perfect little life, with children, a successful husband and a white picket fence. When he left, I felt no loss. In fact, I felt at peace, or as peaceful as my life was at the time being. Walking across the room was traumatic." Rachelle paused before continuing. "I think now, looking back, that I wouldn't have made it to the wedding. It wasn't right. I knew it. Something was missing."

"Do you know what it was?"

"I do now. When you get near me, I don't have to see you. I feel like another part of me is present, like I never was even when I could see. I guess a lot of women would disagree about needing a man that way." Then she looked worried. "I hope that doesn't sound scary to you." She felt the car pull over to the side of the road and he shifted to her. His hands came up to frame her face.

"It doesn't. I know the feeling. When I sent you away, it was the hardest thing I've ever done. I wanted you with me so much. It was like a piece of me was cut out and missing. I thought I was doing what was best for you. Then, when I thought I wouldn't get to you, nothing else mattered. Without you, part of me would be gone forever. I need you with me."

"I want to be with you. You're all I need," she said softly, a smile radiated across her face.

"Then will you marry me tomorrow?"

"Tomorrow?"

"Yes, as soon as we're done at the doctor's office, I want to get a license. I'll call Conrad to see if he can marry us."

Surprise rolled over her. "Britt."

"Rachelle, I know it's sudden, but I don't think it would be a good idea for us to announce it now. There's no telling what the nut would do, but I want you staying with me." He cradled her cheek and kissed her. "I know you just agreed to marry me."

"Yes." The word slipped out of her mouth. Once out, she knew it was right.

It was Britt's turn to be shocked. "Yes?"

"Yes, I'll marry you as soon as we can arrange it."

"We can call your family now." He reached for his cell phone.

"They're out of town. My brother-in-law's family had

a wedding, and they all went to it and turned it into a vacation."

"I remember you saying that. We can have another ceremony later if you want."

"I'll think about it, but it really isn't important to me."

"You name what you want and it's yours."

"You!" She leaned forward. He was there for the kiss. Wrapping his arms around her, their passion grew taking them into a world of their own. The world shattered along with the back and front windows of the car.

"Down!" Britt forced her head between the seats, shoved the car into gear and took off in a race for their lives.

"Britt?"

"Just stay down."

"Was that the windshield?"

"Yes." He shifted to see through the fractured glass.

"Someone shot at us."

"Would you like to guess who?"

"I could guess it in one if I just knew the name."

"You and me both." Frustration poured from him. "Here." She felt his cell phone pressed into her hand. "Stay down but call the police!"

Rachelle fumbled with the phone as Britt rounded a corner. It seemed like forever before someone answered though it was only seconds. "Someone is shooting at us." She gave her name. "Where are we?" she yelled as they went around another corner.

Britt gave the street names as he watched for someone following them around the corner. Rachelle relayed information, and two minutes later, they met up with the first group of officers and pulled over. They were still sitting in the same place an hour later when Detective Todd showed up.

"I thought I was going to have a quiet weekend," the detective greeted them.

"What can we say," Britt shrugged, his arm remaining around Rachelle as they sat on the hood of his car.

"Sorry, I don't have much to give you. They haven't found the bullet so we're pretty much stuck at a dead end. Except that we can count on it being our guy. He's becoming more unstable though. This was a personal attack, and the gun is a switch. I will suggest that you don't stop along any more roads just to sit and talk."

"Good idea."

"You want something positive?"

"Definitely."

"Well, if this guy is as good with the gun as we think he is, I believe he wasn't really trying to kill you. This is all conjecture, but I think it was just his way of letting you know he was watching."

"Or you could be wrong. He's a bad shot and just doesn't care which one of us he hit," Britt came back.

"Right. Anyway, you're free to go. I'll have an officer give you a ride home. We'll have to impound your car."

"Not like I can drive it with the windshield like that."

"I'm amazed you made it this far without running into anything."

"Desperate times. Is it all right if I get Rachelle's suitcase out of the trunk?"

"Sure."

Rachelle stayed by the detective. A minute later Britt was back. She heard keys rattle and she guessed Britt had tossed them over. "You ready to go?"

She stepped to him as he took her hand. Moving with him had become as natural as breathing, even though her nerves were still all jumbled. She clung to his arm, pressing close, offering comfort as well as taking as she had been for the last hour. "You're not going to send me away are you?"

Brit found himself smiling again despite what had happened. "No, we're getting married tomorrow as planned."

They were getting in the police car when Britt's cell phone, which was still in Rachelle's pocket, rang. "Just answer it," he said, releasing her arm.

"Hello," she said, then waited when no one said anything. Figuring that whoever it was, was confused by a female voice, she was about to say it was Britt's phone when the voice answered. "So Clairbourne's having angels answering his personal phone, but I forgot you're not an angel. What else do you answer to?"

"Why are you trying to hurt Britt?"

"You know why, but you didn't listen. He took her away from me," the voice whined. "He took you away, too."

"I was never yours. I don't even know you. Or have we met?"

There was a pause. "You could only think about him. Just like …"

"Aubrey." Rachelle finished, when he stopped.

"Yes, she was beautiful and always got what she wanted. She always had me. She always came back to me. But with him, she wasn't coming back." The voice changed back to harsh tones. "And just to prove to you, that you should have stayed away from him. I left another surprise in Clairbourne's big building. He has four hours to find it, or someone will die."

"Please don't do this. I know Aubrey hurt you. I'm sorry. Let me help you. It wasn't Britt Clairbourne's fault. Please."

"It was him," the man yelled. "He has to pay. He has to. All will be mine. All mine." The voice quieted. "Even you." The words turned sing song. "And it all will come tumbling down."

Rachelle became aware of Britt holding her when his hand came up to take the phone from her.

"What did he say?" Todd asked. He was close and she realized both he and Britt had been trying to listen to the conversation.

"He has a bomb in the administration building. We have four hours to find it, or someone will die."

"I'll get a team over there. If I can have your cell phone, I'll get someone to see if they can trace the call. Are you sure about it being the administration building?"

"He said the 'big building.' The big building would be the main headquarters building."

"It makes sense. He's playing with us, giving us a time frame. But, if he's doing like the psychologist said, he's working a pattern, and if we discount the attempts taken at you, those are personal aggravations coming through. They're throwing him off. Which Dr. Lewis also thinks he blames you for. He started at the receiving bay, and then the warehouse, the quad was in between." The detective began to think out loud, "The main office or just outside your office. The next place would be inside your office, which he should be leaving for last … or the main lobby."

"But what about the hit and run on Mr. Mason? That wasn't at Clairbourne or on us." Rachelle had to ask.

"Yes, but you were there. And he almost succeeded driving a wedge between you two, which was a blow to Clairbourne, and a boost to our guy's ego."

"He knows every move I make," Britt bit out.

Rachelle's hand settled on his arm.

Britt laid his hand over hers. "Come on. I'll go with your theory."

"You don't need to come yet," Todd said.

"It's my company. I'll be there as soon as I find somewhere safe for Rachelle."

"I'm staying with you. You promised you wouldn't send me away again," she countered firmly as if she could see his objection coming. "Just look at the trouble I got in last time you left me. You just said he seems to know everything you do. He'll know if you leave me. He'll come after me. You know that."

"Brat."

Rachelle laughed, knowing she had won.

"Right by my side."

"No place else."

"What am I getting myself into?" He grumbled so she could hear him as he helped her into the detective's car.

Chapter Thirteen

Three hours and fifty minutes later, frustration was rising in everyone. No bomb had been found in the main lobby, around Britt's office, or the design area. Sweeps had been made of the whole building, but there was nothing.

"I don't like it," Britt said, his arm around Rachelle as they stood in the main lobby. It was dark outside the windows that stretched from the floor to the opulent ceiling thirty feet above, on the east and west sides.

"It looks like he's just toying with us." Todd shook his head.

"I don't think so. He wanted us here," Rachelle spoke up. "I think you were right about the lobby too. It makes sense."

"We've checked every square inch."

Britt's eyes scanned the room that was the size of a small basketball court. It was a large open area with elevators on both sides. A dozen couches made up seating in the center. The only other thing besides a few planters and a sculpture was a large receptionist's desk. But he agreed with Rachelle. "It's here. It's like what Dr. Lewis said. He's very methodical. That's why the company first. It's a symbol of power. He has to weaken Clairbourne. Each time he's getting more showy. It has to be here." It hit him that the detective had told him they couldn't find anything once before. It had been in the warehouse right before the bomb had taken out the overhead crane cable almost smashing several people under the box it had been moving. It had been set high, out of the range of the dogs.

Britt looked up at the lighting and high windows. Rachelle's words came back to his mind, 'he wanted us here.' He wanted them here. Britt glanced at his watch. Two minutes and the four hours would be up.

He looked up again. "Get everyone out," he said, and then yelled it. "Get everyone out! Now! It's here, up there. He wanted people here, people who are trying to help me. He wants to show what will happen to those who help me. Get everyone out of here, now!"

Todd got what he was saying. "Everyone out! Clear it, now!" he gave the order. The men in the room looked around, but all headed for the doors.

Britt started to lead Rachelle out then looked at the clock on the wall. The hand on the clock was almost straight up. The second hand was just past the thirty. "Hang on," he said as he turned to Rachelle. Wrapping his arms around her legs, he lifted her up over his shoulder. Rachelle squeaked in surprise but didn't fight him. Britt ran for the door as the other officers picked up the pace. Everyone was running now.

Halfway across the quad they all slowed, moving together in a group, many turning to the building, while still backing up.

"Is everyone clear?" The call came out.

"All clear," an officer in full protective gear and a headset reported back a second later.

Britt set Rachelle on her feet, and she clung to his arms as she steadied herself.

"Are you all right?" he asked.

"Yes, just give me a little more warning next time you do that."

The explosion ripped the air making it impossible for

him to answer, and for the second time that night, windows blasted out around them. This time it was in a shower of glass that would have shredded anyone close. Britt spun Rachelle away shielding her with his body though, fortunately, no glass reached where they'd stopped.

In just seconds it was over, leaving everyone staring back in disbelief. A few lights survived in the lobby, showing not a single upper window remained intact. The ground glistened like it was covered with diamonds.

"Is everyone okay?" Todd yelled, echoed by the man in charge wearing the headset.

Britt ran his hands over Rachelle then pulled her tight against him. "You're okay," he kissed her hard needing to prove to himself that she was, in fact, unharmed.

"Clairbourne?"

"We're all right." He kept Rachelle wrapped in his arms.

"What happened?" Rachelle asked against his chest.

"The windows all blew out." He kissed her on the head, staring back at the building, hardly able to take in what he saw.

"Britt?" There was a question in Rachelle's voice, and he knew she was picking up a mood change in him.

"You realize with this maniac," he paused, "you could be left a widow before your honeymoon's over?"

Her hand came up to his lips. "Don't talk like that."

"We have to face it. I'm being selfish wanting to spend every minute I have left with you, but you have got to understand the chances you're taking before we're married."

Rachelle nodded her head against his chest. "I learned something in my accident. There are no guarantees in life. Things can change in an instant. I want to have all the time I can have with you, whether it be a day or a century."

"I'm going for the century." A smile came back to his face, and he vowed that this maniac was not going to take a minute of their time together from them.

He pressed her back tight against him. Everything was all right with Rachelle. His mind shifted back to the foray of activity around him. "Will you stay with me while I talk to Todd then make arrangements with security to close off this part of the building until clean up and repairs can be done?"

CR80

It was late when the detective finally gave them a ride to Britt's apartment. Passing the security guard, Britt directed Rachelle into the elevator. Setting her suitcase on the floor as the doors closed, he pulled her to him. Rachelle's arms came instinctively around his waist, resting her head on his chest. It was becoming his favorite stance. He relished the feel of her, amazed how much he liked the touch of her, just to hold her.

"What would I do without you?" He groaned, not needing an answer. "I've been alone so long and didn't even realize it." It was true. He hadn't realized he never had much physical contact when he was growing up, not since his mother had died. He had been an only child. His father worked long hours and kept to himself. He had fallen into the same role himself.

She shifted, turning her face to his, sliding her hands up over his shoulders, along his neck to caress his cheek. "I love you." The feelings behind her words were evident on her face. "I've been lonely too. I think it's been harder than not being able to see, because I know I'm missing something but don't know what it is. Not what I feel for you. This, I've never had." She kissed him. "I'm so glad to have found you."

He kissed her back. "I know what you mean. Tomorrow you're mine." He kissed her again as the doors opened. He had to push the door open button to keep it from closing on them before taking her arm and picking up the suitcase. "I'll call Dr. Christensen in the morning and find out how the tests are going and then I'll call Conrad."

The door across the hall opened and closed as a man stepped out. Britt steered Rachelle to the side but paid little attention until the man stopped. "Rachelle?"

She froze.

"You look incredible. I didn't know you were out and about. You should have called."

"Why? What possibility we had was long over."

"Rachelle," Britt called her attention, studying the handsome man who had the polish of someone who had stepped out of a men's magazine.

"Sorry, Britt, this is Richard Johnson. Richard, this is Britton Clairbourne."

"Clairbourne, so it really was you I saw in the picture. I couldn't believe it."

Britt watched the man's eyes run over him ending at the suitcase in his hand. Britt stiffened at the look the man gave it.

"I guess something has changed." Her ex-fiancé smirked. "You were too tight to give it before."

Britt dropped the suitcase and released Rachelle, stepping toward the man.

"Britt." Rachelle reached out, flailing to catch his arm.

"You're still blind." The man gaped, stepping back as if it were contagious.

Britt stopped at her touch and turned back to her.

She stood straight, regal. "That's right."

The man looked at her then back to Britt. "But why?" His eyes dropped to the suitcase. "Then again, I guess it doesn't matter."

Rachelle caught his meaning and gasped. Britt started to shake off her hand, but she stopped him again. "He isn't worth the trouble he would cause. He's the type that would sue you. He's very self-centered. I can't believe I didn't see it for a long time. But he's right. It really doesn't matter to a truly strong, confident man. A man who looks beyond pretenses." She turned away. Britt held back a second, glaring at the other man before he picked up her suitcase once more and led her to his door.

"Do your parents know where you're spending the night?" The man managed enough bravado to yell after them before the door closed him out.

"You can ask me now what I ever saw in him. I can hear the question running through your mind."

"I was trying not to pry." A smile lit his face.

"For a man that was about to get charged with assault back there, you sound pretty calm and happy."

"I am. You never loved him."

"No, I tried to convince myself I did because everyone expected it, but I never did. How did you know?"

"You had no reaction to meeting him except as if it was an old acquaintance. There was no emotion. If you had ever loved him, there would have been pain or anger there. I would have known it, like I know love when you touch me. You don't hide or turn off your emotions. They are too much a part of you."

"Is that so?" She felt the need to challenge him.

"Yes," he said firmly.

"Then how do I feel about you?" She tilted her head up.

"That's easy." He took a step toward her, and she moved back against the wall. "You love me."

"I already told you that."

"Yes," Britt raised his hands putting them on either side of her head. "But what you didn't say was you're mine. That was probably what made Richard so mad. He knew you were never his. With his ego, that must be difficult to accept. It's probably eating at him right now." Britt's lips brushed the edge of her mouth. "He's wondering just what he let get away."

His mouth caressed the other side of her mouth. Her

knees went weak, but he held her up, pressed between the wall and his body. "He's wondering what we're doing and dying of jealousy." Britt took full possession of her lips, drinking in as she gave herself over to him.

With a groan he pushed back, dropped his forehead to rest on hers while he took deep breaths. "I'd be lying if I said I didn't wish we were doing what he thinks. Off to bed." He stepped back.

"Britt?"

"Tomorrow, Rachelle. Tomorrow you'll be mine, and we'll rejoice in it." He led her to her room then dropped her hand.

Rachelle turned expecting him to kiss her, but he moved back.

"Tomorrow," the word was repeated, sounding something between a promise and a threat. Rachelle heard the door across the hall shut and knew Britt was gone. She felt a second of sadness being away from him then was cheered knowing he didn't like it any better. More excitement shot through her. Tomorrow night, he wouldn't leave her at the door but take her to his room, their room. A rush of nervousness hit her which slid right back to excitement. The problems of the day were forgotten when she went to sleep.

જ્જી

As usual Rachelle's internal alarm clock went off early, but Britt was already in the kitchen when she entered.

"Good morning." Britt rose from the table coming to her. "Ready for a busy day?"

"Yes."

"No second thoughts?"

"About marrying you, no. I want this more than anything."

"I feel guilty rushing you." He caught hold of her fingers.

"You're not. This is the way I want it."

"I'm afraid your family might not think that, but I'm glad. I've already called Conrad. We'll meet him in his chambers at one."

"You called him this early?"

"He's an early riser, likes to get a game of golf in before work. Why don't you get some breakfast? I have to swing by the office for about fifteen minutes then we have an appointment to pick up rings before your doctor's appointment, then the license. After the wedding, we'll go somewhere nice for a late lunch." He paused a second. "I wish I could take you somewhere for a honeymoon."

She smiled and stepped to him. "That's not necessary."

"After your surgery, I'll take you anywhere you want."

"I just want to see you."

"Who would have guessed," he teased making her blush.

"That wasn't what I meant."

"But you're thinking it now." He laughed wickedly.

"You like doing that to me."

"You have that right."

"You know to make it fair tonight, I should blindfold you."

"That's fine. I plan to have every inch of you memorized by then."

"Britt." She blushed, shocked at how free their talk had become.

"I won't deny that I want you, that I'm hunger for you. I plan on making love to you as soon as I can and still appear partly civilized."

In one sentence he took her breath and made her laugh.

ᑕᔕᗞ

Rachelle clamped down on the hand Britt slid into hers. Her heart pounded in her chest so loud she thought it should echo off the wall. Britt stoked his free hand up and down her arm but it did nothing to relax her. Unable to wait any longer, she asked the question she feared. "What's the prognosis?" They were surprised when the specialist arrived at the doctor's office while they were there.

"I'd like to operate next Thursday morning."

"Thursday," Rachelle repeated stunned.

"Yes. I had my team already arranged, but the man we were going to operate on is having health problems. I had just decided to cancel the team then Dr. Christensen sent me your charts. Instead, I just put it on hold. You're a perfect candidate, Miss Harris. You're young, in excellent health. It's been long enough since your accident that the swelling is down except in the affected area."

"See here." Rachelle knew the doctor was showing Britt and Dr. Christensen her x-rays. "This is the scan after her accident, and this is one they took a week ago. This is the area we're looking at, where the blockage is. I can't give any guarantee of course. The body, especially the brain and eyes, can be a tricky thing, but I would say the odds are very good. At least fifty-fifty."

Rachelle swallowed unable to believe what he was saying.

Britt called her name, but it seemed to be from a long ways off. She turned to him. "I can't believe that I might be able to see." She felt Britt's lips brush her cheek.

"I know Dr. Christensen went over the risks, but I'll go over them again to make it clear because, with every surgery, there are risks, even minor ones. I'd like you to think it over today and give me your answer tomorrow, the next day at the latest. I know I'm rushing you, but if I go to the next scheduled opening when I have the staff together in this area, it's not for two months."

"We're getting married this afternoon," she said more to herself.

"We can postpone it." Britt gave her hand a squeeze.

"No," she gasped.

"I don't see any reason why not to get married now," the doctor said. "I would just ask that you be careful and not get pregnant."

"I'll take care of that," Britt assured.

"Then I'll say congratulations. This must be quite a day and to add this appointment."

"This is worth it. Rachelle is worth it. She's very special to me."

"I can see that, and I hope to have her seeing again too."

Three hours later Rachelle's heels echoed on the marble tile as she and Britt were shown into the judge's chambers. The smell of wood polish was so strong that the room was probably all done in woods – dark woods would fit the man; mahogany. There would be a bookcase full of books and a large painting on the wall. There was a warmer feel on one side where she guessed light filled the room from a window there. Britt's hair would shine in the light.

Then, as Britt took her hands in his, her thoughts focused on one thing, him, and how absolutely right it was marrying him. She didn't need to see the surroundings. Everything she needed was in her heart and what she heard when Britt said I do. Rachelle about burst, so happy, she almost missed the question asked of her.

Britt had never seen anything as beautiful as Rachelle smiled at him. Sun beamed through the window and bathed her in light. She glistened, but the countenance of her face out shone the sunshine. Love really did radiate, because that was the only way he could describe her. And it was all for him.

"Yes, I do." The words were a soft promise that brightened her face more. There was such an absolute rightness as Conrad pronounced them husband and wife. Then it was time to seal it with a kiss.

He felt her tremble against him, releasing a rush of desire. The caveman in him urged him to pack her off to his cave and make ravenous love to her. The civilized gentleman in him barely kept it together. Stepping back from his new bride, he turned to receive congratulations.

"My hands are trembling." Rachelle laughed lightly as he guided her in signing the certificate.

"That's all right. I think the judge makes a good witness that it was really you that I married."

"I hope you know what you just got yourself into."

"I have no doubts." He slid his arm once more around her as he pressed his lips to hers.

"Hey, none of that, you got your kiss," the judge joked. "Only one kiss per customer, besides it's my turn to kiss the bride." He placed a fatherly kiss on her cheek and then whispered in her ear. "Keep him on his toes, you hear. He's a good man."

"I know," she whispered back.

"What are you saying to my wife?"

"Just making sure she wouldn't rather run away with me."

"Not a chance, she's mine, and even if I didn't object, Sarah would."

"That's true even after twenty-two years she's insisting that I'm hers."

"She must be a smart woman." Rachelle smiled back.

"I tell her that all the time." There was a knock on the door. "Well, I hate to break this up, but duty calls."

"Thanks again, Conrad." Britt shook his hand, "and I really appreciate you keeping this secret."

"Don't worry, I understand the importance and hope the police get this guy soon."

"So do I. You don't mind keeping those papers until I get a hold of Samuel?"

"Not at all, everything that's needed is there."

"Is something wrong?"

"No, sweetheart, there's just some legal papers I wanted him to hang on to until my lawyer gets back from vacation and can handle them. Shall we go?"

"Yes. Good-bye Judge. Thank you."

"You're most welcome. This was a treat for me. I don't get to do enough of the pleasant things around here."

CR8O

"Where would you like to eat?" Britt asked as he escorted her to the car.

"I don't think I could eat." She let it slip out.

"Are you all right?"

"I'm fine." She paused, excited and nervous, maybe in shock. "I can't believe we're really married. It seems so unbelievable. I keep expecting to wake up and find I dreamed it all."

"Well, when you wake up, it will be beside me, and you'll know you're not dreaming."

He saw the color rise in her cheeks and knew her thoughts had slid to their wedding night. The caveman was back. "Come on, let's pick up something to eat and go home."

Home, the word brought a rush. From now on, her home would always be with Britt. "Yes, please. I would like that better."

Rachelle listened as he ordered dinner from one of the nicest restaurants in town. "I didn't know they did take out."

"They do if you tip good enough, and besides the manager owes me one."

Twenty-five minutes later, Britt parked the car and came around to get her out. "Mmm, something smells good." He caught her by surprise with a hard kiss.

"I think it's dinner."

"You think so? Let me see." He kissed her thoroughly again. "I love being able to do that." He purred with satisfaction.

"Anytime," Rachelle agreed leaning against him.

"Let's go upstairs before I take you up on that. Will you hold this a second?" He handed her the sack of food before swinging her up in his arms. "It's tradition." He headed for the elevator, juggling her as he pushed the button.

"I don't think it's meant that you have to carry me all the way up the elevator."

"Maybe, but I like having you in my arms and besides," he paused slightly, "I'm trying to impress you with my strength and stamina. How am I doing?"

"Great, but I was already impressed." She placed a kiss on his cheek.

"Good answer." He took the kiss to her mouth and was still kissing when the elevator opened again.

"Mmm," she purred. "I'm really beginning to enjoy being married."

"You ain't seen nothin' yet." Wickedness filled his voice as he carried her over the threshold. "We're home Mrs. Clairbourne." He placed her on the floor with a great deal of reluctance. "If you'd like to freshen up, I'll set the table."

There was a slight pause then she stepped away. "I'll be just a moment."

Britt watched her touch the corner of the room for reference before moving off toward the bedroom.

He wanted to follow her in the greatest way. Patience, he told himself to give her time. "You're not some stallion who has the scent of a mare." But he sure felt like it, he acknowledged, forcing himself to turn toward the kitchen. He stopped to douse his face with cold water. "What I need is a cold shower." He murmured to himself. "Patience, patience."

Chapter Fourteen

The smell of sweet peas greeted her senses drawing her toward Britt's bed. Love flooded every pore of her body when she found the bouquet on the nightstand. She was tempted to go to the kitchen and throw her arms around him and tell him to forget about eating. That would certainly surprise him, and Britt could use a few good surprises in his life. She hurried to freshen up, assured of her actions until she hit the hall, literally. Her self-confidence failed. Her footsteps faltered.

Rachelle tripped barely catching a door frame to keep from going down.

She clung to the wall to steady herself and had to fight down a wave of tears that tried to slip past the euphoria she'd been feeling. *Oh, that would have been a graceful entrance, so appealing. Falling and breaking something and ending up in the hospital an hour after getting married.* She took another deep breath to force her nervousness down.

It took a full minute to gather enough courage to move forward. By the time she made it to the dining room, she decided that as a seductress she was totally lacking. Fortunately, Britt wasn't there, and she had another minute to decide that maybe it would be better to get through dinner then she could consider a seduction. At the sound of him entering from the kitchen, she asked. "May I help?"

Britt stopped at the sight of his wife. His wife; it hit him with such a jolt that he nearly dropped to his knees. She was so incredible and she was his. "I can always use help." He finally found his voice,

"What can I do?"

Let me make love to you. Britt almost groaned aloud as the thought ran through his mind.

"If you'll just put the silverware on the table while I bring in the food."

Five minutes later he was almost at the point of begging, watching her put a bite in her mouth. He never knew eating could be so erotic, but as pleasure lit her face, his temperature spiked.

"Mmmm, this is wonderful."

He nearly groaned aloud. "Yes. Taste the beef. Their chef does an amazing job on it." He held out a bite to her and watched her lips close around it.

"Oh, that is delicious."

Britt managed a few bites but eating was impossible. His concentration was not on food. He watched Rachelle for a full two minutes as she picked delicately at her food but didn't seem to eat any. "Is there something wrong? You're not eating."

"No, I'm just," she broke off and blushed. "You're not eating either."

"I was wondering if you'd mind if I lied and told you it was dark and time for bed."

"There's no need to lie, just say it's time for bed." There was shyness in her tone, but desire came through stronger.

Britt was out of his chair before she finished the sentence. Her arms were stretched out reaching for him in unison of his sliding under her, lifting her from the chair.

"Rachelle." He buried his face against her neck,

running kisses along the delicate skin. Her head tilted back over his arm, giving him better access. He was feeding ravenously on her and had no idea how he made it down the hall to his bed with Rachelle returning his kisses and whispering words of love. He went down on the bed with her in his arms.

CRBO

Later, they finally enjoyed their dinner. Since he'd thoughtfully ordered two of each entrées and desserts, the leftovers made a great, late-night snack to replenish their energy. By morning they we're still starving.

Making breakfast had never been so much fun as doing it with Rachelle. Britt got in her way on purpose for an excuse to slide his arms around her and sneak a kiss. After the third sneak attack, it became a challenge to see who could out maneuver the other, and the rewards kept drawing out longer and longer. It was amazing they didn't burn anything. They were just about halfway through eating, and Britt was debating if he could convince her that it was dark out and carry her back to bed and make love to her again in the morning light when the door-chime rang.

"I better get that." Britt looked over her satin draped frame. The robe highlighted her figure to perfection.

As he approached the door, he became alert to the trouble still lurking. He peered through the peephole studying the two men in the hall. The first was tall, sandy haired, there was something familiar about him, but Britt was certain they hadn't met. The second man he, unfortunately, couldn't say the same. He had met the blonde man just two nights ago about twenty feet from where he was now standing. Then it hit him where he recognized the first man from. He'd seen his picture in Rachelle's apartment. He was Rachelle's brother, David Harris.

With a bit of reluctance, Britt unlocked the door and

opened it. "Good morning." He tried to put on a friendly demeanor, realizing his first contact with Rachelle's family was going to be with him only wearing his pants. "I presume you're here to see Rachelle, though I'm not sure what he's doing here." Britt motioned to Rachelle's ex-fiancé.

"Then you don't deny she's here. I couldn't believe it when Richard said he saw her entering here with you and a suitcase."

Before anything could be said, Rachelle stepped into the doorway. "David, what are you doing here?" She hurried into the room, leaving the two men momentarily speechless when they saw her in her robe. "You were supposed to still be in California for Becca's wedding. Mom said you were going to stay there for another week."

"They had trouble with one of my projects, and I had to come back early. Then I got a message from Richard. What are you doing here?"

"David, it's all right …"

Richard cut her off before she could finish. "We can tell what you've been doing." His demeanor changed suddenly, and he stepped forward reaching for her. "I'm sorry, darling. I realize this is all my fault. I know I hurt you badly, but in my defense, I was in shock, confused and in denial. But I love you, and I want you back. I'm willing to forgive you and forget your indiscretion."

"Well." Rachelle pulled back, crossing her arms in front of her. "I'm not." Her shoulders stiffened.

"Believe me, it's understandable. You're on the rebound, lost and alone. It was much the same for me."

"I don't care how it was for you. This is totally different."

"Darling." Richard stepped forward. "I know you're convincing yourself that you love him, and he will step up and take care of you. Do the right thing and all, but believe me, he's using you. A man like him can have any woman he wants. He doesn't need a defective one."

"That's enough," Britt's voice sliced through. "I was letting you blab on because it was amusing but–"

"Britt, no." This time it was Rachelle that cut the conversation. "Thank you, but I can handle this." She shifted back toward Richard. "I am not defective, nor am I now or was I ever heartbroken over you. I never loved you."

"Now, darling, you don't mean that."

"I do. I was hurt when you abandoned me when I needed you most, but I was not heartbroken. I was marrying you because everyone convinced me how perfect we were together, how wonderful you were and how fortunate I was. I wanted to be loved, and I thought you loved me."

"I do love you and you don't mean that."

"She does," Britt countered.

"Stay out of this. You don't know what you're talking about, and it doesn't concern you."

"Wrong on both accounts, I am part of this more than you are."

"You're just taking advantage of her," Richard blurted.

"He is not." Rachelle came to Britt's defense.

"Thank you," Britt whispered and Rachelle beamed back.

"Really. How long have you known him?"

"Almost three weeks."

"Rachelle," her brother sounded aghast.

"And you're already in his bed. I had no clue you were so easy."

"That's it," Britt stepped forward his fist clinched.

"Britt," Rachelle stopped him reaching out her hand. Whether she heard him move to figure out where he was or she sensed him, he didn't know but he changed directions, catching her outstretched fingers, bringing them to his lips in a deliberate show before he moved behind her encircling her with his arm.

"Let her go," David burst out.

"David, it's all right."

"It's not all right. This man is taking advantage of you, and you're helpless to do anything about it."

"She's not helpless," Britt said firmly.

"I'm not helpless." They said in unison, and Britt squeezed her shoulders.

David snorted. "Get your hands off her. I want to know your intentions. She was innocent until you got your hands on her."

"I am very aware of that." Britt was starting to enjoy this but was trying to keep it in.

David had no such compulsion. "Then I expect you to step up and do the right thing."

"Heavens," Rachelle groaned.

"That's not necessary," Britt started to explain but was cut off.

"I think it is. You might be a rich and powerful man, but if it got around that you're seducing an innocent, helpless, blind woman, I'm sure it would do some damage."

"I'm not helpless," Rachelle exploded. "Britt did not seduce me." Then she blushed wiping all the anger from her face. Her voice lowered to a soothing tone. "David, if you'll just listen there's nothing to be concerned about with me or my reputation. Britt and I are married."

"What!" Her brother's reaction exploded from him.

Britt raised her hand to his lips, placing a kiss on her knuckles before extending it out for them to see the rings that were proof of their vows. "Rachelle and I are married."

"Are you certain?" her brother gaped.

"Yes." She smiled.

"I mean are you sure it was legal?"

"Yes." Instead of getting mad she looked about to laugh. "Yes, we were married by Judge Kinade in his chambers at the courthouse."

"You married her. Why?" Richard floundered.

"Because she's beautiful, intelligent, kind and mainly because I love her."

"But, but." The man, who at one time was to be her husband, was at a loss for words, and he was forgotten.

"You love him." Her brother was stunned. "You really married him."

"Yes, to both."

"But why?" He didn't finish, there was no need. "You did it in secret because of the trouble that's happening."

"Yes, we decided it would be better to keep it quiet," Rachelle said.

Britt picked up her explanation looking at Richard. "It can't get out. Rachelle's safety is paramount. He can destroy everything else I have. As long as Rachelle's my wife, it doesn't matter."

"Then why marry her? Why not send her away?"

"I tried, but he went after her."

"What?"

"I'm okay. Britt got there to rescue me in time."

"So we decided the best way is to keep her with me. So we moved up our wedding plans. And I mean it when I say it better not get out. I don't want this hitting the newspaper." He looked to Richard.

"It won't, will it, Richard?" This time the anger in her brother's tone was directed some place other than Britt.

"I won't tell a soul, I promise."

"Good," Britt said forcefully. "I'll see you to the door." He released Rachelle and moved to the entry, not giving the man a choice but to follow.

After a second of silence, David finally spoke. "Married, it's hard to believe."

"I know but don't be angry. It was my choice. If I wanted a big wedding, Britt would have waited. I hope Mom and Dad and everyone won't be too upset. We may have another ceremony later depending on how things turn out."

"It's just such a surprise. I think everyone will be okay after they get over the initial shock. Joann mentioned you said you went out to dinner with him, but she said it wasn't serious. Then we left, and the last couple days no one caught you at your apartment when they called. All we had were the messages you'd leave for us."

"Sorry. The man causing problems found out about us and went after me. I'm okay." She hurried and added knowing he was about to jump on that. "Britt's watching over me. That's one of the reasons we got married in secret."

"I understand." Her brother moved to her, placing his arms around her. "You are happy."

Rachelle relaxed finally feeling his acceptance. "Yes, I love Britt. I know it was fast, but I love him and feel he loves me."

"All right then, I can accept that."

"There is one more thing I have to tell you. Thursday, I'm going into surgery. There's a specialist who has looked over my records, and he feels I'm a good candidate. It's not a sure thing but a lot better odds than before."

"Rachelle." David hugged her. She didn't see him look over her to Britt or the look of gratitude that gave Britt his first tingling of acceptance.

"She has a fifty percent chance of success." Britt stepped forward.

"Rachelle, that's amazing."

"It's not a sure thing," she added cautiously and Britt understood that was her way of keeping it in perspective so if it wasn't successful, she wouldn't be crushed.

"But still, it's better odds. This time you really have a chance. Have you told Mom and Dad yet?"

"No, I just found out, and I didn't want to drop either bombshell on them as just a message."

Her brother nodded, then for her benefit added. "I can understand that. They're going to be so excited. They've tried to figure out ways to come up with the money for you. The bank just won't help."

"They don't need to worry about that. I talked to the insurance company," Britt put in.

David nodded in understanding again. "So what's with this psycho guy attacking your company? I saw a little about it on the TV before we left. You know Joann did say you sounded a little different when you talked about Clair … Britt."

"Why don't we move into the kitchen, and you can join us for breakfast, and we'll tell you everything? It started with Rachelle answering the phone and taking the first message when he called."

"Yeah, Joann knew about that."

"To make it short, it didn't take me long to realize how incredible she is. It was a nice surprise to find out Rachelle was falling in love with me, too. My plan wasn't to hurry her, but the psycho developed an obsession on her, and she became a target. I tried to send her away, but he already figured out she was important to me and still went after her. So the best way to keep her safe seemed to be to keep her with me."

Now that her brother decided he wasn't taking advantage of his sister, Britt felt that they got along well. They talked for almost an hour until he had to get ready to go into the office.

Chapter Fifteen

Rachelle came awake with the phone ringing. She felt Britt shift, then the arm that rested over her waist moved as he slid away. A feeling of unease seeped in as the warmth of his body faded. There was a click of the light switch before he answered the phone. The unease was swamped by a wave of dread, and she reached for him. Tension radiated from him. His arm was like touching tempered steel. She wanted to stroke away the rigidness but didn't get the chance.

"I'll be there in about twenty minutes." He swung his legs off the bed, and Rachelle heard the phone drop to the nightstand.

"Britt?"

The mattress sank as he knelt back down. He caught her hand bringing it to his lips. "I'm sorry it woke you. Go back to sleep."

"What's happened?" Her trepidation climbed.

"They had signs of a break-in at one of the warehouses. I need to go check on it for a few minutes. It shouldn't be long."

"I'll come." She tried to slide from under the covers, but he held her down.

"There's no need. Just go back to sleep. You'll be safe here. I'll alert security in the hall." He kissed her, getting off the bed again.

Rachelle followed him up. "I'm coming with you."

"Rachelle."

"No, please don't try to leave me behind."

"It won't be like last time, I promise, you'll be safe."

"I'm not worried about me. I'm worried about you. Please, Britt, I have a bad feeling about this." As she said the words, she knew it was true. She was afraid, afraid that if he walked out the door he would never come back.

Maybe it was just tension from three days of not hearing from the psycho, maybe it was the frustration of not being able to locate the voice though she had talked to almost every man in the company, or maybe it was just the nagging feeling that they were missing something, but she knew something was going to happen. She didn't want to be away from him. She knew Britt was experiencing similar sensations. It had been in the way he kept her close, the way he touched her, the way he had made love to her. It was as if he was afraid she would be snatched away from him at any minute.

"Please Britt." The silence was deafening then she heard him move to her. His hands framed her face. "I love you." He kissed her. "Stay right by me and you follow exactly what I say."

Twenty minutes later they pulled to a stop. When Britt didn't move to turn off the car, Rachelle broke the silence that they had driven there in. "What's wrong?"

"I'm not sure. There's a security car here but that's it. I expected more. I think I'm going to drive back to the main building then call security and the police from there." He shifted the car in reverse and started to back up then stopped.

"Wait a minute, there's Carlton. He's at the side door. The others must be parked on the other side of the building." He pulled the car forward before he turned it off and came around to get her.

"Stay close," he said as he wrapped an arm around her.

He tensed when he caught Carlton's sneer as he looked at Rachelle. He knew the man was thinking they had just come from bed, but he didn't like the derogatory gleam in his brother-in-law's eye. He was going to have to tell his family soon that they were married. Right now it was a private pleasure he held tight in his heart.

"Britt." His brother-in-law acknowledged him while ignoring Rachelle.

"Carlton, I didn't expect to see you here."

"I decided that I might be able to help when they called the house. So I headed over and then tried to reach you."

"Where is everyone?"

"In the upper office." He held the door for them, letting them enter first.

Lights flooded the building, but it didn't feel right. Rachelle clung to his side. There was a slight tremor in her touch. She was as nervous as he was.

"It's so quiet," she whispered, leaning into him.

As soon as she said the words, he knew that was what was nagging him. The building was totally silent. It didn't fit. Even if the men waited in the back office, there should have been some kind of noise, not an echoing nothingness.

"You made good time to beat us here."

"I had just come in, and there wasn't any traffic," his brother-in-law answered.

"I wonder why security called the house? They usually call my cell." His mind was starting to think of things, and he didn't like what it was coming up with.

"Maybe it was turned off or the battery's dead."

Britt knew neither was true.

"Why don't you check it?" the man suggested.

Britt slid his hand in his pocket fingering the phone. "I left it in the car." He stopped with Rachelle beside him. "Carlton, why don't you go on, I want to go back and get it. Come on Rachelle." He started to turn. Carlton moved in front of him. For some reason, Britt wasn't surprised to see the gun in his hand.

"Hand me the phone." He motioned with the gun. "Or I may have to shoot Miss Harris."

Britt heard and felt Rachelle's gasp. He was tempted to make a dive for him but knew before he reached Carlton, the gun would go off, and at the distance, there was no way it would miss him or Rachelle. Britt pulled his cell phone from his pocket and tossed it to the side hoping Carlton would follow the motion. He didn't. "Yours too, Miss Harris."

"I don't have a phone."

"Tsk, tsk, then what's that in your pocket?"

"My sonar." She lifted out the palm size device showing it before dropping it back in her pocket.

"What is this, Carlton?" Britt drew the attention back to him.

"I think we both know that's a dumb question. Keep walking back toward the stairs."

"Why are you doing this?"

"I think you can figure it out too. I know how you feel about me. You'd like to get rid of me. There's no way you would ever let me move up. And now with her ..." He motioned to Rachelle. "I'm afraid things are in for a change, and Tiffany may not be set to inherit after you. I dare not wait. It's just an added bonus that you brought Miss Harris with you. I wasn't expecting that you would bring her here."

"So you've been planning on getting rid of me for a while."

"I had thought of it but didn't think I'd have to worry about it for a while. That was until at the house last weekend. I realized I couldn't wait."

"You'll never get away with this."

"That sounds so cliché, but I think we both know I will. The police are looking for a psycho. They'll never look at me."

Britt scanned the area trying to see something that would give them a chance. He wished he'd insisted that Rachelle stay home. He wanted her away from there. Never had he figured Carlton was the one behind all that was happening. He never seemed like he had it in him to play the games. He always seemed more like the type to take advantage of things. Oh, he'd plot and scheme, but not to take direct action, especially if it was on the messy side, which murdering them would be.

He had to think. He couldn't let Carlton kill them. He wasn't going to give up on his life with Rachelle. He wasn't going to give up on her now that he'd finally found her. Only there was nothing he could see that would help.

"Keep moving," Carlton ordered, pulling his attention back to the man behind him.

"Carlton—"

"Now!" Carlton snapped and Rachelle jumped.

Britt eyed a stack of packing crates they just passed and wondered about trying the old trick that always worked in the movies of tipping something over on the bad guy, but again, there was just no way he could do it before Carlton shot him. He needed a distraction. As if Rachelle agreed with the thought, he felt her give a gentle squeeze on his hand letting him know she was with him. He glanced her way, amazed at her calmness. She didn't question him at all. The look on her face was of total confidence. She was not going to give up her life with him either, and she would back him or help him in any way she could.

Britt glanced back at the crates. Maybe he could do something like the movie move if Rachelle could help him with a little distraction. He shifted his fingers in her hand. When she gave him a little squeeze to acknowledge the move, he was sure she was with him. He straightened two fingers and made a walking movement on them, then tried to demo one of his fingers stumbling and dropping to a knee. When no squeeze came, he made it again. This time Rachelle closed her hand up over his, letting him know she understood what he meant. Britt held her hand tight, judging the distance. He gave a slight jerk on her hand, and Rachelle reacted immediately. Stumbling, she dropped to one knee.

This time Carlton did react. His attention turned to her. He cursed. "Get her up."

Britt was already moving but in the other direction, throwing his weight into the stack of crates. Pain spiked through his shoulder on contact, but it had the desired effect, the heavy containers tumbled. A shot echoed through the building as Carlton jerked back out of the way. Britt expected to feel a bullet rip into his flesh instead the sound thudded into the containers that fell on his brother-in-law. Britt's first instinct was to rush him, but one look at the gun swinging back his direction had him grabbing Rachelle's hands, pulling her up. She ran with him, following him like he was leading her in a dance. He tugged her around some equipment just as another shot sounded, and the bullet hit with a metallic twang.

Britt pulled Rachelle around another set of crates, giving her an extra tug at the last second that kept her from running into them, still she didn't say anything. She trusted him to lead her. He slowed their pace as they approached the back wall, drawing her to a stop behind a pile of casings. For the first time since they entered the warehouse, he got a good look at her face. Fear shown there.

"It'll be all right," he whispered, then unable to stop himself he pulled her to him and gave her a hard kiss. Rachelle clung to his side while he forced his eyes away to search for a way out. A wave of despair hit. The door that they entered was almost at the opposite end of the warehouse. The main entrance with the loading doors was at the far end.

He went over the layout in his mind. There was an

emergency exit half way along the wall behind them. The question was, did Carlton know about it, and would he be waiting there for them to make their escape?

Britt listened. Silence again echoed in the warehouse, giving no clue which direction to go. The slight sound on metal steps was like a beacon, telling Britt, Carlton was climbing the stairs to the upper level toward the office. The balcony was in clear view, as they would be when Carlton reached the top. The building was planned that way, so a person up there could get a view of the whole warehouse, especially if he moved out on the cat-walks. The strong lighting illuminated every corner. They would be like ducks in a shooting gallery if they didn't get out of there before Carlton reached the top.

"Come on," Britt whispered. "We've got to move."

They raced for the closest exit. Britt knew Carlton had to be close to the top but didn't dare to glance that way. His attention focused on the path to the door and anything that might trip Rachelle. He released his hold when they reached the door shoving against it. He might as well have hit a brick wall. There was no budge in the door. He pushed again, though he already knew it wasn't going to move. It had been jammed.

"Britt." For the first time Rachelle spoke, she kept her voice low, but there was a touch of panic in his name. He pulled her down behind a stack of pallets.

"The door's barred. I'm afraid the others will be too. We got to make it to the door we came in."

"Okay."

"Carlton has to be on the upper catwalk. From there he can see everything."

She nodded, biting the edge of her lip. "Let's go."

Britt knew she understood their odds of making it as well as he did, but she wasn't any more willing to give up than he was.

He brought her hand to his lips before tucking it back

to his side. Their pace was slower this time, Britt moving them with as much shelter as he could. They had made it only about twenty feet when the first shot burst from above. Britt shoved Rachelle down behind some shelving, flattening his body over hers

"Britt." Terror screamed in her voice.

"Are you hit?" Panic shot through him at the thought of her getting shot.

"No."

He again forced himself to be calm and think. "We'll never make it to the door. We're too visible, and he knows where we are."

"What are we going to do?"

"We can't stay here. It's only a matter of time until he picks us off." He shifted his weight feeling the sonar jab into his leg.

He looked back at the wall by the exit. There was no exit sign above the door, but the breakers were there. The warehouse only had a few high windows, and with the cloudy night sky outside, there wouldn't be any moonlight to filter in. If the lights went out, it would be dark in the building. Carlton wouldn't be able to see them.

He glanced back at the breakers making up his mind. "Stay here."

"Britt."

"Don't worry. I'm not going to leave you. I'm just going to do something about all the lights. The breakers are on the wall."

"No, he'll see you."

"He'll be over us in a minute. This is our only chance." He rolled to a crouch before she could object again. He knew there was little chance of making the breaker and flipping it before Carlton saw him, but it really was the only chance he and Rachelle had.

"Stay down," he ordered. Coming up, he sprinted for the box. A shot sounded. Rachelle screamed. The bullet hit far behind him. He slid into the wall by the breaker-box, pulling open the panel. The next shot sounded followed closely by another shot before he could touch the switches. Pain sliced across his shoulder. In front of him, the box sparked. Britt stumbled back and threw up his arms to cover his face as the power box sparked again. Then the lights went off. The whole warehouse fell into darkness. Carlton's shot did what he didn't get a chance to do.

"Britt." Rachelle's cry led him back toward her.

"Rachelle," he said her name when he couldn't locate her in the void. "Where are you? The lights are out." It was blacker than he expected. No light at all filtered in from above.

"Here."

He heard her move but was still unable to see her. Then she touched him and he locked his arms around her. Amazed at the relief he felt in her. He had only been in total darkness for seconds, but he felt a wave of helplessness and a gripping fear knowing Carlton was still out there waiting to kill them, and he couldn't see to protect Rachelle.

"Are you all right?" She clung to him.

"Yes, it's just so dark I can't see anything." He held her to him, aware of the stickiness running down his chest. "Can you lead us out of here?"

"Maybe. I'm not sure where the door is. I lost the point of reference when we were running."

Britt thought for a minute trying to get his bearings. "It's that way." He took her hand and pointed the direction he thought was the way they entered. "At least, if we go that way, we will eventually run into the wall and can follow it to the door, but there are a lot of things to maneuver around."

⊗⊗⊗

"I can handle that." Rachelle pulled the little sonar

from her pocket, turned it on then fitted it into her palm. She could feel Britt pressed against her. She was also aware of the tightness in his voice. He was in pain. Though he had been standing straight, and she felt no injury when she held him, she was sure he had been hurt. She prayed that since she couldn't feel it, that it wasn't bad. But she had to get them out of there as fast as she could.

She never thought in her life she would be grateful for being blind, but at that moment, she was. Darkness was an element she could handle now. She had proven it to herself over the last few months. She forced a calming breath into her lungs and focused on the direction they wanted to go and the little device in her hand.

Stealth was more important than speed, making it easy for her to have time to detect objects and move around them. Several times they had to make turns and back track as the aisle they were on ended, but she kept the point of reference in her mind, hoping that it was the right way. It felt like they had been moving for hours though it had only been minutes when they reached the wall.

Beside her she heard Britt sigh softly. He leaned over and brushed a kiss against her cheek. "Good, the door should be toward the left, but there are pallets and machinery that we'll have to go around. There's wide open area about ten feet square if that will help you locate it."

"It will."

"Remind me to have some emergency lighting installed in here. I didn't realize there wasn't any. This building is only used for spare building parts that are not in production at the moment." She could hear the frustration in his words. He was feeling helpless, which was totally foreign to him. He didn't like it.

"I love you." She leaned forward to kiss him. When she touched his shoulder, he jerked slightly, and she felt wetness. "Britt." Fear laced through her.

"It's nothing, either a bullet just grazed me or I cut it

on a sharp corner."

"We should stop the bleeding."

"It's mostly stopped on its own. Don't worry about it. We've got to get out of here."

Rachelle wanted to check it out but he was right. The best move was to get out of there and get help. Placing his hand back on her waist, she started to move. They had only gone about ten feet when they heard a scraping noise somewhere over head and froze. Britt pressed his body against her, forcing her back against a stack of crates. They stayed there in silence listening to the person move.

Rachelle could hear the faltering on the steps as Carlton slid his feet along, testing each step as if he was afraid the footing would disappear in front of him. She knew he was using the railing of the catwalk as a guide but was confused as to where he was at. She felt a wave of satisfaction, when she heard what was obviously Carlton's toe hitting one of the railing posts and almost tripping.

They waited as the sounds moved away, than a minute longer before they started to walk again. They had only gone about twenty feet, when they heard some more rustling sounds from above, something clanked on metal. A scream pierced the air. It cut off with a crash and the clatter of falling boxes, somewhere toward the center of the warehouse.

Rachelle tried to muffle the gasp that escaped and grasped Britt's arm. He pulled her to him again. "What was that?" she whispered, but she felt like she knew. It just seemed too impossible.

"I'm not sure. Let's get out of here." He kissed her on the top of her head. "We have to be getting close."

Rachelle had to force herself to step back from the shelter of his arms. Then it took her a second to get her thoughts off the scream they heard and on to the sonar. It was another thirty feet when she detected the open area. She almost cried out with relief when her finger touched the cold metal door. When Britt pushed it opened, tears did slip from her eyes. Beside her she heard Britt sigh, and knew he could finally see.

"You are amazing." He grabbed her up kissing her thoroughly before putting her back down. "Let's get to the main building. We can call the police and wait there."

Rachelle was more than willing.

Twenty minutes later they sat by the security desk in the main building waiting while the police checked out the warehouse. Rachelle clung to Britt's hand as the paramedics tended his shoulder. He refused to let her out of his reach even as he drove to the main building and made the call to the police.

"How is he?" The question startled her, but she recognized the voice of Detective Todd.

The voice that answered was the same paramedic that described it to her a minute earlier and assured her it was hardly more than a scratch, though at Britt's intake of breath as they worked on it she thought Britt might debate the scratch comparison.

"Not bad. He still should go to the hospital to have it checked out and get some antibiotics, but all in all, I'd say he was mighty fortunate."

"Are you done with him then?"

"Just one more piece of tape should do it. I'll say again, he should still go to the hospital. The bleeding has stopped, and they really can't stitch it, but it should be tended more thoroughly. You don't want to risk the possibility of infection."

"I'll see he gets a ride to the hospital when we're done."

The police officer fell silent for a moment. Rachelle figured he was waiting for the paramedic to finish up. It was Britt that broke the silence.

"Did you catch him?"

"We found him." There was a long pause. "He's dead.

He fell from the catwalk. He landed in some machinery, and it looks like it broke his neck. We'll have to wait for the medical examiner to give us the final verdict. For now, I have to ask you some questions since you were the only ones in the building, but I'm afraid I need to do this separately."

Britt's hold on Rachelle's hand tightened. She clung to him not wanting to be taken from him either, though wasn't given much choice. "This is Officer Hayes, she'll stay with you while I talk to Mr. Clairbourne. Then I'll come and talk to you. I'm sorry but it shouldn't take too long."

It felt like it took forever. Rachelle had nothing to do but count the seconds as she waited. She could hear several mutterings, but no one ever came close enough to hear what was being said. Rachelle was getting antsy by the time Todd returned.

"Sorry to take so long. Is it all right if I record our conversation?"

"Yes."

"Thank you, it makes it easier. Can you tell me what happened?"

Rachelle went through every detail. Step by step as close as she could remember it.

"So neither you nor Mr. Clairbourne went up on the catwalk?" he probed.

"No. I'm sure he meant to kill us up there. Britt knocked something over before we got to the stairs."

"You did an excellent job making a distraction."

"It was Britt's idea."

"Still, I must say you did amazing. He said you stayed calm the whole time."

"I'm not sure calm is the word I would use. But I fought not to panic. I knew that wouldn't help Britt and that he'd figure out a way to get us out of there, though I was terrified the whole time."

"You both handled the situation well. Britt never went

up on the cat walk?"

Rachelle didn't miss the way he slid the question back in again. "No."

"He was with you the whole time?"

"Yes, the farthest we were ever separated was when he went to cut the power, and then it wasn't too far, because I could hear him clearly, even though he was being quiet. I would say within ten or twelve feet."

"That was a smart move. It probably saved your lives. Well, that should be it. I'll get Mr. Clairbourne over here." The detective must have motioned when he first started the sentence because Britt reach her about the same time he ended it. Rachelle knew he was there an instant before he slid his arms around her and pulled her to him. She was more than willing to cuddle into him and relished the fact that they were safe. Mindful of his shoulder, she wrapped her arm around his waist.

His hand came up to cradle her face. "You all right?"

"Yes, but we should get you to the doctor."

"I'm fine."

She leaned forward and kissed his lips, silencing him. "You're going to the doctor then I'll take you home and take care of you." She kissed him again, letting him know his care would be tender and loving.

"I'll go to the doctor." He sounded almost eager.

"I'll get someone to drive you over," Todd spoke up.

Rachelle had forgotten about the man's presence and had to fight down a blush.

"I have to stay here and wrap this up. It's nice that it's all over. I have to admit. I never figured it would be Reese. We checked into him briefly, but he didn't fit the profile at all. It's hard to believe he could keep up the constant act on the phone. It was very convincing. He had the psychologist totally fooled. And Dr. Lewis is usually right on."

It took a second for Rachelle to get what he was talking about. When she did, she started shaking her head and pulled back from Britt.

"Wait a minute. It wasn't Carlton. The man on the phone wasn't Carlton. It wasn't the same voice."

"Rachelle."

"No." For the first time that evening, Rachelle felt herself becoming hysterical. "It wasn't him. I know his voice. It wasn't Carlton. It wasn't. He's not the one after Britt."

Britt pulled her to him. "It's okay."

She tried to shake her head again but was held too tight against his shoulder, and when she moved, he sucked in a painful breath. "Britt." She stilled.

"It's all right, Miss Harris. We'll check it out thoroughly. I promise you."

This time she did manage to step back. "It's Mrs. Clairbourne. And I'm telling you, no matter how it looks, Carlton is not your man. The voice was wrong. It was not the same voice."

"He was having allergies." It was Britt that tried to pacify her with the comment.

"It still wasn't him. I heard him before. The tones in their voices are different." There was silence for a moment. She knew the men were exchanging looks. She also knew they both thought they had gotten who was behind everything. Rachelle wished she could believe it, but she knew, to the very center of her soul, they were wrong.

"I promise you we'll check it out," Todd repeated. "I'll be in touch."

"Rachelle goes into the hospital in two days. Well, actually, I guess it's the day after tomorrow. They're going to restore her sight."

"Congratulations. And congratulations on your marriage."

Rachelle couldn't manage a reply. She heard the man move off.

"Britt, I think we'd better postpone the surgery.

There's too much happening, with this guy after you, and now you're going to have to handle telling your sister about Carlton. Think how she's going to take that he tried to kill you. There's going to be the funeral. And on top of that, when they find out we're married ... it's not a good time."

"No, we're not going to postpone your surgery. I don't care what else happens. I want you to have the surgery now." The firmness that was in his tone was in the kiss that took her by surprise. His hands were on either side of her head, gripping her gently when he broke the kiss and laid his forehead to hers. His voice was husky as he spoke. "For a brief time there tonight, I couldn't see anything. I know you have adjusted to it, but I don't want you to have to be in that darkness any longer than you have to if there's something that can be done. I would give anything for you to see. Please don't say again you want to postpone."

The tightness in his voice sounded almost like a combination of fear and pleading. All Rachelle knew was she couldn't deny his request. She would go ahead with the surgery. She just prayed they'd realize the psycho was still out there. At least with the surgery coming, she figured it wouldn't be hard to keep Britt with her at all times.

"Will you stay with me from now on? I want every second I can spend with you."

"Every second, I'm yours."

She felt a little relief. She would know the man if she heard him come close. She could at least be on guard until the police realized they had the wrong man.

Chapter Sixteen

Rachelle felt the lips brush against her cheek. They touched her lips and lingered. Her mind crept from the haze that still lingered in her body from the anesthesia. By the time she managed to work herself to be fully awake Britt was gone, but his scent curled around her, pressing away the sterile hospital smell. She felt peace.

She had been drifting in and out of consciousness for hours, aware of her surroundings but not really there. Earlier she had heard Britt and the doctors talking. They were saying that the operation went extremely well, that they were quite confident of the chance of success. They still cautioned patience, and they'd have to wait and see.

See, would she see? She clung to the possibilities. Waking up in the morning and looking over at Britt lying beside her, the sun streaming over his rich dark hair, across his shoulders. She wanted to watch her hands as they moved over him. She wanted to see him on horseback and walking down the street or hall. She hadn't told him she could recognize him just by how he moved. He had a strong, confident stride that was amazingly quiet, and fluid. He wasn't one of those men that clomped around but more like a panther gliding through the jungle. Yes, a panther was an apt description of Britt. She always had a thing for the large powerful cats. She remembered as a child she had asked for one for Christmas. Her parents had given her a stuffed one. Well, now she had a real one of her own.

Rachelle tried to tell herself not to get her hopes up too high, but it was as impossible as trying to stop the earth from turning. Her heart burned. She wanted to see if Britt's face shown with the love she felt in his touch.

She heard someone slip into the room, and the nurse checking the monitors beside her. It was funny how she could remember the sounds after all these months. But sounds were what she had clung to. Sounds, her mind locked on the word and went deeper to voices dissecting into tones and patterns, flow, pitches. They had been what she relied on. She knew them. And she knew that Carlton might have tried to kill them, but he hadn't been the caller. She had talked to him, heard him behind the words.

She wondered how she could convince the police that it wasn't him. She had tried several times over the last day and a half. The problem was there had been no other calls or trouble, and they had found a small piece of the explosive cord that had been used on the lobby windows in Carlton's car.

Britt tried to tell her not to worry about it. That the police would handle it and all she was to be concerned with was her surgery and where she wanted him to take her after it was over. His focus had shifted to her the last few days. She knew he was worried about her. He tried to be positive, but she could hear the fear that the surgery wouldn't be successful in his voice. Not that he was worried that he might be stuck with a blind wife, but that she would be disappointed all over again.

She wasn't sure how to convince him she'd be all right if she didn't recover her sight. She wanted to see again. She dreamed of it, but she would be all right. She no longer worried about fitting in Britt's world being blind. His love had taken her past that. In fact, now she realized that her blindness had been a blessing in a way. It put her in position to meet Britt. And if she had to have her choice between getting her sight and Britt, it would be Britt. She would tell him that when he came back.

The thought was just through her mind when she heard the door open again. It seemed too soon for the nurse to be back, and she caught the smell of sweat. Whoever it was, it was not Britt. The smell was definitely not right for him. It was pungent to her. She couldn't place the smell to anyone she knew off hand, but there was something that tingled familiarity.

Rachelle heard the door pressed closed then the sound of something shifted on the floor. She almost decided that it must be the cleaning person then realized there was no smell of the heavy cleaner that usually accompanied them.

"Who's there?" Fear burst within her. She groped for the call button, but the controls on the bed were unfamiliar to her. Before her fingers found it, a hand clamped down on her wrist.

"You're awake. I didn't expect that."

Fear flared to terror. Rachelle felt as if her heart would stop. This voice was the voice she knew. This was the voice that wanted to destroy Britt. It was him. The cry almost made it out, but his other hand cut it off, leaving only a whimper.

"I know you're not surprised to hear me. You never believed I was dead, but they wouldn't believe you. They were so easy to fool. They're all fools thinking they could stop me. They can't. I'm going to destroy Clairbourne, and you're going to help me. You're going to be at the center of the final blow. He's going to watch you die before I kill him. He will beg for me to kill him."

Rachelle clawed at the hand on her mouth, and tried to hit but there was no power or coordination behind her movement. Her strength faded within seconds.

"Now, now, Angel Voice, you're going to hurt yourself." He dropped her hand, and she tried to pull away as she felt his hand stroke her cheek. A shiver of revulsion ran through her, and she felt tears slip free.

"You're crying. That's good. Aubrey cried for him. She wanted him to come for her. You want him to come for you too, don't you? You think he can save you but he can't. You should never have turned to him. You should have never given yourself to him. I know you've been with him. I've been there all the time. Just outside the door when he took your innocence. You should have listened.

"Why do angels fall? Aubrey, she wasn't an angel. She liked to do wicked things, but you weren't like that. He turned you. He has to die. I'm going to stop him. I'm sorry you have to die too. You never should've turned to him. You never should have fallen."

The hand ran over her cheek again. Rachelle tried to knock it away. She slapped his hands. There was the sound of tape being pulled free. For an instant the hand over her mouth disappeared, but before she could get a sound out it was covered by a wide piece of duct tape, trapping her mouth closed as firmly as his hand did.

There was another sound of tape being pulled free. She pictured the strips attached to his pants. When he grabbed her wrist, she tried to jerk it free but he just pulled it back. The sticky material stuck to her skin. Rachelle held her other arm out so he couldn't grab it. Bumping the side railing, she tried again for the call button. He just hit her hand away. Instead of grabbing it and taping her wrists together like she thought, he taped one wrist to the bed then reached for the other.

"We need to take this out." She felt a tug on the tape holding her IV. There was a stab of pain in her wrist from it. "Now, don't fight. I know what I'm doing. I had lots of training. Isn't it funny, they train you how to take care of life as well as destroy it? Did you know I was the one that responded when my bomb missed you?"

The shiver Rachelle felt was not from the sting of the

IV as he slid from her arm. She tried to pull back but he held it firm applying pressure to the swab before he put a strip of tape over it with what almost seemed excessive care.

"I was glad it missed you, but yet I was mad. You stayed with him. Why? I warned you. I would have cared for you. But you were helping him trying to find me; trying to find my voice."

Rachelle couldn't help but jerk at his words. He knew she could find him from his voice.

"What's wrong? Does it surprise you that I knew? I told you I knew everything. I was always there, watching over both of you, protecting you from myself." He let out a low laugh, and she felt sick. It all came together. He was protecting them, he was everywhere. He was a security guard.

"Yes, you understand now. Sometimes it was hard not to talk around you because everyone else might have noticed if I sounded plugged up with allergies when I hadn't been earlier. Then again, maybe they wouldn't, but you would have recognized my voice if I didn't talk like this." His voice changed, and she knew who it was. The security guard from the main desk, the day they found the bomb outside Britt's office, the one with allergies. Ward ... Warren that was it. He had been around other times too she knew. He was one of the guards at her apartment and the hotel.

"I got the idea from Carlton. He was always complaining about allergies. Isn't it funny that he would try to kill Clairbourne? I couldn't let him do that, though. Only I can kill Clairbourne. Only I can."

On that, he fell silent. Her hand was released from the bed then trapped so fast she hardly knew it happened. Rachelle tried to scream when he lifted her from the bed. No sound made it past the thick tape. She felt the wheelchair under her, and she experienced a rush of hope.

He wasn't going to kill her here, now. And there was no way he could get her out of the hospital without being seen and stopped. He paused to slip booties on her feet before raising them to the footrests. Rachelle kicked out in defiance. He simply caught her ankle, holding it down while the tape was wrapped around her ankle fastening it to the chair.

The hand that came out of the darkness to brush back her hair frightened her. The gauze he wrapped around her jaw to match the one over her eyes terrified her. He tucked a light blanket around her, covering her legs and draped over her arms.

She heard the shifting sound over by the door again, then his voice. "Now to get the nurses out of the way."

The second the words were out, the emergency beeper went off outside at the nurses' desk. She heard the nurse rush past her room. There was a second wait. "So easy. Time to go." He opened the door and simply wheeled her out.

Five minutes later, she sagged in defeat. She couldn't believe he had just rolled her out of the hospital into a waiting medical transport van. He secured the chair and drove off. She had a brief hope in the elevator when someone must have motioned to her. Warren had made the comment of taking her down to the patio to enjoy the evening air. Rachelle tried to draw attention, but it had been no use. The elevator doors opened, and he just strolled out with her.

Rachelle couldn't believe she could have fallen asleep, but the next thing she knew the van pulled to a stop. Her mind screamed 'no' but the words couldn't make it out. The not knowing what was happening was agonizing. Tears slipped from her eyes dampening the bandages. He was going to kill her. She knew that and she didn't want to die, but worse, he was going to use her to draw Britt into a trap to kill him.

Pain as she never knew filled her. She didn't want Britt to die. She wanted to see him and live. She didn't know how much time passed before Warren came to move her again, this time out of the van and up the elevator.

When the doors opened, she knew that they were at Clairbourne Industries. Keys rattled and a door opened. She caught the scent of Britt in the air. Britt's office, her brain accepted that as logical. This was where it had to end, the point that it was spiraling down to. And all she could do was cry in silence, in darkness, as insanity moved around her preparing his evil plan.

Rachelle could only guess, but she was certain he positioned her by Britt's desk in front of the large window. She wanted to scream, but there was no way to do it with the bandaging.

"Are you crying? Why are you crying? This was your choice." There was a childlike tone to his voice. "I tried to warn you. I would have kept you safe, but you turned to him. I would have loved you. I would have." He placed something in her lap. Rachelle tried to buck it off, but a strong hand pushed her back in the seat. There were more sounds of tape, this time being torn off the roll. He wrapped it around her waist and the chair, securing what she guessed was a bomb her. Again, the wrapping over her eyes soaked up the tears. The waiting for Britt to come started.

❧

"Mr. Clairbourne, I'm sorry to have to ask you to come here tonight." Detective Todd greeted Britt with a handshake at the door. "I understand you were at the hospital with your wife. How is she doing?"

"It went well but she's still groggy from the anesthesia. She's highly reactive to it. I want to get back as soon as I can."

"I understand, but believe me this is important. It looks like your wife was right. There's no way your brother-in-law could be behind the bombings. At first, when we couldn't find where he had any knowledge of explosives, we turned to the preface that he hired someone to do that, but we still couldn't make it connect. Now we think he decided that the caller wasn't going to kill you or that we would catch him first, so he decided to kill you himself while he had someone to blame it on. And to be honest, if it weren't for your wife's conviction that we had the wrong man, we might not have looked so deeply. She's very convincing, and she never missed identifying any of us."

"So Carlton isn't behind the bombings."

"No, and there's more. The medical examiner thinks he was thrown off the catwalk."

Britt couldn't keep back the breath that rushed from him.

"There was skin under his nails and other signs of a struggle, but from what you and your wife said, you didn't have any direct contact with him, and since there were no scratches evident on you when you were checked out, that supports that. But, from the angle he fell it looks like he had help."

"So you think that the caller killed him? Why?"

The detective nodded. "I talked to Dr. Lewis. She said it would be a strong possibility that our guy would stop Carlton from killing you because he would want to do it himself. As she said, 'like a jealous kid with a toy.' You are his, only he can kill you. It goes to the power thing he has going."

"Then he's still out there. I need to get back to Rachelle." He pulled out his phone. "I'll get my security over there now."

"Wait, the hospital has security. Your wife will be fine, but security's the problem. It's why we wanted you down here personally. You said that, at the warehouse, the only car you saw was a security car. Carlton had parked his car a ways away so it wouldn't be seen, but I kept thinking about the security car and ran a check on the security personnel again, looking deeper this time." He opened a folder and handed it to Britt.

An icy chill filled him as he stared down at the familiar face of the photo. He knew the security man, Dustin Warren.

"His name is Isaac Warren."

"Isaac, I thought it was Dustin."

"Dustin was his older brother. I'm not quite sure how he managed to pull it off, but he exchanged ID with his brother. They looked quite a bit alike. They were both in the military, Special Forces."

"You keep talking in the past tense." A sinking feeling settled deep within him.

"His brother died three years ago. Isaac … broke after he found out. He went ballistic. It took six guys to hold him until they could get a medic to sedate him. After evaluation, he was found too unstable to return to active duty and was released. He was supposed to get further psychiatric help, but after a time, stopped that." Todd let it hang.

There was no need to say he should have continued it. Todd started up again. "About a year and a half ago, he was living with an Ann Hill, Aubrey Ann Hill. They met at the psychiatrist office, both patients. During the day, Ann worked as a secretary to Clairbourne Industries, at night, Aubrey liked to come out to play stripper.

"Anyway, to cut to it, we talked to her doctor, since she's dead, and it was pertinent to a murder investigation, he agreed. The main thing he told us was that she had developed a fixation on you. Seems she substituted in your office while one of the secretaries was out on medical leave. She decided she wanted you. Made her own fantasies that you would marry her. When the secretary came back, she went back to her old position. She quit, thinking you'd come after her, pleading for her back and declaring your love. After that she disappeared. Doctor didn't know what happened to her, she just quit coming, then she turned up dead. He figured she killed herself. He didn't know she was living with Warren. Warren started working at Clairbourne at the time she was there. We don't know how he managed to hide his information. I think it's possible that Aubrey changed it. She was very good with computers."

"He was assigned to Rachelle's security at her apartment and at her hotel. He must have heard that she could identify the voice right off and was careful not to speak around her."

Before Todd could answer, Britt's phone rang. He pulled it out and looked at the caller ID. "It's the hospital. I have to take this. This is Britt Clairbourne," he answered and his life faded away. "I'm at the police station now. We'll be right there." His words sounded as hollow as he felt. He had to concentrate just to breathe. Pain filled him as he looked up at the detective.

"Rachelle's missing. The nurse went in to check on her, and she wasn't in her room and her IV had been unhooked. They've checked the whole floor, she's not there. They're checking the hospital now. He's got her. He's taken her." It tore him apart as the words came out. Britt wished the detective would object but he didn't. The grave look that settled over the man attested that he believed the same thing.

"I'll get officers over there now. I'll drive you."

They made it down the stairs and into the parking lot when Britt's phone rang again. This time he didn't stop to look at the ID before he accepted the connection. His body had shifted from shock to action. "Yes."

"Have you missed your fallen angel yet? Will you let her die like Aubrey did? It's time for hide-n-seek. But you better come alone, or she'll go to pieces without you. Do you think she might still make it to heaven?" The phone went dead in his ear. Britt pressed the button, bringing the phone number back up and froze. Without explanation, he looked to Todd. "He has her in my office."

"I'll get the swat team over there."

"No." Britt gripped the man's hand as he reached for his radio. "He's monitoring the police radio." Britt's mind was again functioning at top speed. "He knew that I knew she was missing. He must have been listening when you had officers sent to the hospital. He's special ops, good with electronics, and his time on my security has given him a lot of access to them. He'd be expecting something like that."

Todd was quiet a minute, thinking over everything. "You're right, he's monitoring the radio. I'll call it in on the phone, and we'll plan it for communication silence. They still have the building plans you supplied earlier. It won't take long to set up."

"We don't have the time. He's expecting me in about ten minutes. He called me from my office phone. He let me know on purpose where he was. He'll know how long it'll take me to get there and do something to her if I don't get there on time. I'm not going to let that happen. I'll try to buy you some time, but I'm going there now." Britt could see the detective thinking, he knew he was probably debating on arresting him for his own safety, but Todd also knew what he was saying was true.

Todd shook his head in resignation. "If you get killed, it will be my badge, but you're right. The best bet we have is to let you go."

"I take full responsibility if I die." It was easy for Britt to say because, if Rachelle died he didn't want to live either, but he was going to do his best to see that didn't happen.

The man shook his head again. "Okay, but let's get you a little prepared. Take off your shirt."

Todd had the Kevlar vest out of his truck before Britt had his shirt off. He helped him strap it on. "Before you go in call my number. I'll mute the call, but we'll be able to hear everything. I'll give you a police escort until a couple blocks away to make up for lost time, then peel off and come in with the swat team.

Britt raced through the streets following the flashing lights and praying Rachelle was all right. She was still so drugged up when he kissed her at the hospital. Several times, when she was coming in and out of consciousness, she had whispered that she loved him. He hoped she remembered his return of love. Was she even conscious now? Did she know what was happening? Was she in pain? She should be back in the hospital. She should be safe. He never should have left her. He just hadn't expected her to be in danger. He had wanted it to be over so bad so he could concentrate on her.

Ahead, the police car pulled over. Britt forced himself to slow down and drive the last two blocks at a legal speed, though he wanted to press the pedal to the floor. His control slipped once he pulled in the parking lot and he ran into the building. He took the stairs instead of waiting for the elevator. A sinister silence met him when he opened the door, but he knew he was at the right place. The entire floor was pitch-black except the sliver of light that cut under the door to his office.

Britt debated on stealth then tossed it aside and strode forward. Still nothing prepared him for the sight when he opened his door. Light pooled around Rachelle. She was strapped down to a wheelchair. The large glass window behind his desk formed an ominous shadow around her. Her head was almost totally covered in bandages, but he had no doubt it was her by the way her head tilted up, as if she sensed his presence. For all the carefully crafted setting, the most terrifying thing was the numbers that counted down on the bundle strapped to her lap. One minute thirty-eight went to thirty-seven, thirty-six before he could move.

Unable to stop himself, Britt rushed forward coming

down by the wheelchair. "Rachelle." He studied the bomb, wondering how he was going to get it off her or if he even dared try. The question was would the police get there in time? With this guy's tendency to blow up things the bomb squad would be coming. But when the clock read one minute and seventeen seconds, Britt made up his mind he didn't have time to wait. He raised his hands to study the wiring then froze as the voice sounded behind him.

"You made good time. You had a minute and a half left, but do you really think you can save her?" Isaac Warren stepped out of the shadows. He pressed a button on a devise in his hand and the countdown stopped. "You didn't even bring the police. I'm impressed, but you never would have made it up here with them. I figured on that contingency."

"I'm here, Isaac," Britt used his name on purpose. "Let her go."

The man visibly jerked. "That's not my name."

"It is."

The cry that burst from the man was pained, and Britt knew he found one of the keys. "Going by your dead brother's name won't bring him back, just like what you're doing won't bring back Aubrey. Rachelle did nothing to hurt her. I did nothing. I hardly knew Aubrey."

"You lie, she said you loved her. You took her away."

"No. I didn't know Aubrey or Ann except to greet her when I went through the office. I'm sorry if I hurt her by not paying attention and that she hurt you–"

"No, you did know her. She talked about the way you treated her. She told me that you would invite her into your office and had private lunches served, with champagne and caviar, then you would make love to her on your desk."

"That is not true," Britt said sharply. "Not any of it. I've never taken advantage of any of the women that work here. I've never had sex with anyone in my office, and I've never done a champagne and caviar lunch. I don't like champagne or caviar. It was all a fantasy, Aubrey's fantasy." He dropped the last sentence to a soothing tone.

"No, you lie." There was pleading in his words.

"No, you know Aubrey liked fantasy. She was fantasy, Ann's fantasy."

"No." The cry cut through the shadow a second before the shot did.

Britt threw himself over Rachelle. A muffled whimper escaped from beneath the bandage. Behind her, the window cracked, but it didn't shatter. Now that Britt had his hands on Rachelle, he found it impossible to release her.

"It's all right," he whispered to her. "He hit the window." He could feel the panic in her and ran his hands over her to ease her. When he felt the strap that fastened on the bomb, he froze then carefully ran his fingers over it to feel for a wire that might be booby-trapped. The wire was hard to find because it looped down where the strap had been tightened to her. In an instant he made up his mind. Working by feel, he started to loosen the strap.

"Isaac, Ann was sick," Britt started to talk, praying for time.

"No." This time the objection was whimpered.

Britt glanced back but kept his fingers working on the tape. "She needed help. You knew that. You tried to help her. The doctor where you met tried to help her."

"No, he just wanted her also. Just like all men. They all wanted her, but she loved me until you came along."

There was another shot. Britt jerked, tightening his hold on Rachelle again, this one was closer, smashing another hole in the window. Rachelle strained against the tape holding her arms. Britt clamped his hands over them to keep her from hurting herself. "Easy." This time it was the duct tape he went to work on, using his body to shield her while he felt around her ankle for the end and start to work it free. He was on her other ankle before the man behind him started to talk again.

"You're not denying it." The voice was back to a conversational tone.

"You won't believe me if I do. Or you do believe me, but you don't want to face it. Like you don't want to face that your brother is dead." As soon as the words were out, Britt knew he miscalculated.

"He's not dead." The words were punctuated by a bullet slamming into his side, the force driving him against Rachelle. His cheek pressed against the explosive, but he couldn't pull back. Britt felt like he'd been hit in the side by a sledge hammer. He had to fight to breathe. It was several seconds before the shock eased enough for him to realize that, at least, there wasn't any blood running from his body, which meant the vest had done its job. Mentally, he sent his thanks to Todd for thinking of the vest then prayed for breath, wondering if he still didn't have a broken rib.

The bomb shifted against his cheek as Rachelle struggled against the tape holding her arms in a frantic attempt to get to him. The hand he moved up and down her leg wasn't too steady, but she calmed under his touch. He turned his head slightly and kissed her fingers before managing to push back enough to start working on her wrists. Each movement brought new pain to his side, but he had to get Rachelle free. She was too vulnerable in the chair, too easy of a target. If the bullet would have been two inches to the side, it would have missed him and hit her.

"I'm sorry about your brother, Isaac," Britt started to talk again in a low soothing voice. Hoping to ease the tension in Rachelle as much as keep Isaac distracted. He wondered how much longer it would be before the swat team was there. "I'm sorry he was killed. I'm sorry about Ann, Aubrey. I'm sorry they died, but I had nothing to do with it. Rachelle had nothing to do with it. She's innocent."

"No." The man's voice was filled with tears. "She

turned to you. I would've kept her safe. But she turned to you, helped you. I could have loved her. She could have been mine but she gave herself to you." Rage started to build in his voice. "She's not innocent. She's just like Aubrey, giving herself to other men."

Britt only had an instant to make the decision. "No, she's not like Aubrey."

"She slept with you."

"She's my wife. Do you understand that? She is my wife."

The room was so silent Britt could've sworn he heard his heartbeat, wondering if he made a mistake again.

"You're lying again."

"I'm not."

"Then where's her ring?"

"It's in my pocket. I have it because she was in the hospital. Would you like to see it?" Britt turned to face him and slowly slid his hand in his pocket and drew out two rings. "Mine," he slid one on his finger, "and Rachelle's." He pulled the last of the tape free, raised her hand and eased the ring into place, kissing it before he moved it for the man to see. "I never loved Ann, never had anything to do with her, but I do love Rachelle."

The man shook his head, but Britt continued talking. "Rachelle helped me because she's a good person and because she loves me. Are you going to make her suffer because Aubrey lied to you?"

The gun lowered until his arm hung limp.

"You need to let Rachelle go. She never lied. She is innocent. You have to protect the innocent." When the man didn't move, Britt raised Rachelle to her feet. She wasn't steady. He had to hold her and the bomb that hung loosely at her hips. Britt wondered if he could get her out of it and if she could manage to walk out of the room. He needed to get her out of there then maybe he could do something about Isaac.

A light flashed on Isaac's belt. He jerked, but instead of bringing up the gun, he raised the remote for the bomb. "You lied," he cried as he pressed the button reactivating the countdown, at the same time Britt dove for him, impacting with him before he could bring the gun up. Britt went for the remote while slamming the man against the wall.

Pain slashed through Britt's head as Isaac brought the gun down catching him in a glancing blow, but Britt held on, slamming the hand against the wall trying to break the grip on the remote. Out of the corner of his eye, he saw the gun coming down again. He barely got a hand up to stop the next hit. Isaac pushed off the wall, lowering his head. Isaac ran into Britt connecting with his shoulder driving him back. Pain rocketed through Britt's body and he went down. But keeping his hold, he brought the man down with him. It was luck that had him coming up on top. Britt slammed his fist into the man's jaw, and Isaac went still.

Not waiting to see if Isaac was unconscious, Britt dove for the remote, only to find it broken. Glancing to Rachelle, she sagged against the corner of his desk. The counter was down to nineteen seconds. It took one second to reach her.

"Raise your hands." She obeyed as he gripped the webbing, pulling it up her body, over her head. His first instinct was to throw her over his shoulder as he had done before, but with the time at fourteen seconds, he doubted they could get far enough away to be safe.

He dropped the bomb to the desk, not taking time to think if anyone might be below. He grabbed up the wheelchair and smashed it against the window. The cracks made by the bullets in the safety glass made it impossible for the window to withstand the hit, and the glass shattered out. In one fluid motion he released the wheelchair, swung back, snatched up the bomb and flung it out the window. The blast came seconds after it disappeared from sight. Britt didn't care though. He had Rachelle in his arms, and that was all that was important.

He held her to him pressing his lips down her face, sometimes catching bandages, sometime skin. It didn't matter, he had her.

He forgot about Isaac until he saw the movement. Britt shoved Rachelle behind him shielding her with his body as Isaac's hand came up with the gun. Three shots echoed through the office, but this time, no blows impacted into his body.

Isaac's form dropped like a marionette cut from its strings. The man in the doorway kept his gun trained on the man who had threatened everything Britt loved. Isaac didn't move.

Britt's attention went back to Rachelle. "It's all over." He kissed her again. "Let's get this off." He unwrapped the gauze from around her mouth then carefully removed the duct tape he found under it. He kissed her lips tenderly when he reached them.

"Britt," she whispered against him, doing her own seeking of his lips for assurance.

"It's over," Britt said again. "It's really over this time. The police have him."

She sighed and rested her head against his shoulder.

"Are you okay?"

"Yes, just so happy to have you. I love you. I was afraid I would never get to tell you that again." Though he couldn't see them, the sound of tears was heavy in her voice.

"I know what you mean. I was afraid of the same thing."

"I want to see you. I need to see you." She reached up clawing at her bandages.

Britt caught her hands, bringing them to his lips, kissing them before laying her palms against his cheek, pressing her fingers there. "Patience, love." He kissed her again. "Now is not the time, it's too soon. We need to get you back to the hospital, see me this way for now."

He helped her make the first motions with her fingers before she took over tracing each curve of his face. Her lips followed her fingers then her hands dropped to his chest and stopped.

"A vest, you're wearing a vest. You really are all right."

"A little bruised is all, thanks to Detective Todd."

She pressed against him, placing a kiss over his heart. She clung to him a moment before she kissed him again. "Detective Todd," she said out loud.

"Yes, Mrs. Clairbourne."

Britt knew the man wouldn't question how she knew he was in the room though he hadn't spoken to her.

"Thank you so much."

"For what?" The man was clearly confused.

"For watching over Britt when I couldn't." Rachelle pressed her lips to Britt's once more. "Though, I hope to be able to do a better job of it in the near future."

Epilogue

Rachelle's face glowed with happiness, as she looked up at him. He had tried to make it the best Christmas for her ever, but she had made it for him. Each day was incredible with her. She opened his eyes with her delight of seeing things again, giving him an appreciation for things he had never known.

He laughed when he raised the lid of the box and removed the stuffed teddy bear. "It's cute." He looked at her delighted face. "But, I hope you don't think he'll take your place. It might be soft but I happen to like cuddling you."

"Good." She beamed back. "Then you'll have to find someone else to give it to."

It took him about two seconds to realize she what was talking about. His gaze dropped to her stomach, and she laughed out loud.

"You're pregnant." He reached for her.

The rest of the gifts were forgotten as they celebrated the special gift they had given each other.

ABOUT THE AUTHOR

I grew up in a small town in Wyoming loving the outdoors, sports, art, and reading Hardy Boys books. After reading them all at least a half dozen times, I started writing my own stories.

Thirty years ago I married a wonderful, honorable man. I'm mother of five children and grandmother of six boys. I love traveling. Through my husband's work and vacations, I have visited much of the United States, all over Eastern Europe, Canada, Mexico, China, Thailand, Cambodia and Australia, giving me many intriguing locations and experiences for my stories.

I am a storyteller. I write the classic hero story because I think there's a need for more heroes, love, and adventure in our lives. I'm not out to change the world with my writing; I'm just hoping to make your day a little better.

Hope you enjoy,
Alysia S. Knight

Feel free to visit me through my website
www.alysiasknight.com

If you enjoyed Blind Witness please look for my next book releasing soon.

Beauty and the Chief

This fairy tale gets mixed up. When the Beast can't get women to love him, he kills them. Beauty, interior designer Jillian Taylor, becomes his next intended victim when, while running with her dog, she interrupts his ritual killing. Jillian catches the eye of another suitor, Police Chief Mark Richards, a man of honor, raising his son alone after being abandoned by a wife who loves show and status more than them. When Mark sees the truly good woman, under what he is afraid is all glamour, love begins to grow. The real question is − will Mark be able to save Beauty from the Beast to make his own happily ever after come true?